Salted

Away

Cyberworld Publishing

www.cyberworldpublishing.com

ISBN 978-0-9808011-5-6

Cyberworld Publishing
Jindalee St, Toronto, Australia

Koniotis Mysteries Series

Each book in this series stands alone, but they are also all connected in various ways and form the different parts of one story.

Salted Away

Koniotis Mysteries - Book Two

by Gina Drew

Caitlyn's map of sites visited in this book

Kyrenia

Karpas Pen.

Kantara Cast.

Bellapais

Boğaz

Pendaktylos Pass

arion

Buffavento Cast.

Salamis

NICOSIA

kedonittsia

FAMAGUSTA

Buffer Zone

Dhekel

Ayia Napa

LARNACA

Khipokitia

Zygi

C Y P R U S

Nicosia locations shown on Caitlyn's map

A. OLD NICOSIA
B. LAIKI YITONIA
C. TURKISH ZONE
D. MAKEDONITISSA VALLEY
E. ACROPOLIS
F. MAIN UN BASE
G. STROVOLOS

1. Border Crossing Checkpoint
2. Ledra Palace Hotel
3. House of Representatives
4. Municipal Theatre
5. Cyprus Museum
6. Canadian High Commission
7. Dunsford Flat
8. Sirail Hotel
9. Ziya's Office
10. Ziya Flat
11. Russian Embassy
12. American Embassy
13. Kykko Monastery -- Nicosia Branch
14. Koniotis House
15. Hilton Hotel
16. Bristow Flat
17. Makedonitissa Monastery
18. International Fair Grounds
19. Makarios Stadium
20. Piccard House
21. Stepanov House
22. Hamilton Flat
23. Cypriot Police Headquarters
24. Famagusta Gate

Caitlyn's map of the Cypriot city of Nicosia

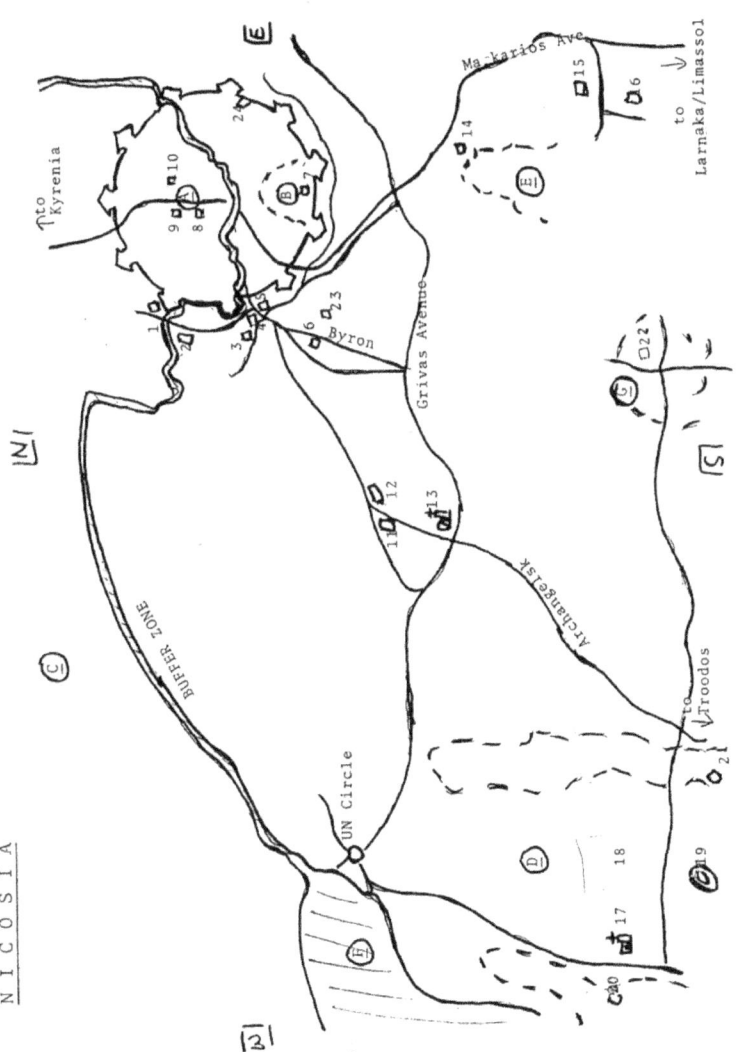

Primary Characters:

Peggy Bingham—Rich American collector of antiquities

Sarah Bristow—American embassy military attaché

Justin Chamberlain—American art collector and exporter of ill repute

Erica Christos—A Belgian soprano

Paul Conte—American embassy political officer

Antonis Demetriou—Greek Theatro Ena actor

John Dunsford—Canadian high commission political officer

Father Nikolay—Russian Orthodox monk, Kykko Greek Orthodox Monastery

Sophie Gianni—Italian belly dancer

Ginger Hamilton—Much-married wife of Willie Hamilton

Willie Hamilton—Retired British army major; report for the *Cyprus Mail*

Dieṭrich Kleist—German forger of artifacts

Caitlyn Spencer Koniotis—American archaeologist in Cyprus; wife of Takis Koniotis

Takis Koniotis—Chief of Cypriot police department International Investigations Unit

Mikhail Lukenov—Russian embassy intelligence official

Eleni Piccard—Cypriot; Shipping and handicraft industry CEO

Helmut Roentgen—Artifact smuggler

Maria Solonos—Assistant to Takis Koniotis at Cypriot police department International Investigations Unit

Sergey Stepanov—Well-connected Russian businessman

Alec Stuart—British high commission political officer

Tansul—Resourceful Turkish Cypriot police department assistant

Mehmet Tosun—Slippery merchant of indeterminate origin

The Knife—Villain of the piece

Alvarez de Toledo—Parasailing Spanish ambassador

Andriko Visiliou—Chief archaeologist at Kaliana dig

Safa Ziya—Turkish Cypriot police senior investigator

Prologue

Brussels, Late April 1983

The woman was clawing at the spymaster's arm in panic. The Knife shrugged her off and swung around to escape her grasp, only to be assailed with the sweaty merchant's face. The breath of the fat little Lebanese—caused by who knew what oriental spice—normally would've been enough to repel the spymaster into another room. Just now, however, the strong aroma served to jolt him back to the problem at hand.

He turned back to the woman. "What makes you think the operation has been compromised?"

"Sophie Gianni. She's downstairs in my auto. The Italian representative burst into her flat this evening. He slapped her around and questioned her about going through his briefcase and who she'd been talking to."

"So?"

"She . . ." The woman's nerves almost gave way. The Knife did not take bad news well. "She says he'd been closely questioned by security officials earlier today about information leaks. He was sure that the document that had been leaked had never been out of his safe except when he'd mistakenly put it in his briefcase when he'd visited her last week."

"Shit. But that doesn't mean we're blown. We'll just have to isolate her involvement from the rest of operation and see to it that she doesn't get caught up in another interrogation. Where's your car?"

The woman shuddered and hesitated before ending all hope for Sophie. She was fully aware of what the agent was capable of doing to maintain the operation. Her hesitation gave the Lebanese merchant the opportunity to speak.

"But that's not all, exalted one. The situation has gone to hell in a purse, just as she said. We've got to clear out now."

"What do you mean, Jallud? Come to the point—if you have a point. Pull yourself together. There's no need for panic."

The merchant was so worked up he was unable to form the necessary words. He had pulled out a string of worry beads and was rubbing them vigorously across his closed eyes.

"He means the Gianni woman isn't the only problem," the woman interjected. "He has the German code clerk outside. It looks like the other side is moving against us across the board."

"No, No," she added hastily as the Knife visibly tensed up and seemed ready to lash out, "our autos aren't close enough for the two to see each other."

"Go on. Why do you think Ackerman has been compromised as well?"

"Jallud told me that Ackerman came to him not more than an hour ago. One of his friends—one of the night shift code clerks—called him this morning and warned him not to show up for work.

The security officer had been in the code room all night, pulling records and asking who had been on duty when this and that message had been transmitted. As the night wore on, they were narrowing in on Ackerman."

"So, that's two limbs we need to lop off. Then we should be all right."

"But will we?" the woman persisted. "Don't you remember that your Danish source asked you about Ackerman and whether he was involved? Your agents don't appear to be as isolated from each other as you thought. If the agents still in place get wind of the deaths or disappearances of others in the network, won't they panic? Isn't this all beginning to unravel? Don't you think it's time to cut and run?"

The Knife retreated into contemplation, a state of thought that was interrupted by the jangling of the bell at the street door below the second-floor apartment.

The spymaster went to the window, slitted the drapes, and looked into the street below.

"Damn. It's that love-struck boy. And he looks all atwitter. Someone must have put a flare up his backside, as well."

A spilt second of sorting through options and the Knife let out a heavy sigh. "I guess you're right. Let's put our plan of retreat into effect. You both know what to do. Get Gianni and Ackerman moving first and then go ahead with the others. Leave by the back door. I'll tend to the general's son."

"So, what do I tell Ackerman is happening?" Jallud had suddenly found his voice.

"We've told each of them all from the beginning that we had a retirement plan for them. Just tell them they'll like where they're going. Once they get there, they should be pleased enough."

"But I don't understand? They don't know each other, and you've worked so hard to keep them apart. Why are they all—?"

"They don't need to understand. And neither do you." The Knife quite obviously was beginning to lose patience. "The center set up the retirement arrangements. And the center has its own forms of retirement for used-up spies or those who don't cooperate. You'd best not forget that."

Chapter One

Cyprus, Late Fall 1996

"Retired with what?" The cool blonde suddenly focused her attention completely on the American embassy political officer, Paul Conte. She had lost interest in the discussion between Paul Conte and her new husband, Takis Konitois, who was a police official with the International Crimes Unit. She had been enjoying watching the beams of sunlight playing on the snow patches beneath the pines beyond the Forest Park Hotel's terrace room. She would never cease to be amazed that snow began to fall on the Troodos Mountains long before the beaches, less than an hour's drive away, were abandoned for the winter.

"Retired with prejudice. Salted away and then, as they call it, retired with prejudice."

"And just what is that supposed to mean?"

"If you'd been paying the least bit of attention to the conversation, Cait, you would've known that I was explaining to Takis—and thought I was explaining to you as well—why I'd been so busy of late. Why were you staring into the forest so hard? Were you using your psychic powers to determine where to locate your next brilliant archaeological dig?"

Caitlyn reddened. She knew Paul was playfully baiting her again. She could tell this not only because of his swipe at her well-publicized discovery of a major Neolithic site in a valley leading to the sea from Mount Olympus, but also because he had called her Cait. She had told him in no uncertain terms that no one but her family back in Virginia used that pet name for her. But Paul still called her that from time to time just to get a rise from her.

Well, it wouldn't work this time. She just smiled blithely and returned to the topic at hand. "I believe you were explaining the meaning of those strange terms to me."

"Salted away and retired with prejudice? Ah, yes. That's popping up to embarrass the Russians and their former East European dupes, because they were impolitic enough to throw in the towel on the cold war. Actually those terms were ones those of us in the State Department had already established in a tongue-in-cheek way. Our own intelligence agencies never admitted to isolating and killing off their agents who failed or who changed sides. So, when we heard that someone had just disappeared and our friends in intelligence said they'd retired, we quipped among ourselves that they'd been salted away so they could be retired with prejudice—ergo killed off. Got it?"

"Yes, very funny," Caitlyn said with as flat a tone and as little expression as she could muster. She knew the only way to avoid follow-up puns from her friend was not to encourage his twisted flights of humor too much. "So how are you involved in that? You told me that you're a treasury agent, not an intelligence agent."

"Yes, of course, I'd never lie to you, fair lady. But, as I was saying, with the end of the cold war, the records of the Soviet and Eastern Bloc spy agencies are becoming public. Now we're learning not only about all of their spy operations, but also how they were done, and who did them—including, in some cases, leaders still in the current governments. Because of this, we fear there'll be a bloodbath among former Russian spies in an attempt by Moscow and friends to try to avoid egg on their faces. All of us in the Western embassies— not just the intelligence officers—are racing to analyze all of the information these records and former agents can give us concerning the Russians' intelligence operations and networks before they can get Pandora's box closed again."

"You do have a way with tired clichés," Caitlyn responded. Paul gave her that wounded puppy dog look, and she relented by flashing him one of her dazzling smiles.

Cutting into the banter between his table companions, Takis Koniotis interjected, "And you were saying that you thought my office would see increased business along this line because of all the Russians who are coming into Cyprus?"

"You betcha," Conte answered. "Your government probably put together your special unit just in time. I think you're going to be swamped with Russian refugees who want to spill the beans about Russian operations and Russian agents who are going to want to shut them up before they can."

As Koniotis was absorbing this unwelcome possibility, his cell phone started to jangle. Within moments, he and Caitlyn, because she had driven up to the Troodos with him from Nicosia for lunch, were, almost prophetically, off to check on a dead Russian.

In less than an hour, they had maneuvered from one Troodos peak top to another and arrived in the forecourt of the very isolated, but also very rich, Greek Orthodox Kykko monastery.

"We found him over here early this morning, on top of this covered well in the central courtyard. We notified the police in Nicosia immediately, but it took them a while to locate you," explained the abbot, as he quickly guided the couple through the heavily frescoed walls of the open corridors leading to the monks' quarters. "He evidently fell from up there. That balconied corridor is just outside Father Nikolay's cell."

"You think he slipped and fell over the cloister railing in the night?" Koniotis queried. Both he and Caitlyn looked up and were almost blinded by the sunlight being reflected off the gold inlay of the intricate frescoes.

"No, I wish it were so, but I'm afraid this was no accident—for a couple of reasons."

As Koniotis examined the body more closely, he understood. The priest had suffered several very nasty knife wounds.

"You said there were a couple of reasons this wasn't an accident. The wounds are self-explanatory, but you know something else about what happened here?"

The abbot hesitated for a moment, evidently struggling with his response. "I suppose it's proper for me to talk about this. Father Nikolay didn't say he was coming to me in confidence last evening. Shortly after our dinner and before evening prayers, he visited me in great consternation. Father Nikolay had come to us from northern Europe, where he had been assigned as a representative of the Russian Orthodox Church to the European Council of Churches headquarters

19

in Belgium. There had been some trouble for him there—I never asked exactly what—and he had come here on prolonged retreat. He had been a very quiet man, but a very good and devout addition to our order. But, as I was saying, he came to my study in a very bad state last evening. He said he had seen someone from his past among the visitors to the monastery yesterday afternoon—someone he kept referring to by a distressingly violent nickname I can't seem to recall at the moment—and he was in fear for his life.

"I'm afraid I wasn't much help to him. The matters he was talking about are completely out of the realm of my experience. Something about his past as a courier of information, apparently some sort of activity that was highly secret and dangerous. I first suggested that we call in the authorities, but that just seemed to upset Father Nikolay more. I then suggested that he go back to his cell and try to achieve a calmer state through prayer and that I also would contemplate further on what could be done for him. But I didn't see him at evening prayer, and then I'm afraid I got caught up in other pressing matters. I resolved to talk with him again first thing this morning, but I was awakened with the news that he was dead."

During the abbot's explanation, Caitlyn had been exploring the ground beneath the second-floor corridor from which the priest had fallen. A couple of scraps of paper caught her attention. She was surprised to see litter here, since the monastery buildings and courtyards seemed to have been meticulously groomed. What she found were three scattered Cypriot pound notes and a couple of tattered business cards.

Amazing, she thought, as she focused on one of the cards. It was such a small world. The card was for the antiquities business a college friend of hers had established here on Cyprus after deciding that the study of archaeology at the University of Michigan was not to his liking.

She rose and walked toward the well. "Takis, look what I—"

But Takis was preoccupied with a find of his own, and Caitlyn slipped the banknotes and business cards into her coat pocket and gave her full attention to what Takis held in his hand.

"What's this? Some sort of material. I found it clutched in the priest's hand."

"It looks like silk or satin," the abbot observed. "Much too fancy for our order, I'm afraid. I doubt whether it came from here."

"Why, it's shaped like a pocket. It looks just like a pocket from the inside of a men's jacket. I'll bet the priest put up a fight and tore this off his attacker. Oh, very good! There's a label on it. Pennsylvania Avenue. Now what could that mean?"

"Pennsylvania Avenue? Is that what it says?" Caitlyn asked.

Takis handed her the scrap of material.

"I know that brand. That's an exclusive tailor in Washington, D.C. My father has suits made there."

"So, it's off an American men's suit," Takis declared. "Now we're getting somewhere."

"Well, either a man's or a woman's suit," Caitlyn said. "They tailor business clothes for both men and women."

But Takis wasn't listening. He'd turned to the abbot and suggested that they go up to where Father Nikolay had gone over the railing. To Caitlyn, he said. "Could you go out and watch for the site investigation team? It should be arriving from Nicosia just about now, and we need to have detailed photos before the scene is contaminated."

"As we walk, perhaps you can try to remember the name the priest had used for the man who disturbed the. We can try . . ." Takis's voice trailed off as he and the abbot walked away from Caitlyn along the balcony.

Caitlyn was pleased that Takis had asked for her help and bustled off to the monastery's forecourt without another thought for her find and was quickly occupied with directing the arriving police teams to the crime scene.

* * * *

"Oo, gorna show some leg for the locals, Pretty Rita?" The pleasantly inebriated UN officer nearly fell off his bar stool as he playfully reached for his hostess.

"Don't yer wish, Love?" Rita countered with a hearty chuckle. She simultaneously twirled beyond his reach, pushed her wind-blown caftan back down over her meaty calves, and lifted her gaze to the Kyrenia Mountains looming above her seaside establishment. The statuesque, outgoing Brit expatriate was grateful for the unseasonably warm air current coming down from southern Europe and swirling off the slopes of the mountain range paralleling the Turkish-held northern coast of the island.

The chill of the previous week had promised an early snow on the higher Troodos peaks in the Greek zone to the south. But Rita's on the Rocks, a favorite seaside retreat for the island's foreign diplomatic corps, which had free access between the Greek and Turkish zones of the island, was enjoying a late-season revival of business far into November. The attraction of Rita's for the local foreign community, if the great earth mother herself was discounted, was its gathering of all of the essentials for life in a neat little package. It offered food, drink, sun, nonjudgmental conviviality, and the Mediterranean. And it was located outside the travel pattern of most of the tourists who visited northern Cyprus' Turkish Cypriot Republic.

Under the threat that this could be the last good sun tan day of the year for all but the northern European tourists, who would be out soaking up the ultraviolet rays even on New Year's Day, members of the diplomatic corps had poured into Rita's like lemmings. Now the sun was disappearing behind the westernmost Kyrenia Range peak. This caused a chill to set in across the pool area and prompted most of the families to either start packing up for the return journey to Nicosia, or to huddle closer into the bar kiosk. The exodus from Rita's was heralded by the last of the snorkelers coming up from the sea.

Most likely as a reaction to the inevitable closing of the season, the bar was becoming the boisterous beacon for most of those who remained. After carefully assessing the probable consumption capabilities of the remaining patrons, who were huddled in the closing circle of waning sunlight around the bar, Rita hauled her bosoms onto the bar top, grabbed up six empty liquor bottles, and headed toward the kitchen hut. As she entered the shadows of the grape arbor-covered restaurant patio that jutted off from the pool and bar area, she detected the murmurings of two men she'd forgotten were still lingering over an early dinner. The waves lapping on the side of the rocky slope overlooking the snorkeling cove made the men's unusually intense conversation unintelligible.

Rita started toward her guests for a little chat. The older of the two, the tall, gangling, red-haired, and unpressed Alec Stuart was a

23

favorite of hers. If she hadn't known that he was a political officer with the British high commission, the British embassy on Cyprus, she would have taken him for a free-soul, beach bum. Just her sort of man. She would've been uncustomarily speechless if she'd known that he was also the senior British intelligence agent on the island.

Something in the way they were hunched over their table and casting furtive looks at the bar brought Rita up short. If she didn't know about Stuart's real profession, she certainly had her suspicions of his tablemate's purposes on the island. In contrast to Stuart, the American embassy officer, Paul Conte—political officer by name, although Rita suspected his responsibilities were much more secretive than that—looked very fit and official, and, in Rita's not so humble opinion, always seemed ready to be fired off toward any danger.

The mere thought of what those two might be up to caused Rita to veer off toward the kitchen. En route, she tossed the empty liquor bottles into a large barrel and patted a wisp of stray jasmine back into the foliage of the arbor above the passage to the kitchen. Usually when these two were here at the same time, they were squared off and trading jibes. Whenever this happened, those gathered around the pool and bar playfully admonished Stuart to be careful of the well-muscled, tightly strung American. To Rita's view, however, in all probability Stuart would have been capable of folding Conte in two with little effort and stuffing the cocky American in his back pocket if he so desired.

Something in the aura of their meeting today caused Rita to sense that this wasn't a good time for her to bring attention to the two by engaging them in her usual boisterous banter. But she was afraid that others would notice them, and her regard for Stuart caused her to catch his eye as she moved into the shadows of the kitchen and to incline her head toward the bar area with a warning glance.

"I guess we're not going to be treated to the world according to Rita this evening," the American observed.

"That's just as well," Stuart concurred. "I agreed it would be a good idea for us to compare notes on our current cases. But I didn't agree it would be wise for us to do it here. This is one of the few places we can meet in public, and we've been careful not to be chums here. We may be making an unwise spectacle of ourselves. It's a shame you can't act like you're drunk."

"As opposed to you, of course," Conte retorted only half jokingly. "You're usually so pissed that all the regulars think that's your constant condition."

Stuart ignored the jibe. "What I wanted to check with you today was whether your embassy was also seeing a greater influx of Russians to the island. The Russians we're interested in are accompanied by large sums of cash of questionable origin. We're also concerned with the increase in the importation of European and East Asian 'artistes' and 'maids.' We're sure that's creating a prostitution situation that Cyprus has never encountered before. It's already bad enough that the island is divided by a belligerent border between the Greek and Turkish populations and that both sides blame us for their bloody political division in 1974. We don't need Russians or increased international crime to be thrown into the mix."

"Yeah," Conte answered. "I had lunch with Takis Koniotis today. Just as I was telling him that his newly created International Investigations Unit was probably about to be inundated with a crime wave, he was called away to investigate the death of a Russian monk.

25

These poor Cypriots. They've led such a crime-free existence, which is a good thing, since the island is divided between the Greeks and the Turks. But, both ethnic groups are so stubborn and so filled with mutual hatred that I don't think there's a chance in hell they'd cooperate to counter a mutual crime threat. It'll be a real headache to keep major crime under control here such as the Russian mafia is capable of, and probably is already putting into motion, and these naïve Cypriots are ripe for the plucking."

"The killing of a Russian priest, you say? I hope that doesn't keep Koniotis's unit from noticing Sergey Stepanov. He appeared here in the first wave of well-funded entrepreneurs from Moscow and has already established ties to the upper levels of the Greek Cypriot business community. Like many of the others, he came with enough cash to put together an off-shore charter tour and tourist agency, which is already offering four return-trip flights weekly between Moscow and Cyprus. Having established his own transportation, it's going to be a real headache to control his activities."

"Yes, we've already focused in on Mr. Stepanov ourselves," said Conte. "I agree he's going to need extra attention. We've tried to check up on him. But it's like he just dropped into Cyprus out of the sky. We haven't been able to find him in any of the intelligence data banks. Even Moscow has refused to verify his existence—this despite the fact he frequently travels around Europe and Russia on a Russian passport and has been observed entering the Russian embassy in Nicosia far more than his business interests would seem to warrant. And now we've found that Stepanov may be even better networked and protected than we imagined."

"What do you mean?" Stuart leaned in closer.

26

"I was at Larnaca airport this morning, and I saw Stepanov waltzing through the terminal, big as life—with Eleni Piccard on his arm."

Stuart gave out a low whistle.

Eleni Piccard was the Greek Cypriot widow of a French businessman who had spread his family's shipping empire to Cyprus in the mid-1960s and who'd disappeared during the 1974 conflict that had divided the island into Greek and Turkish zones. She was one of the richest and most powerful people in Cyprus. In addition to the shipping companies, her conglomerate owned several major tourist hotels on the southern coast and the country's only large handicrafts export company.

"Well, I don't know about you," said Conte, "But I've tried to stay out of her way since we helped implicate her in those drug and arms smuggling, money laundering, and terrorism cases earlier this year. I didn't have any more to do with revealing how she was manipulating that situation for her own gain than Caitlyn Spencer did. But, whereas Caitlyn and Eleni are still real pals, I got burned badly by her reaction to my involvement."

"Me too," agreed Stuart. "I'm just glad she didn't use her clout here to get me recalled to London. She's just a little slip of a woman, but she sure has a bad temper and is prone to wreak serious vengeance. And now, if Stepanov is moving under her protection—"

The discussion was thrown into suspension by a general hubbub that was rising from the bar area and that did not, in any way, resemble the progressive marinating of the regular party closers. The attention of the bar group was directed down toward the cove. Both Stuart and Conte focused on the commotion, but Conte was the first

27

to react. In an instant he was over the low wall running between the restaurant patio and the edge of the rocks going down to the sea. Stuart followed at a somewhat less explosive pace—but well before those at the bar started down the pathway leading from the pool to the sea.

The body was being churned up against the rocks at the base of the slope into the sea. She was on her back, her long, blonde hair fanned out all around her head and catching the last rays of the sun as it set behind the Kyrenia Mountains.

With effort, Conte and Stuart hauled the body high enough on the slope so that no further harm could be done by the surf and the jagged rocks. However, enough damage had already been done that the two could not readily discern the cause of death.

This is really strange, Conte was thinking to himself somewhat nonsensically.

The appearance of a drowned woman with long, blonde hair in an almost-deserted Turkish Cypriot cove was certainly strange. But this wasn't what had triggered Conte's thought. He was more perplexed by why a tall, very dead blonde, who had been washed up on these rocks, was decked out in an elaborate belly dancing costume.

As he was mulling this thought, the first wave of the bar crowd was reaching the water's edge, and an hysterical scream was suddenly knifing through the still of the night.

* * * *

"Knife wounds. Very deep and broad knife wounds," concluded the all-business Turkish Cypriot police official, Safa Ziya, shortly after she had arrived on the scene. By now night had fallen, and the body of the blonde woman had been laid out on a lounge chair and pulled behind the kiosk bar, where the multicolored lights in the rafters set a garish scene.

"She hasn't been in the water long, it would seem. She must have been washed down from the direction of Kyrenia. Interesting dress. Looks like a costume from one of the cheap clubs up the coast. She doesn't look like a Cypriot—either Turkish or Greek. Now, Mr. Stuart and Mr. Conte, while we're waiting for the medical examiner, suppose you tell me again how it came that two foreign diplomats were involved in such an intriguing find here in the Turkish Cypriot Republic."

Chapter Two

Maria Solonos, Takis Koniotis's young deputy, was blinded by the morning sun exploding through her superior's office window. Although the weather did cool off somewhat in the winter months in Cyprus, the sun seemed more, not less intense when the air turned crisp. At first she thought no one was in the untidy room, as there was a sharply defined light-dark edge between the beam of sunlight bouncing off a multitude of dust particles and the shadows beyond the light's reach. Then, as she recovered from the dazzling light, Maria could see a familiar, handsome profile, a bent arm, a creased pant leg, and a trail of cigarette smoke just at the edge of the window sill.

"Are you staring at that huge Turkish flag painted on the mountainside again, Takis?" she asked accusingly. "You know that's there just to bait us because we can't visit the north. I know that it's especially hard for those families, like yours, that were driven from the northern coast, but brooding about it only serves the Turks' purposes. And just look at you," she continued. "You didn't shave this morning. You're not thinking of trying to grow a beard again, are you? I doubt the minister will consider that appropriate for the first chief of the newly formed International Investigations Division—even if your new American wife likes the idea."

Koniotis's chair whirled back around from the window with an outraged squeak. But the view of the monumental piles of paper and folders on his desk was only a little less depressing than the teasing symbol of the Turks' occupation of the northern third of his Greek homeland.

"Hell, is there any way I can get out of this seminar? And, no, I'm not trying to grow a beard; I came straight here from Kykko monastery yesterday. I was too busy to go home last night."

"Seminars like this go with your new, fancy title—and much better you than me." Maria Solonos lifted two law books from the only chair in the room other than Koniotis's own complaining swivel chair, blew a cloud of dust from their surfaces, and deftly pushed them back into place in a nearby bookcase. Giving the seat a cursory swipe with a file she had brought into the room, she deposited her petite frame on the chair, and, with a satisfying plop, added the file to the mound on the desk in front of her colleague.

"When it rains, it pours," she pronounced in a prim tone. "Our case file is building quickly, but I very much doubt the minister will let you wriggle away from leading our group to the bicommunal seminar. If you weren't going, he'd have to go himself, and you know that's not going to happen. Tell me what happened at Kykko, and I'll fill you in on a new case that came in while you were playing in the Troodos snow yesterday. Soon you won't have a thought to give to your meeting Monday with the Canadians and Turkish Cypriots at the Ledra Palace."

Koniotis stood, stretched, and leaned against the window molding. He kept the flagrant mountainside painting in his peripheral vision while he told his deputy about the Russian priest. The strong light on his half-turned face caused Maria to be struck with how tired her friend and boss looked. Although he was not yet thirty-two, the formation over the past year of a special police unit to deal with all crime in the Cypriot Republic that in any way involved a foreign national had taken its toll on his typically Greek classic, dark good looks. Maria found herself half wondering whether his recent marriage to a foreign woman with a strong will and her own professional position was benefiting him. She hadn't thought of him marrying anyone who wouldn't completely subordinate her needs to his—which had been the principle reason Maria hadn't tried to land him. He was such a perfectionist and was persistent and ruthless in his pursuit of criminals, which was, of course, why he had risen to the position of chief of this unit. Well, no, she thought, the reason he had risen in the ranks had resulted more from his brilliant hunches and the thorough research of his work team on several high-profile cases. And the reason he was now chief of this unit was because its creation had been his idea from the beginning. Since the Cypriots themselves, representing a small, long-insulated population of strongly family-centered culture, were extraordinarily law abiding, nearly half of all the serious crime in the republic did involve a foreign element.

Takis briefly and efficiently filled Maria in on the murder of the Russian Orthodox priest at Kykko and on the victim's mysterious discussion with the abbot about having seen someone he eventually remembered the priest having called "the Knife."

"Stabbed, you say?" noted Maria. "Was the knife found?"

"You mean the murder weapon, not the suspected perpetrator, I presume? No, nothing was found at the scene that would have made such an entry wound. The lab reported about an hour ago that the weapon might have been some sort of special hunting knife. We did find some interesting evidence at the scene, however. The priest was clutching a scrap of expensive material with an American tailor's label attached to it. Chances are good he pulled it off his attacker. The nationality of the victim and a foreign connection to what little evidence we found tosses this case on our pile. You'll need to check with the American embassy and see what you can find out about the tailor's customers."

"Done," Maria responded as she made a note on her pad. "Speaking of our caseload, just to be on the safe side, perhaps we should have the pattern of the priest's wounds checked against those of the boatman involved in the Spanish diplomat's death."

"Another death connected with the Alvarez de Toledo case?"

"Yes, that's what the new file I brought in is about. I guess the case wasn't already spectacular enough. It's not every day a former Spanish general, who was an ambassador to Cyprus in the mid-1970s, dives into the façade of the Coral Bay resort hotel when his parasail line snaps. But while you were in the mountains yesterday, I was out on the Paphos resort coast connecting what we thought might have been a recreational accident with murder. Just two days after the Spaniard died, the boatman who had been leading out the parasail line in that incident was found knifed to death in a speedboat at anchor in the hotel's cove. Our people examined the line again and found that it had been cut nearly through at the point at which it had snapped. So, now we have another high-profile case . The ambassador's death now looks like murder, and it looks like the boatman was involved in—"

She was interrupted by the ringing of the telephone. When Koniotis replaced the receiver, he reached out for the folder Maria had brought into the room and placed it inside the Kykko murder folder that had been resting on his desktop.

"That was the medical examiner. We don't have to ask them to compare the knife wounds on the Russian and the boatman. The examiner noticed the similarities himself and has done the comparison. The wounds are very distinctive—and identical. It looks very much like we might be dealing with a serial killer here. You'd best start setting up a special team to tackle these killings."

Maria rose to leave. "Don't let this upset your weekend plans, though," Takis said with a deceptively light tone as she reached the door. He was becoming increasingly aware that Maria seemed always to be in the office and to be churning away on her research. Since his recent marriage, he had started to become aware of his tendency to ignore the needs of others and to drive himself and his colleagues too hard.

Maria flashed him a questioning look.

"I won't be working this case round the clock myself," Koniotis said. "My wife is dragging me to a couple of concerts in the next few days. And if I can't get out of this police force bicommunal seminar next week, I won't be doing much case solving for a while." His voice trailed off. He hated the thought that he'd be doing less than his full share of work on this developing case.

"Thanks, Takis," Maria responded. "But don't worry about me this weekend. I have a date."

"Anyone I know?"

"Probably not. He's a professional actor and you're a cultural Philistine. You can meet and inspect him, though. We'll see you at the concert Tuesday night. Your wife and I have already compared social schedules."

After she had left, Koniotis returned to stewing about the seminar he didn't want to attend. This was all his wife's fault. She'd been pressuring him to be open to dialogue with his Turkish Cypriot counterparts across the buffer zone. Therefore, when his superiors had asked him to attend a bicommunal seminar on police methods that was being sponsored in the coming two weeks by the Canadian high commission, Koniotis had accepted in a moment of weakness. It had been a moment of insanity.

Well, he hadn't had two murders of foreigners to solve when he had agreed to attend the seminar. Koniotis grimaced as he remembered that he had not only agreed to attend but also that his superiors had then stuck him with the responsibility for coordinating Greek Cypriot participation with the Canadian political officer, John Dunsford. Grimly, Koniotis reached for the telephone to cancel his attendance.

He jabbed at the buttons on the telephone. Talking to each other is a waste of time. Nothing the Turks say can be trusted, he thought bitterly.

But then he cut the line just as it was beginning to ring. That was exactly what he had said that had prompted his wife to argue that life here would never get better as long as the two communities perpetuated their differences.

"Oh, Hell!" he exclaimed to the stone walls. Then to himself: "I haven't changed my mind, but I can't face off the wife without showing I've made an effort."

He gently returned the telephone receiver to its cradle. As his concentration deepened with the restful creaking rhythm of his swivel chair, he started digging for the two foreigner murder cases files that had inexplicably already disappeared from sight on his desk.

* * * *

Safa Ziya shivered as she exited the police vehicle after it had plowed down toward the coast as far as the rocky slope would permit. She was about as far away from civilization in northern Cyprus as one could get. Cold wind was whipping across the narrow Karpas Peninsula, which jutted out of the northeastern corner of the island toward the great underbelly of the Turkish mainland. The isolated strand of sea oat -laced scrabble rock that led down to the blue-green Mediterranean looked starkly pure and peaceful. But the memories it brought back to Safa were just too painful.

It was in just such a setting that she had left her family and departed for America to take up her American embassy-sponsored berth at the University of Texas at Austin. She had still been working hard at her studies when the troubles of 1974 hit in Cyprus that had left her with no close relatives, all lost in the brutal and swift pogroms that the two major ethnic communities on the island had wreaked on each other. By the time she had returned to the Turkish zone of Cyprus, she was all alone in the world—a war-scarred orphan who was not a beauty, who was a little too heavy, and who was terribly self-conscious about a slightly crippled leg.

The detective who had driven her to the scene exited the police car and pointed out the old abandoned Greek Orthodox chapel peeking out of the tall grass at the edge of the rocky beach below. The windows of the building had once been boarded up. But most of the boards had been pried off over the past two decades and lay helter-skelter on the ground below the sills, their jutting rusty nails offering better protection against unwelcome entry than the boards on the windows had ever done. Many of the tiles had come off the small rooftop dome, and a corner of the roof had collapsed. Another policeman was stationed at the thick wooden door that now hung precariously on one hinge.

Safa Ziya shivered once, pulled up the lapels of her coat to try to offer her ears protection from the raw wind racing across the sea from Turkey, and then started making her way between boulders and stunted fig trees toward the chapel. When she reached the beaten-down area of weeds and gravel in front the church's door, she looked up, only to find herself shivering once more.

For the hundreds of years that this little chapel had served the local Greek Orthodox residents, it's stucco walls had been ceremoniously whitewashed twice a day. This ritual quite obviously had ended when the Turkish forces swept onto the northern beaches in 1974, however, as no one had bothered to whitewash the walls since that time to erase the telltale signs of dried blood along the wall next to the chapel's door. This had obviously been one of many mass execution sites along this forlorn section of the coast.

Ziya, her thoughts very much on the her lost family, almost turned to stumble back to the car. But she was a professional, and she was the chief homicide investigator for the Turkish Cypriot Republic.

So, she squared her shoulders, acknowledged the terse, but respectful, welcome of the policeman stationed at the door, and, beckoning him to follow her, entered the building.

The chapel was flooded with light coming from an open aperture at the apex of the dome, between the loose boards on the windows, and from the hole in the corner of the ceiling. Ziya's first impression was of the brilliant colors of what was left of ancient frescoes dancing around all four walls. What hit her next, however, was the unmistakable stench of advanced human decay.

She dug frantically in her coat pockets for a scarf or handkerchief, for anything she could cover her nose with, but before she could pull anything out, the policeman handed her his own handkerchief. Acknowledging his gift with a quick smile, Safa rewarded him with a gesture to wait for her outside, and she was suddenly alone with the moldering artist.

She assumed that the body of what seemed to be a man who had been dead for several days was an artist. He had fallen on top of a small pile of seemingly aged slabs of plaster, some of which were painted with figures that remarkably matched the fragments of frescoes that still adhered to the chapel walls. In his fall, the artist had also scattered tubes of paints and paint brushes.

She examined the body from a short distance long enough to conclude that she recognized the victim and that she probably knew why he had been here if not why he had died here, and then she joined the policeman outside the door. As she exited, she waved the just-arrived forensics team into the building. They had come better equipped to work within the close confines with a decaying body than she had.

"Who found Kleist?" she asked the policeman.

He looked startled. He'd spent considerable time trying to pull information out of the locals to determine who the victim was. In the end, he'd come to terms with the body and pulled the man's wallet to determine that the victim was Dietrich Kleist. But the inspector had known who the victim was in an instant. Her reputation in the department must be well deserved.

"A laborer had been passing earlier today and noticed the door to the church had been forced open. He knew it was against the law to go into any of the Greek churches, but he knew this one was rumored to have famous ancient frescoes in it, so he decided to check to see if anyone had left anything that might be worth something. He found the body and reported immediately to the local military post. He evidently thought it would be better that he be taken for a possible thief than for a murderer. The people around here are terrified of the mainland Turkey soldiers at the military post. But, if I may ask, could you tell me how you knew the victim's name was Dietrich Kleist? Here is his wallet. I found it beside the body."

"Oh, Kleist is well known to us," said Ziya. "He has been arrested several times on suspicion of forging artifacts for sale to foreign art collectors. From the looks of his work in there, he was very good at his forgeries. It was just a matter of time before we caught him. But it looks like his time ran out. I didn't have time to notice. Any idea how he died? I suppose it's too much to hope for that it was a heart attack."

"I doubt it, inspector. It looks like there were at least two knife wounds in his back. He probably didn't even see the attacker.

His back was to the door, and he may have been focused entirely on his painting when he died."

"Well, there isn't any more we can do here today," said Ziya as she pulled her coat tighter about her. The lengthening of the late afternoon shadows had heightened the effect of the cold wind whipping in across the beach. "Please tell the lab people that I'll need a medical report on the victim by tomorrow morning, if possible."

"Yes, inspector, I'll tell them. But they probably won't be pleased that they'll have to work late."

"I'm sure when you've told them the victim is a foreigner, they'll be glad to do the work this evening. They know how sensitive the police chief is about foreigners. In any case, they won't be alone. I'll probably be all evening in the Kyrenia area myself, trying to find out about a dead blonde." She didn't notice the startled look on the policeman's face as she struggled back up through the sea to the waiting car.

Ziya entered her office in the Turkish sector of Nicosia the next morning, pleased with what she had been able to discover the previous evening in Kyrenia and anxious to immerse herself in the Kleist case. She was also expecting the medical tests on the body that had washed up on the cove at Rita's to be awaiting her.

I hope this doesn't reflect a trend, Safa thought, as she tried to slip into her desk without being noticed by her annoying and always nosey office mate. It was very unusual for there to be one, let alone two, pending suspicious death investigations in the Turkish zone that involved foreign nationals.

Safa was irritated to find that neither of the medical tests were on her desk.

An explosive cough from the other desk, accompanied by a hawking sound, broke Safa's train of thought and added to her irritation. She pushed herself up from her desk with a deep sigh and clumped over to the window on her uneven legs. She opened the shutter a bit and looked out on the light traffic circling the Turkish war memorial outside her building. But this only reminded her of the family she had lost without a trace. To avoid the memories, she reviewed what was known in the, possibly related, recent deaths of the two foreigners.

Another revolting sound from the perpetual patient across the room brought Safa back to the present. She felt so isolated in her office. She was generally given the most difficult and sensitive criminal cases to handle but was stuck sharing a small office with this oaf, hadn't received a promotion in years, and was never consulted on police business beyond her own cases. She suspected that all of these indignities resulted from her gender. If mainland Turkey could tolerate having a female prime minister, why couldn't the supposedly more sophisticated Turkish Republic of Cyprus tolerate a female senior police inspector? It seemed that her only ally in police headquarters was the senior research assistant, Tansul. Tansul, knowing ability and interesting cases when she saw them, had voluntarily attached herself to Ziya and was too powerful in the department, being the sister of the chief of police, to be forced to broaden her range of support.

Safa was only really in touch with her work when she was out on the street, free of this stifling office with the male police inspector who hovered silently and disapprovingly on the other side of the small room. Safa had never fully comprehended the function of the man who had shared her space for several years, who had never responded to her with a complete sentence or with any useful information, and who managed to maintain a disgustingly noisy head cold no matter the season.

For an ever-so-brief moment the two office mates made eye contact across the small room. Embarrassed by this, both quickly diverted their eyes and dove into the paperwork on their desktops in a pretense of busyness. Safa labeled a file for the Kleist case and dug a wad of notes out of her purse. She was digging around on her desk for the file on the woman found at Rita's when Tansul entered the room with exaggerated stealth and dropped two sheets of paper in her lap. Safa's office companion looked up with mild curiosity, an effort that caused him to trumpet a sneeze, clamor for a tissue, and abandon all further interest in Tansul and Safa.

In reaching for the material Tansul had delivered, the notes Safa had taken from her purse fluttered to the floor.

"What are these?" asked Tansul, as she helped to retrieve the scraps of papers.

"Notes on my queries in Kyrenia last night," Safa answered. "I was able to find out quite a bit about the victim at Rita's. Her name was Gina Bertelli, an Italian resident of Kyrenia. The belly-dancing costume she had been wearing helped me trace her to Anti's tavern, the seaside restaurant east of Kyrenia. The owner of Anti's confirmed that Bertelli had been working there recently and that, even though she knew next to nothing about real belly dancing, had been a favorite of the growing number of Russian visitors to the north. She's resided on the island for years and didn't seem to have had financial problems. Her belly-dancing stint appears to be the result of boredom more than financial need. Rather strange that she was here, however. We don't have many Italian residents."

"I'll start making foreign queries," Tansul replied in sotto voce to remain beyond the hearing of the official across the room, "but without modern computers and no international connections beyond mainland Turkey, it will take a while."

"I understand the difficulty, Tansul. Thanks for offering to try. Now, what have you brought me?"

"These haven't been released outside the chief's office yet," Tansul whispered conspiratorially. "But I thought you needed to see them as soon as possible. Here on this one, see that it says the woman was killed with a knife that makes a particularly wide wound. Something like a large-bladed butcher knife."

Safa looked up quizzically. "Thank you, Tansul. But why the hush hush about that?"

"The chief is trying to determine just who needs to know this, although you'll surely be left in charge of the cases and will receive the official reports later today. It's potentially quite disturbing, especially for the tourist industry. Look here at the other medical report. The German artist was killed with the same sort of knife."

"Oh, Damn!" Safa exclaimed. "A killer specializing in foreign victims, and I've got to attend that worthless bicommunal seminar. I wonder if I can get out of that." Ignoring the snort from across the room, she reached for the telephone.

* * * *

Mehmet Tosun was nervously fingering his worry beads, as he sat cheek to jowl with piles of Turkish rugs, copperware, fake ivory, silver, and porcelain pseudo antiquities. This dubious treasure trove

43

was ensconced in the small office behind his equally stuffed Nicosia shop near the Turkish side of the only checkpoint between the Greek Cypriot and Turkish Cypriot zones. Roentgen was late. It annoyed Tosun that the man's tardiness should bother him, since he wasn't sure he wanted Roentgen to come at all.

The man mountain shifted his weight to the alternate buttock, took another hefty drag on his Turkish cigarette, and tried to pull his heavy wool suit away from his sweaty body to induce greater air circulation. His presence was only slightly less offensive to the olfactory senses in late November than it would have been in the same setting in high August.

"What a shitty business," Tosun muttered, carefully forming each distinct syllable. "I can't make money without Roentgen, but one of us is for the desert. How can I survive this time?"

Finally Roentgen arrived and was obsequiously welcomed by Tosun's nephew, who was simultaneously looking up and down the street and putting a "closed" sign on the door. Leaving then, the boy locked the door firmly behind him and slipped into the shadows of Memdoluh Asaf Street.

Helmut Roentgen in the flesh wasn't at all what one would've imagined based on the fear his coming had instilled in the Turkish antique shop owner. He was tall, pencil thin, and elegantly dressed in a silk suit. He had an aristocratic bearing that allowed him to move with ease and with flawless, fluid motion. His hands were those of an artist, and he flashed Tosun a boyish smile that could melt the hearts of the marble lions guarding the entrance to the New York public library.

Tosun hopped forward with short steps, a wide, silly grin on his face and both of his arms extended in anticipation of a brotherly

44

bear hug. Roentgen deftly maneuvered a string of copper pots between the shop owner and himself and smoothly changed the shared greeting into a slight bow of the head.

"I'm sorry. I cannot stay long, my friend." The visitor's chilly voice belied the sentiment expressed. "I just wanted to be sure that you realized the American woman will be coming here and that she seems to have become suspicious."

Tosun started to comment at length but was expertly cut off in midsentence.

"That's all I wanted to convey," Roentgen continued in even tones. "I want you to tell her to return home and that her fears are all unfounded. Tell her that we, in fact, find her insinuations somewhat hurtful. If that does not stave off her ire, inform her that she should remain here and you will try to locate me."

He turned to go, but then turned back. "You are to tell her that you understand I am in Vienna, trying to settle—at my own expense—the delivery of the rest of the icons. Under no circumstances are you to tell her I've been in Cyprus this week. Can I trust you to tell her, my friend?"

The last statement, accompanied by a particularly piercing look, did not convey quite the friendly tone the words in which it was voiced would indicate.

Tosun started to launch into another commentary, but Roentgen was already through the door and whistling down the street. The shopkeeper did not find the sounds of Mozart bouncing off the confining walls of the Turkish Cypriot souk at all comforting.

Roentgen didn't even ask about Kleist's last consignment. That was all he could rave about in his previous visit, thought the

45

Lebanese merchant, who was a genuine Turk on about the same par that most of the goods he displayed were genuine antiques. It was more than a slightly bemused shopkeeper who waddled back to his cubbyhole—and to his well-worn worry beads.

Chapter Three

Waiting until the last possible moment, Takis Koniotis wearily trudged away from the Greek Cypriot checkpoint and toward the former Ledra Palace hotel, now locked within the buffer zone of the belligerent border running through the world's only remaining divided capital city. Day tourists and the few foreign residents who are privileged to travel back and forth between the Greek Cypriot and Turkish Cypriot zones of the island could do so only at a single, heavily guarded access point across the Green Line buffer zone. This term had been acquired from the color of the grease pencil the negotiators had used to establish a cease-fire line following the 1974 Turkish invasion of Cyprus. In their transit between very different worlds, the travelers passed between the sixteenth-century Venetian walls of the old city of Nicosia and the forecourt of the once-glorious Ledra Palace Hotel.

Despite years of plundering neglect and of alternately being the prize and the target of war, the long, four-story building still stood as the grand example of British colonial Middle Eastern architecture. But now, rather than being host to royalty and the nerve center for upper-crust official, business, and social life in the British colonial capital of Nicosia, the building served a quite different, if equally momentous, role. It now served as the dormitory for whatever UN member-supplied contingent was currently assigned to patrol the Green Line sector running through Nicosia's old walled city. And its reading room, long the venue for pre-independence negotiations and treaty signings among the British colonial and indigenous Greek and Turkish communities, continued, under the name of the Treaty Room, to be the only place where, under the supervision and protection of the UN forces, representatives of the Greek and Turkish communities came together. Here, the few understandings and agreements that painfully inched toward better relations between the two estranged Cypriot communities were hammered out and inked.

Koniotis hated coming to the Ledra Palace hotel. He hated it because it reminded him of a British colonialist past, with the British just the latest in a long line of occupiers going back through the Ottoman Turks, the Venetians, the medieval Crusaders, the Ptolomies, and the Romans—and that was only its recent history. He hated it because it bore the marks of the Greeks' failure to prevail against the Turkish invaders. But most of all, he hated it for its continued use in outsiders' doomed attempts to get the Greek and Turkish communities to coexist.

His hatred of being forced into the position of attending this bicommunal seminar increased his anger as he walked through the gate of the hotel's compound wall, draped with concertina wire slowly being devoured by brilliantly colored bougainvillea. His anger only increased more when he looked up and saw the pock marks of bullet tracings crisscrossing the building's stone-block face. His anger did not decrease, although he managed to clothe it, when he came face to face with the seminar's host, who had been standing at the building's entrance and looking anxiously about for stray attendees.

John Dunsford, as the recently posted Canadian high commission political officer (and, not incidentally, chief intelligence officer at the mission), was the one responsible for the success of the seminar. The once-handsome face of the fiftyish, balding, bespectacled, long-suffering civil servant betrayed a twitch of middle-aged professional burnout as its owner unsuccessfully tried to suppress a sigh.

"There you are, Takis. I'd just about given up on you. Everyone else is here. We had the usual problem of the Turkish attendees being able to get through their checkpoint, but we finally managed to get them here."

"How nice," Koniotis replied tightly.

His disposition did not improve as he was drawn into the cold, stark Treaty Room. The lighting was gloomy, not helped by the enclosed windows, which had been bricked in years previously when bomb-throwing had been instituted as a favorite form of registering disapproval of peace talks by one faction or the other. Everything else was cold, roughly quarried and pitted ochre-colored stone: the walls, floors, and ceiling. A gigantic fireplace dominated one end of the room. The tension in the chamber was palpable. The Greek Cypriot attendees were huddled to the left of the fireplace. The Turkish Cypriots were to the right. Sitting behind a table immediately in front of the fireplace were the Canadian high commissioner and the team of seminar leaders, who'd been flown in from Ottawa to share the latest techniques of police investigation.

"Today will be a short session taken up with introductions of the participants, the seminar leaders, and the material," Dunsford announced cheerily to the room. After introducing the high commissioner, who spoke at monotonously great length of the Canadian government's and his own respect for the efficient police forces of both communities and good wishes for bicommunal efforts, Dunsford took the floor. "Now we'll introduce the two senior police inspectors present from the two sides of Cyprus, and perhaps they can briefly talk to us about what they hope this seminar will accomplish for their own police force. Greek Cypriot chief of the International Investigations Unit, Takis Koniotis."

Koniotis had not realized he had been expected to give a speech, and he was in no mood to do so. He stood and said, "Thank you, High Commissioner and Mr. Dunsford, for sponsoring this seminar on the latest police investigation techniques. I expect it to be very informative." Then he sat back down.

The silence in the room was stifling. Dunsford had obviously expected Koniotis to talk for several minutes and found himself struggling to down a swallow of hot coffee so that he could regain the floor.

"Yes, well, thank you very much, Takis." Beaming at the leadership team, he continued, "I'm sure our facilitators will, indeed, be very informative. There's much we can all learn about the most modern police techniques and about international cooperation in tracking and apprehending criminals. And, with that, I'll introduce Ms. Safa Ziya, senior investigator with the Turkish Cypriot police, who has a fine reputation of her own as a past professor of the theory of investigative techniques at the University of Texas, Austin, in the United States. Ms. Ziya."

Dunsford had realized that Ziya had been quite angry when she had been held up at the Turkish Cypriot checkpoint, but for the first time he now noticed that she was still highly agitated, her ire only increasing as she spoke.

"I too, on behalf of the Interior Ministry of the Turkish Cypriot Republic, also thank you and the Canadian high commission for sponsoring this seminar. This is my first attendance at a bicommunal event, however, and I certainly hope that my experience in being admitted to the buffer zone is not indicative of how such events are conducted. The guards at the checkpoint had received no instructions to let us through. Obviously, there was a breakdown in communications somewhere. Now, if you and our minister don't really care all that much if we attend this damn seminar, I know that I, for one, can certainly find something else . . ."

Everyone in the room was mesmerized by Ziya's unexpectedly heated, straightforward, and baldy worded speech. Everyone, that is, except Takis Koniotis, who appeared to be totally preoccupied. He seemed not to have even listened to the introduction of his Turkish Cypriot counterpart. His lips were moving in silent discussion within himself, as if he had never left his office and was still reviewing the evidence in one of his stubborn cases.

In the end, the opening session of the seminar proved to be even shorter than Dunsford had anticipated.

"I guess that is that," he said to the Canadian high commissioner as they stood at the entrance of the Ledra Palace and tried to maintain a cheery front as they waved away the last of the

51

participants. "I really didn't think this was going to work anyway. The police are the most hard-nosed of the lot. We probably should concentrate on bicommunal sessions with artists and medical people the way the Americans do."

"We're not the Americans," the high commissioner said breezily. "I thought the session went splendidly. Now, if we get any sense of cooperation from these people at all, we can declare a victory. And if the cooperation doesn't get any better, we can always write it up in dispatches just as we want. I think you need to spend your afternoon getting to those stupid bastards in the Turkish Cypriot ministry on not letting their people through the checkpoint. What incompetence. The police can't even pass the documentation of their own people to their own checkpoint."

"Yes sir," Dunsford said with a tight smile. But the smile faded as soon as the high commissioner had gotten into his Jaguar and roared through the Greek Cypriot checkpoint. Today's session had, in fact, gone just as Dunsford had hoped, as well, and he had been so sure its collapse would put an end to the whole scheme to get the two police departments working together. He had no wish to waste his time on that effort.

* * * *

The sun was retreating behind the dusty peaks that afternoon, quickly bringing a chill to the air in the narrow streets of Lefkara, an old Cypriot mountain village located in the eastern foothills of the Troodos Mountains. The streets of the village were still peppered with tourists, although most of the buses had already started their descent to the arid plain for the half-hour superhighway drive either north to the interior capital city, Nicosia, or south to the industrial seaport of Limassol.

Not far down one of Lefkara's main streets leading from the central Greek Orthodox church one of many alleyways led off to the right. The pathway ran between nearly blank native stone walls, both sides of which could almost be touched by standing in the center of the dirt-covered passage and stretching your arms out. The walls were relieved every ten yards or so by richly carved, highly polished double doors. But the walls, which rose at least two stories, were uniformly windowless. The atmosphere was dark, crisp, and cold. The inevitable question after having passed the third or fourth door was how anyone could move furniture or even the bare necessities of daily life into such an area, where even the smallest car could not go. This thought, invariably, would've barely surfaced just before meeting up with a car that was, amazingly, parked in the alley and making further progress by foot very difficult.

This alley ended in a T junction, beyond which the village once more seemed still as the tomb. Behind a door just beyond the T junction, however, the normal tranquillity of a beautiful little flagstone courtyard, surrounded on three sides by a two-story, single room-deep village house, was being assaulted by a familiar, highly pitched battle of wills. The grapevine-covered wooden balconies above and hibiscus-, oleander-, and bougainvillea-bejeweled flower beds below—in what should have been a haven of quietude—resonated with a distinctly non-Cypriot battle royal.

The Hamiltons, as the neighbors were painfully aware, were at home.

Willie Hamilton—retired Major William J. Hamilton of the British infantry—was sitting in the center of the courtyard and precisely in the center of a rush-seated and carved village chair. He was stripping pink blossoms from a nearby oleander bush and lobbing them at a large, precisely positioned olive oil jar, as if they were hand grenades. It was obvious that he knew how to lob real hand grenades. Precisely placed on the pine trestle table beside him were a newspaper article draft he was proofreading for the third time, a basket of small mountain-grown apples, a nasty-looking hunting knife, and a large, nearly empty bottle of Anglaias brandy. The newspaper article was sustenance for his bank account. The apples were sustenance for his Spartan diet. The hunting knife reflected a long life on campaign in which the major had always had a weapon near at hand. The brandy bottle had made its permanent presence felt shortly after he had married Herself.

Willie twisted his tiny, sinewy, sixty-year-old frame and lifted his striking, blue-gray eyes toward a position on the wall above the oleander bush. The waning light warmed his ruddy cheeks and highlighted his penetrating gaze. This was the laser-sharp stare, matching his laser-sharp wit that enabled him to pierce and pluck out the innermost secrets of those entrapped by his eyes. Perhaps for this reason, he was highly successful in his semiretirement job as the local political affairs columnist for the country's only daily English-language newspaper, the *Cyprus Mail.*

The major let loose with a deep, oft-voiced litany of profane rebuke, which was directed at the balcony overhead on the eastern end of the white-stuccoed building. The latest thrust having gone unparried from the upper floor for a prolonged period, Hamilton's face went even redder. He turned from his attack on the pottery jar to jabbing and carving at his chair arm with the hunting knife in patterns that the original artisan had never imagined. He hated it when Herself strayed from the script and ignored him.

But all of the attention available to Herself, Ginger Hamilton, was just then focused on the model-thin, extremely fair-complexioned, high-cheekboned visage in her mirror. Despite having overachieved her fifty-fifth birthday (she would never tell her age, but everyone guessed it at a glance), Herself was starting to become pleased with what she saw. Ginger was neither purposely ignoring her husband nor changing tactics in their running argument on his favorite subject. Rather, seated, as usual, at her dressing table—her worship center— Mrs. Geneva Nives-Smyth Baldwin Remington Hamilton was now much too involved in the strategic process of achieving the perfect arch to her left eyebrow to continue her bantering with her (latest) husband. Unfortunately, Ginger's eyesight was pretty much shot and she was much too vain to wear eyeglasses, even in private—especially in private—when at her mirror. Therefore, the uneven effect of her surgery on her eyebrows only accentuated her habitual arch expression of slight distaste, an effect she would never realize she had perfected.

She had to hurry the process, which irritated her and only served to make her hand shake. They were already running late for the drive into Nicosia for the choral concert at Famagusta Gate, and Willie hadn't even started to dress. He was still wrapped up in his accusations about her relations with the Greek actor, Antonis.

Ah, Tony. Ginger smiled, which, of course, caused her to turn to admire herself in the mirror. The sight, however, did not please her, and she dug her talons into the makeup brushes in search of the proper scalpel to save the masterpiece.

"He can just lump it about Antonis. We were friends—yes, and lovers. Lovers . . . ," this directed in a stage whisper at the balcony from which the bellowing from below had not abated ". . . long before I ever met *you*."

Soon thereafter, the major, tired of battle, took a last swig of brandy. With a deft swing of his hand, he placed a comma and struck out a phrase in his article draft and tottered toward the outside staircase leading to his own bedroom on the western side of the courtyard.

The neighbors on all sides breathed a sigh of relief. Andreas had made a definite mistake in selling his family's ancestral home to these foreigners after his mother had died. They had made the little courtyard home beautiful, of course—in a foreign, sugarcoated way. Luckily, however, they did not spend much time at their fantasy village retreat. They had made no effort to fold into the Lefkara community. This was just as well. Unending generations of Hamiltons could live in their little make-believe Lefkara courtyard and they would ever remain transient foreigners to the rest of the village.

No one—in Lefkara or Nicosia—would have been surprised to have found the Hamiltons locked in verbal battle. Not that it was not grudgingly acknowledged that they were both champions at the games and were quite entertaining in the right venue. And no one would have been surprised to discover that the favorite topic of the hour was Ginger's infidelities—her past ones, her present ones, her future ones, or her dreamed ones (alas, at her age, now mostly the latter). Those who were perpetually kind noted that the couple had only been fighting like this for the past five years. But at these times there was always some wag present more than willing to point out that they had only been married for four.

Chapter Four

The Hamiltons' red Morris Mini was rocking with the strains of mouth-to-mouth combat as it rolled up to and over the curb directly in front of the main Famagusta Gate entrance. Willie proceeded to park strategically between two stone planters, which had been placed to ensure that no one tried to park where he had just done so. He cheerily popped out of the driver's door, tossed a mutilated card with the word "Press" smudged on it on his dashboard, and moved toward the entrance at the right of the large wooden gates. Ginger Hamilton had already swept from her side of the automobile into the beckoning light of the doorway before Willie had gotten his door shut.

Famagusta Gate, now the cultural arts center for Nicosia, was originally constructed as the most elaborate of three city gates into the medieval walled city. Each gate was commonly known by the name of the city its road led toward. The dry-moated city walls had been constructed in a circular pattern, broken by eleven arrow-pointed bastions, by the Venetians in the late 1560s to protect against an anticipated attack by the Ottoman sultan. Famagusta Gate was the only one of the three entrances to have survived the foreseen assault largely intact. The gate now was (barely) in the Greek zone in the eastern side of the city, just as Paphos Gate was now (barely) in the Greek zone—and near the Ledra Palace Hotel checkpoint—on the western side. The northern-most Kyrenia Gate was fully in the Turkish zone of the city.

The term "gate" was somewhat misleading when applied to Famagusta Gate, as it consisted of a wide passageway sloping gently down from the interior street, through thick stone-covered earthworks, and out to the floor of the dry moat. The interior space had only recently been restored for use as an art gallery, concert, and lecture hall.

On this night, the city's artistic community was out in full force. The Nicosia Singers were performing their autumn concert in the hall formed from a central domed chamber and passageway, paintings by local artists were being exhibited in side chambers, and the British Council was providing a preconcert cocktail party in the exhibit halls.

Willie Hamilton entered directly from the street into the western exhibit hall, too late to see where his wife had escaped to. The first familiar face he focused on was that of Takis Koniotis. The police inspector was engaged in bantering conversation nearby with what the major referred to—sometimes even in his *Cyprus Mail* column—as the diplomatic community's "intelligent" set. This was Willie's own little pun, as he also knew them off the record as representatives of the intelligence organizations of various embassies in town.

"I need to try to pry something out of Koniotis for Thursday's edition," Hamilton thought, as he quickly forgot he'd been looking for his errant wife and got down to business. He was not here to look at artwork or to attend a concert.

As he sidled up to the embassy group, he sized up the characters. Koniotis seemed to be trying to have a side chat with Alec Stuart of the British high commission and Paul Conte of the American embassy, who were dressed in identical shirts and ties. Mikhail Lukenov of the Russian embassy, in turn, was—quite unsuccessfully—trying to hone in on this sotto voce discussion without appearing to do so. Simultaneously, he was trying to act as if he was part of the conversation American embassy defense attaché Sarah Bristow and the Canadian embassy's John Dunsford were having. Neither of them seemed at all aware that the Russian was supposedly part of their discussion.

Slipping a drink from a passing tray as he approached, Hamilton assessed his quarry. An interesting pair, Bristow and Dunsford. I'll have to pay greater attention to those two.

He knew that they had both arrived on the island within the last couple of months. Bristow, to the dismay of the somewhat chauvinistic Cypriots, had been posted to the island as the American embassy's chief military representative—a position that they normally respected even more than that of the American ambassador. A full colonel in the U.S. Artillery Corps, Bristow had obviously been a brilliant and capable officer to have made this rank even in her own armed services. Hamilton had to admit that she intrigued him, not the least because, as he had found out the first time they'd met, Bristow, like him, had, in addition to the artillery training, been trained as a commando—something that no woman had been permitted to do in his day. She was a trim-figured, pleasantly featured brunette, who was always dressed in well-tailored, if not imaginative or even slightly provocative, clothes. Although no delicate beauty, Bristow had a wonderful smile and a fine sense of humor, which did not prevent her, however, from speaking her mind and getting straight to the relevant point. Despite the assumed problems of a woman operating on an equal basis with Greek military officers, it had not taken her long to gain the begrudged respect of her Cypriot and UN counterparts alike.

"But what," Hamilton wondered, "does she see in the Canadian's spy chief? They've been keeping company ever since she arrived. I understand they served in Europe somewhere together. But Dunsford looks like he's well past his prime—and doesn't care."

"Ah, Gentlemen," Willie interjected himself into the Koniotis group, "I didn't realize we had a dress code this evening."

Alec Stuart laughed. "Oh, You must be referring to our matching outfits. Paul and I aren't about to have a cat fight over each assuming we had bought a Paris original for this party. Nothing sinister here; all aboveboard and what—we're just both singing in the choir."

"Well, I'll just scratch the suggestion of a social faux pas out of my report, then," Hamilton bantered back, as he erased an imaginary entry from an imaginary notebook with the very real swizzle stick from his gin and tonic.

Then, taking Koniotis gently by the sleeve and drawing him further into the chamber, he said, "Perhaps you stardust twins won't mind if I take Takis off for a little chat?"

Mikhail Lukenov took one shuffling step toward the departing pair but then drew back in consternation and frustration, as the separate pairs of Stuart and Conte, and Bristow and Dunsford resumed their quiet discussions.

"Takis, about these deaths of Alvarez and the Russian monk—" Hamilton started.

"I'm sorry, Willie. We really don't have much on either of these two cases yet. And you know I release everything I can when I can—but then only to all at the same time."

"But, can you just confirm—?"

"Ah, there she is," Koniotis closed the interrogation, as the pair drifted toward another group that was gathered around a strongly drawn pastel drawing by a member of a dominant Cypriot artistic family, Lonia Efthyvoulou. "I don't believe you've met my wife yet."

Hamilton willingly dropped his original line of questioning for the opportunity to meet Koniotis's newly acquired—and somewhat mysterious—bride. As they approached, he could see she was in the company of a group Hamilton thought of as the "giver and user circle." This group was composed of both those who gave money to the Cypriot arts and archaeological research and those who used the money.

"Darling, I would like you to meet the *Cyprus Mail*'s most tenacious bloodhound, Major William Hamilton," said Koniotis, as he smoothly moved into the group that was gathered around the Efthyvoulou pastel.

"Very pleased to meet you, Mrs. Koniotis."

"Please, call me Caitlyn," answered Takis's wife, with a genuine smile, a soft, silky voice, and a friendly squeeze of the arm.

Hamilton was instantaneously won over to the American. Caitlyn Spencer Koniotis was a stunning, willowy, honey-blonde beauty who, tonight, was wearing a silky, stark-white cocktail dress. The simple lines of the dress belied the admiring glances it and its model were receiving from all corners of the room.

There was a story here, and Hamilton had been dying to meet the new Mrs. Koniotis for the entire month the couple had been married. A highly successful archaeologist, she had arrived in Cyprus a few years earlier on an American grant. She had come to help excavate a Neolithic dig in the little village of Kaliana in the lower reaches of the Solea Valley, which provided the main access from the central plain up to Mount Olympus in the Troodos Mountains. Within weeks she had been responsible, through a process of deductive reasoning, for, indeed, finding a site from the earliest Neolithic period in the lower Solea Valley. But at her initiative they had found what they were looking for at a location on the slope across the valley from Kaliana rather than at the original dig site. She also—and this was what interested Hamilton most—had somehow been involved in the closing down of international crimes networks that had been in operation on the island. These cases had implicated many important people, both in the foreign community and in the upper reaches of Cypriot society.

What really had the foreign community abuzz, however, was that she had seemed to be closely squired by the American, Paul Conte, when she first had arrived, but last month she had unexpectedly married Takis Koniotis.

"Must have been some sort of connection with the international crime cases she was involved in shortly after she got here," thought Hamilton. Koniotis and his division were credited with breaking those cases.

But, those cases were hushed up immediately and effectively. Hamilton's mind continued searching for a story lead. A couple of leading citizens, an American embassy officer, a couple of terrorists, and a UN official had died under suspicious circumstances. In addition, the French ambassador had been hustled out of the country.

As he had turned to frame a question for Mrs. Koniotis, he discovered that she was already being swept away by her husband. He sighed and began to take in the remaining people in this grouping. There were Andriko Visiliou, Cyprus University archaeology professor and director of the Kaliana dig, and his wife. And at the center of the conversation was Justin Chamberlain, a flamboyant American art and artifact collector, and exporter of somewhat questionable repute.

Hamilton's gaze continued around the group, and he suddenly felt a chill go up his spine and beads of perspiration pop out on his brow. At Chamberlain's side, not fully focused on the banter, stood the object of Hamilton's sudden attack of nerves. She and her escort were whispering to each other. Facing Willie was Eleni Piccard. Facing Eleni, with his back to Willie, was her recently acquired companion, Sergey Stepanov.

Ah, the apparent primary mover in the shutdown on information on the investigations last spring, thought Hamilton, as he tried madly to control his apprehension and to contribute to the light cocktail conversation.

As quickly as he could, however—and having eventually spied his wife across the exhibit hall, he abandoned the cocktail party pleasantries and backpeddled from the group.

I want to keep my foreign work permit, he thought grimly as he departed. There is certainly a good story or two in the business activities of Piccard—and especially now that the Russian, with his reported Russian mafia connections, has been added to the equation. But the stakes in this are too high for my blood.

It was not that Hamilton was a coward. In fact, he had recently written a series of articles on the murky connections between certain business interests on the island and Middle East sources, which had led to several threats against his life. None of these threats had slowed him down. But none of these companies had a fraction of the economic and political clout that the Piccard holdings enjoyed in the country.

Hamilton completely forgot about Eleni Piccard, however, as he focused on his own wife and the man to whom she was speaking—not, apparently, in quite the intimate tone he would have expected under the circumstances.

"Demetriou!" Hamilton almost exploded and only the continued chit chat about him assured him that he had not screamed the hated name aloud. He increased his pace as he sliced through the crowd, his fists bunched for action. Of all the nerve. So that's why Ginger wanted to come along to this concert. To meet up with that damned Greek actor.

But something in Ginger's stance arrested his anger as he approached the group. She looked absolutely crushed, although it was apparent she was trying desperately to hide it.

"Darling," Mrs. Hamilton said, "I'd like you to formally meet my old friend, Antonis Demetriou, at last." And then almost as a purposefully disdainful afterthought, " . . . and his . . . date . . . for the evening, Ms. Maria Solonos."

Willie Hamilton, of course, knew that Maria Solonos was an associate of Takis Koniotis. He was furiously struggling with just what to say next, whether as newspaper man or betrayed husband—or triumphant husband of a rejected wandering shrew—when the lights began to flicker to call the concert goers to their seats.

As everyone was moving into the hall, Hamilton chanced to see the Russian, Mikhail Lukenov, almost take a pratfall, as he tried to follow the various Western allies intelligence officials. The sight caused him to stifle a chuckle.

Completely misunderstanding the source of Willie's laugh—which then only added to his mirth—Ginger flashed her umpteenth husband a look that would have melted a less experienced soldier down into his combat boots.

* * * *

"Well, I'll be damned!"

Across the buffer zone, as the piano and violin were tuning up for the opening of the Nicosia Singer's concert, Safa Ziya put down the telephone receiver and her book. She struggled up from her scruffy, overstuffed chair and limped toward her kitchen to make a cup of tea. She had been reading a dull book in an effort to start the process toward an early night to bed when the department called her at home.

"Well, I'm not likely to get much sleep tonight," she told herself. "This is both progress and a dark alley."

What the research lab had thought could not wait—particularly since Ziya would, she was afraid to say, be attending the second session of the bicommunal police seminar the next morning—was news that unaccountably linked the two recent foreign murder

66

victims. The Italian belly dancer, Gina Bertelli, and the German artist, Detrich Kleist, had both, but separately, entered northern Cyprus—by ferry to Kyrenia from Izmir, Turkey, rather than the normal route for foreign visitors, which would be by plane from Istanbul—in the same month, May 1987. And more interesting and puzzling, they both had accounts at the same local bank, accounts that were both being fed from the same Belgian bank.

Too close to be coincidence, Ziya thought, as she stirred too much milk into her tea, followed by too much sugar.

"To hell with the budget. I'll have to ask for a full international background report on these two."

She moved back to the telephone and stumbled against a table just as the lights went out—right on schedule for the programmed electricity conservation blackout for the entire Turkish zone area of Nicosia.

"Shit! Ouch! Shit!"

* * * *

The Nicosia Singers had not changed their repertoire. Claudio Monteverdi's *Beatus Vir*, the centerpiece of the classical segment of the concert, was in full voice. The choir's soprano soloist, Erica Christos, was lilting down the scale in angelic accompaniment to the soloists for the other parts:

"Ex-al-ta-bi-tur in Glo . . . ri . . . oof."

There was a popping noise, and, as the lights went out, the Belgian-born soprano was sinking to the floor.

Pandemonium broke out, followed after a minute or two by a return of the lights.

The narrow aisle of the central passageway was clogged with people falling over people, all trying to move someplace other than where they had been when the lights had gone out.

Paul Conte was kneeling in front of the choir platform, cradling the lifeless body of Erica Christos in his arms. Takis Koniotis, Alec Stuart, and Maria Solonos were pushing chairs aside at the edges of the passageway to make their way down to the domed chamber. It would have been impossible to try to wade through the tide of people in the center aisle. They reached Paul Conte's side almost simultaneously.

The American diplomat looked stunned. He was muttering "She's dead" over and over, like a broken record.

He looked up. Alec Stuart was the first one he focused on. With a sharp, accusatory tone Conte demanded, "Where were you? You were supposed to be standing with me in the choir. Where were you when this happened?"

"I was out in front of the building, Paul. I'm sorry," Stuart answered quietly and with what seemed like a sense of embarrassment. "I'd gone out for a last smoke before we had to go up on the risers, and I saw a tow truck working on moving Willie Hamilton's Mini. I was sweet-talking them just to leave it there. As far as I could determine, there wasn't a single auto in sight that was legally parked. So I missed getting in for the concert."

Just then Willie Hamilton joined the group. He was huffing from the exertion, and it took him a moment to direct their attention to the window that overlooked the domed chamber from the western exhibit hall.

John Dunsford stood in the window, holding a small handgun by the barrel with a handkerchief. When he saw that he had the group's attention, he pointed off toward the hall's back wall and called, "The light panel is up here too. I just turned them back on."

Although, he was listening and took in everything that was being said, Takis Koniotis was looking out into the hall. He was studying those who were now riveted to where they were standing when the lights returned, looking down toward the crumpled soprano in horror. Koniotis was unable to detect the presence of either Eleni Piccard or her companion, Sergey Stepanov; Mikhail Lukenov; Sarah Bristow; or the worrying art dealer, Justin Chamberlain. He looked up at the western window and noticed now, for the first time, that the Greek actor, Demetriou, was also standing there at Dunsford's side.

"What am I missing here?" Koniotis thought. "Think!"

Turning back to look at the dead soprano, he mentally added, "And what secrets might be going to the grave with you, I wonder?"

Chapter Five

Takis Koniotis was still disgruntled Tuesday morning as he sat through the second attempt to open the bicommunal seminar at the Ledra Palace Hotel. It wasn't that he distrusted having Maria Solonos organizing the investigation of the shooting the previous evening of the singer, Erica Christos. But he deeply resented having been told that his superiors wanted nothing to stand in the way of his attendance at this seminar.

"This useless seminar," Koniotis corrected his thoughts bitterly. "I can't wait for the next break, so I can call Maria and find out what she's learned."

John Dunsford, as the moderator, was reintroducing the purpose of the seminar.

"He looks none the worse for wear for what happened last night," thought Koniotis. "But, then, this isn't his problem."

Dunsford was trying to discuss crime detection on the island as being a common problem that both sides faced and that could be controlled best through cooperation across the zones. However, the Canadian himself didn't seem all that interested in the topic and thus was not carrying the seminar participants with him.

"Let's just get on with the morning's speakers," Koniotis mentally urged. "The faster that's over, the faster I can get back to the office."

He looked over at his Turkish Cypriot counterparts. His attention was arrested by a largish and slightly lumpy, but intelligent-looking woman who was being treated with deference by the other Turkish Cypriot police officers arrayed around her.

"She looks just about as interested in all of this as I am," he noted to himself. "Well, at least we have that in common. Now, what did Dunsford say her name was? I must have been a million miles away when he was introducing her yesterday morning."

With difficulty, he focused his attention back on Dunsford's preliminary remarks, which were warming up now that he had gotten past the formalities of the seminar opening. Dunsford was discussing some specifics on the current issues of common concern between the two communities. He had mentioned the issues of drugs and arms smuggling and of money laundering—with a few recent examples of how the division of the island had exacerbated these problems. He had then introduced the topics of artifact smuggling and the rise in the influx of Russian businessmen of questionable financial backing.

Before he could check himself, Koniotis blurted out, "Yes, yes, these are very serious concerns. But what insistently faces me today is a developing pattern of foreigners being knocked off."

Suddenly, from across the room, Safa Ziya's head snapped up out of the daze she had been in as the result of a sleepless night, and she exclaimed: "You, too?"

Dunsford broke in nervously, "All in due course, certainly, Mr. Koniotis, Ms. Ziya, but our speakers this morning are covering drug smuggling. So, we'll now begin—"

"Ms. Ziya?" Koniotis cut in. "Is that Ms. Safa Ziya?"

"Why, yes," Dunsford answered, slightly perturbed. "Safa Ziya. I introduced her to the entire group yesterday."

"Oh, yes, I know you did," Koniotis responded contritely. "In fact I was just thinking that I had not fully absorbed that introduction. I apologize, Ms. Ziya. I had no idea it was you I was meeting, even though I knew you were working in the north in some capacity. I went to Texas at Austin too. You were still a legend there when I attended."

"Well, that's wonderful," Dunsford broke in, giving very little indication he thought it was wonderful. "You two will have to become better acquainted at the break. Unfortunately, we are getting off schedule, so we'll have to . . ."

"Safa Ziya. Here. And my counterpart on the Turkish side," Koniotis was mulling in his mind. He looked across the room at the Turkish Cypriot investigator with a new appreciation in his eyes—to find that she was looking at him as well in an attitude of intense consideration.

* * * *

She again found herself on the acropolis terrace, looking past the columns and into the loggia, where her older sister, Phyllis, was secretly entertaining. The wind was blowing Phyllis's diaphanous chiton around her tiny frame and was competing with the music from the lyre that was being strummed in the background. Someone stirred in the shadows at the other end of the loggia. Acamas again. Phyllis was singing to him, her arms stretched wide. But then the sweet notes of her song were drowned by a growing rumble. Phyllis looked around in the direction of her unseen sister, and the flash of recognition once again jolted the younger woman to the quick. The earth trembled and then buckled, and the columns fell inward, in swirling dust.

Caitlyn Koniotis shook her head vigorously and reached up to push the blonde curls away from her face. That vision again. She would have written this off to a bad flashback to the previous evening, except that she'd had this same trance several times before. One of these days she would have to tell Eleni that she kept appearing in her daydreams, although her name in the dream appeared to be Phyllis. This one wasn't at all pleasant, though. Caitlyn wondered what it meant, but the very unpleasantness of the vision caused her to do what she could to dismiss her momentary break in concentration. One more shake of the head and she was fully back in the present.

"There. That's the last of that pottery lot to be carbon dated," Caitlyn told herself. "This find isn't as old as we had thought it was."

She had been working intensively in her workroom at the Cyprus Museum since early morning. She was trying to become completely absorbed in her work as an archaeological researcher for the Cyprus Antiquities Department in order to shut out the events of the previous evening. She had not known Erica Christos, but that did not mitigate the shock of having been at the Famagusta Gate concert when the singer had been shot. The fact that her husband, Takis, would probably have to investigate the case made it all the more worrying to Caitlyn. The singer had been married to a Cypriot but had herself been a Belgian citizen.

Caitlyn sat back in her chair and took a few sips from the cup of tea she had just warmed up. She felt less concerned now by the

73

recurrence of her periodic, disturbing visions of a strangely familiar ancient past. She'd had such vivid imaginings, as she called them, for as long as she could remember—and for some reason she couldn't explain to anyone, they had aided her in her archaeological work. When at a dig, she was often able to surface glimpses of the everyday ancient life in the area being excavated, and this sometimes helped her to focus the dig in the most rewarding locale. This was exactly what had happened at the Kaliana dig here on the island a few years previously, when she had been able to pinpoint a major archaeological find. But her visions had become more frequent and more real— almost as if she could make direct connections to ancient ancestors— during her time here on Cyprus. And when she subsequently learned that she had indeed had ancestors who'd lived on Cyprus, she had decided that she was where she would stay. In the end, that had been a less shocking decision for her and for her family and friends than had been the whirlwind courtship that had led to her marriage to Takis Koniotis.

Her vision this morning, a disturbing one that she had experienced on several occasions in the recent month, had suspended her absorption in the intricate dating tests long enough for her to remember that she had intended to call Justin Chamberlain this morning. She hated getting involved, but Justin was an old friend. If what she had been told was true, he needed to be warned about operating on the edge of propriety. When she had taken off her coat upon arrival at work this morning, she had also found the business cards she had picked up in the Kykko Monastery courtyard. She wanted to ask Justin how his card had come to be there. She also needed to remember to tell Takis what she had learned about the piece of material he had taken from the hand of the murdered priest.

"Well, it can't be helped," she thought, as she steeled her resolve and reached for the telephone.

The precise, cultured voice that responded on the other end of the line contained a mixture of both the playful and of a sense of superiority.

"Why hello, Caitlyn. So nice of you to call. We did not get nearly enough time to ourselves to talk about old times last evening before that inconsiderate bang. I've heard of tone-sensitive music critics, but I didn't think the soloist was that off key."

When Caitlyn didn't respond to his little joke, he smoothly switched gears. "I was so surprised to learn you were staying on in Cyprus. And simply flabbergasted to learn you had married. And to a policeman, too. A bit middle class, though, wouldn't you say? I didn't think your procreation clock was ticking that hysterically."

Unable to suppress a laugh, Caitlyn said, "No, I wouldn't say, and you are as snobby as ever to suggest it."

Caitlyn was very tolerant toward Justin's outrageous statements and his flamboyant air of superiority. They had gone to the University of Michigan together, both majoring in archaeology and ancient art. Justin had been brilliant and had helped Caitlyn gain an appreciation of and love for the area of studies that went considerably beyond academics. She knew he could be insufferable—and was usually considered so by those who did not know him well. But she also knew that his air of superiority and occasional tasteless comments hid a defensive shell. Under that shell, he was a vulnerable child with the soul of an artist and a feeling of inferiority that had resulted from a broken home. His father had been a highly decorated American army general who was always away on campaign, and his mother was the alcoholic, self-centered daughter of a British peer. She had frequently been away on some sort of conquest of her own, as well. Caitlyn and Justin had initially grown close because Caitlyn's father was also American and her mother wasn't. The difference between Caitlyn's and Justin's upbringing was that her parents had always been there for her, when his parents rarely were there for him, and her parents had hearts big enough and nerves steady enough to take Justin in as well during university vacations.

It was at least partially because of Justin, who had already established a branch of his art import-export business in Cyprus in the late 1980s, that Caitlyn had settled on the research study grant that had originally brought her to Cyprus.

"Justin," Caitlyn honed in, purposefully putting a serious, motherly edge on her voice, "both Professor Visiliou and Paul Conte have separately told me that they heard you were getting involved in some questionable artifact shipments. Say it isn't so."

"It isn't so, my friend."

"That came back much too easily, Justin. Please, you must be careful. You have no need to get into this activity. It's almost as though you want to destroy your life and reputation."

"Please don't worry about me, Caitlyn. I'm a big boy now."

"Also, Justin, I saw you talking privately with Eleni Piccard last evening in the exhibit hall. Please be careful of her. She has been involved in some questionable dealings as well, and you only multiply the speculation about yourself when you are seen with her."

"Methinks the lady protests too much," laughed Chamberlain. "You, yourself, have been thick as thieves with Eleni. Didn't her Ledra Foundation sponsor your dig at Kaliana? And didn't she take you under her wing from the very beginning? And haven't you told me repeatedly about the strange affinity you have for the woman? Lord knows why you believe it, but don't you fantasize that you and Eleni were connected somehow in ancient times?"

"Yes, yes, that's all true," Caitlyn responded with exasperation. She was very glad he couldn't see the blush rising to her face, and she suddenly felt very vulnerable for having shared these thoughts with him. "But we also both got mixed up in a couple of international crime cases shortly after I came here. And, whereas I was involuntarily drawn in by being with the wrong people in the wrong places, Eleni was knowingly using the situation—and her own shipping corporation—to promote her own interests.

"Please heed this friendly warning," Caitlyn continued. "Eleni's shipping interests are being closely scrutinized. And it isn't just illegal to smuggle artifacts out of Cyprus. It is immoral to do so as well, and it is against all of the ethics we were taught at the university. I don't want to stand by and see you ruin your life. But I also could not close my eyes to the type of operations I'm told you may be involved in."

"I promise, it's all just vengeful lies by bested competitors," Chamberlain responded smoothly. "But, thank you for telling me. I suppose it helps to have a police official in the family. But truly, I'm just an innocent boy scout. Just for you, however, I'll continue being just an innocent boy scout. Howsomever, toodles for now. I have a Roman column to swipe out of the Curium amphitheater in broad daylight and sell to a mafia boss in New York City." And he disconnected the line, as he was prone to do, in a fit of mirth.

Caitlyn sat with the telephone receiver in her hand for several seconds, her eyes misting over. He hadn't even given her a chance to mention the business cards she had found. But eventually she shook off her irritation, replaced the receiver, and reached for another box of ancient (she hoped) pottery shards.

* * * *

Eleni Piccard sat at her office desk, folding and unfolding her delicate hands, her brow knitted in concentration. Her hand wavered over the telephone for the twentieth time that morning. As she stretched her hand out before her, she could see that it was trembling. This was not like her. Her staff could not see her in this condition.

She knew she had resolved not to make contact on this issue. But she had to know. She had to know why, years after everything had been set up, it was all unraveling. Especially now, after what had happened last night. And who was doing the unraveling? Was this all by design—and had this always been the design? Or, in some way, could she help keep everything together—even now?

Which side was she to be on? Hunter or hunted?

She made her decision.

"I will not live in fear like this. I must know the worst."

She lifted the receiver, dialed a number, requested a connection, listened to the response, and slowly replaced the receiver.

Not there; not expected back for some time.

The minutes ticked away on the French clock on the elaborate mantelpiece. Eleni Piccard sat at her desk, folding and unfolding her hands, her brow knitted in consternation.

Mehmet Tosun spied her as she reached the passport desk in the arrival hall below.

"So," he thought, "my informants were correct. She has come." He mopped at the back of his neck with a grimy silk scarf.

The portly merchant was standing on the glassed-in balcony perched above the baggage claim area in the Turkish zone's Ercan Airport.

Peggy Bingham stood out starkly in the hall filled with Turkish vacationers. First, she was an extremely tall, thin, "all-business," obviously Western woman with hawk-like features and mousy brown hair streaked with gray, which was pulled back on her head in a severe bun. Second, rather than engaging in the usual good-natured bantering of the people of the region, she was making mincemeat of a passport control clerk who was not moving at quite the pace she desired.

This was a woman on a mission. She would not have seemed at all out of place if she had stepped ashore just so with the first twelfth-century crusaders to have conquered the Christian country of Cyprus in the name of Christ. The patrician Bostonian's sensibly cut, drab clothes belied her gigantic "old money" fortune and her avid, although, alas, somewhat naïve passion for Greek, Roman, and early Christian church-period antiquities.

After successfully cowing the passport clerk to the point of stripping away his minor-official arrogance, she strode purposefully and scornfully toward the baggage claim bin. Tosun emitted a little squeak and huffed down the balcony stairs into his Volkswagen Beetle for the hurried trip back to his shop.

Tosun obviously knew the route to his shop near Nicosia's border checkpoint by heart and Peggy Bingham had presumably never even been to Cyprus before. However, the merchant had barely gotten back to his door before he spied the avenging angel bearing down on him under full sail, suitcases flapping at her side, from the main street. Still harboring the hope that Bingham's nearness was just a terrible coincidence and that she was hunting some other innocent antiquities forger and smuggler, Tosun shuffled into his dark shop, slammed the door behind him, and dove into his tiny office.

The shop door popped back open almost as soon as it had closed, and Peggy Bingham started to charge in. Some powerful source, however, stopped the battleship dead in the water, just on the threshold to the shop. Ms. Bingham rocked back on her heels, her hand going immediately to her nose. She did not enter the shop, but instantly explored every corner of the room with her piercing, black eyes.

"Mehmet Tosun. I know you're in here. Produce yourself. Now!"

Tosun glided out of his office, his arms wide, his smile stretched from ear to ear.

"Welcome to my humble shop, Dear Lady. What can we help you with today, pray tell?"

"Drop the crap, Tosun. You know who I am, and you know why I'm here. You also knew I was coming. I saw you on the balcony at the airport. Do you think I would have let you anywhere close to the deposit I made without having had you investigated?"

The merchant, the indecent assault on his saintly reputation clearly painted on his face, attempted to rebuild his defenses, "I'm sorry, I don't—"

"Stow it. I don't have time for you. Where is Helmut Roentgen? I'm finished with waiting for the delivery of the icon miniatures. Everywhere I turn to catch up with him, I run into your name. You knew I was coming. I wrote to you looking for him."

"You did not answer my letters," she continued, slowly and deliberately, as if this crime alone condemned Tosun to the hangman and as if she was fully capable of carrying out the sentence herself on the spot.

"Oh, you must be Miss Peggy Bingham," Tosun once again became all smiles and seemed visibly relieved to have this little mystery cleared up. "Welcome, Dear Lady. Of course Helmut and I knew you were coming. Didn't you receive my replies? I have no idea what could have happened to my reply letters. We were waiting for you. Helmut was having just a spot of trouble arranging for the transportation of your icons. He is off in Europe, making all of the last-minute arrangements. All at his own expense, of course. Won't you please sit down and have a tea?"

"No, I will not sit down and have a tea," Peggy Bingham retorted, but in a somewhat mollified tone. "And just when do you expect Mr. Roentgen to return?" she asked suspiciously.

"In just a day or two. We already have you booked at the luxurious Serail Hotel in the main square. We will contact you there by telephone. In the very short time you have to wait, you must visit some of our ancient sites and see some of the other very special antiquities I have available for sale. A special discount just for you, of course. I can make all of the arrangements for your welcome visit. I'm sure you will find much here to have made your trip, unnecessary as it was, worthwhile. Here, let me help you with your luggage."

* * * *

Later that night, the Koniotises were abed, Takis massaging his wife's aching muscles.

"You know it's my turn next," he said teasingly. "I've had a rough day too."

"Oh, did you move about a million tons of ancient soil with only a couple of beads to show for it? I probably shouldn't have tried to go out to that dig this afternoon. There are more than enough eager university interns here this term to handle the digging work."

"Ah, but you told me they were very nice Phoenician beads, which told you all sorts of things about ancient trading patterns at this end of the Mediterranean—the Phoenician's pretty beads in exchange for all of the cedar of Cyprus, with the result that the Phoenicians had the world's greatest navy, and Cyprus became a desert."

"Yes, they were very nice beads. Now it's your turn." The two exchanged positions. "Oh, your muscles are tight. This case of the foreigner murders has gotten a little tense, I take it?"

"Yes, it has. Too many murders and not enough evidence."

"That reminds me," Caitlyn said. "I have a couple of things to tell you about evidence. Now what were they? Oh, yes, I can remember at least one. Your scrap of material the priest was holding."

"Right. That label from that Washington, D.C., tailor. Maria's checked with the American embassy, but they haven't reported back yet."

"Well, they needn't bother now. I called my mother the other day. She lives in Virginia just a couple of hours drive south of Washington—as you'll see when we visit there next summer. She ran up to Washington and checked directly with the tailor. I'm afraid that won't be much help. A simple label won't be enough for them to match the suit to any of their customers, and they do a lot of business with a lot of people going through Washington, which includes a whole range of local and foreign government officials and business people."

"But it's an exclusive tailor, isn't it?"

"Yes, mother said the establishment was quite posh."

"Well, at least we know we're looking for a man who is both well traveled and well heeled."

"Not true," Caitlyn shot back.

"What do you mean?"

"You Greek men are such incorrigible chauvinists. Didn't I say the other day that it could be from a woman's suit as well as a man's? You can't just assume at this point that the killer is a man, can you? Mother confirmed that the tailor does a brisk business with women professionals, as well."

"I suppose you're right, although our Greek women don't go around murdering people."

"Oh, you're such a pig." Caitlyn slapped her husband on the back of the head and was rewarded with a pained exclamation. "You haven't read much Greek mythology, have you? It's always the women who are the most bloody minded."

"Well, at least you didn't use your own brand of mythology to gather this evidence. I expected to be told you had seen it all in one of your quirky visions."

Caitlyn stopped massaging and went very still.

"Honey, what's the matter? I'm sorry, I didn't mean to upset you."

"I probably never should have told you about my imaginings, Takis. I just thought you might understand. They're not that much different from those famous hunches that help you in your cases, and my visions have already helped you in your work. I can't stop them. They just happen. And I don't think I'd want them to stop, even though many of them really scare me. Having mental connections with those from the past isn't really all that much further away from scientific foundation than the connections through DNA that we now fully accept and probably are only beginning to understand. The fact is that I do have some sort of special connection with my ancestors, ones that have only increased since I came to Cyprus and learned that I have roots here. And the fact also is that these visions helped me locate the Kaliana site, helped you solve that case that same year, and pulled me back here to Cyprus after I had left. If it hadn't been for those visions we would not be together now. And I think you have to admit that I could help you even more if you allowed me to work with you more closely on your cases."

She began to quietly cry, and Takis sat up and wrapped his arms around her.

"I'm sorry, Honey. Don't cry. Have you been having that bad dream about the earthquake and the woman being crushed again?"

"Yes. And for some strange reason whenever I think of that woman, I think that someone near me is in some sort of danger. Just getting glimmerings like this is very frightening."

"Hush, hush. It's time for sleep now. I'll try to be more understanding about your imaginings. And, of course you were right to have told me about your visions. We need to share everything that is important to us. You're right, we make a great team," he continued. "Thanks for what you found out about the material. I'll try to keep an open mind about who the killer could be. You're a great help. You said, by the way, that you had something else to tell me about the case. What else?"

But, try as she might, Caitlyn wasn't able to remember what else she was saving to tell Takis. And very soon after they had turned the light out, the two newlyweds had something far more urgent to concern themselves with than the business cards found near where the Russian priest had been murdered.

Chapter Six

It was uncharacteristically gloomy on Thursday morning as the bicommunal seminar started into its fourth day in the Ledra Palace Hotel. The sky over Nicosia was uncommonly overcast, which served principally to remind residents they were approaching winter weather. The lack of sunlight also served to accentuate the bunkerlike feeling inside the Treaty Room.

For the conference plans of the Canadian high commission and moderator John Dunsford, however, the atmosphere inside the seminar group was getting brighter with every passing speaker and discussion period. Following two tension-filled sessions and one uncertain one in which at least the two delegation heads, Takis Koniotis and Safa Ziya, seemed to be warming to each other, Dunsford was now surprised to see that the seminar discussions were becoming progressively more lively and interactive.

Although neither Takis Koniotis nor Safa Ziya had participated much in the early discussions, they exchanged continually warmer looks during the first two hours of the third session. And, almost as if by assignation, in today's session, the two drifted off toward the same quiet corner of the room at the start of the first coffee break of the day.

Seeing the two moving to an intersecting point, John Dunsford stepped toward Koniotis as if to intercept him for a chat. But Dunsford's own movement was arrested by a pair of participants peppering him with procedural questions before he could catch up to the Greek Cypriot policeman.

"I am truly sorry I was so inattentive toward you when we were first introduced," Koniotis said as soon as the two had arrived at a corner next to the room's large stone fireplace. "I had no idea you were the famous Safa Ziya."

"That's quite all right, although I know nothing about being famous," Ziya responded graciously. "I know I look much more like someone's maiden auntie, which, incidentally, I am—or, at least . . ." A twinge of pain crossed her face. ". . . should be—than an American-educated academic. In fact, I can find it very easy to understand your earlier preoccupation if, as you say, you have been burdened with a series of uncommon deaths among those in the foreign community."

"Yes, I'm afraid we have, and it is very perplexing. There was another one just the night before the opening of this seminar, and I was even there at the time. And I was irritated because my superiors forced me to come to the seminar the next morning rather than focusing on investigating the case."

"I know exactly how you feel," said Ziya bitterly.

Koniotis proceeded to review the deaths of the retired Spanish diplomat, the Cypriot who had been on the boat with him, the Russian monk, and the Belgian soprano. "All so strange," he concluded, "with the only common denominator so far to suggest the deaths are related being the foreign nationality of all but the boatman. But it is highly unusual for us to have any murders, let alone totally random murders, or murders of foreigners, so close together in time. But why are you so interested in these cases? You seemed to indicate yesterday morning that you might have a similar problem."

"Yes, I do," Ziya quickly responded, and a full, animated, yet comprehensive and concise description of the deaths of the German artist and the Italian belly dancer poured out. "We are currently operating on the theory that they were murdered because of some mutual connection to an artifact smuggling setup. We already knew Kleist was involved in such a racket. Or perhaps it is all linked to the Russian criminal elements that are beginning to arrive, apparently on both sides of the island. We did find out the two victims were connected. But our facilities are so primitive and our investigation resources so small that the background investigation is moving entirely too slowly."

"You said you did find a connection?" Koniotis honed in.

"Yes, more than one. Both victims arrived on the island by the same route and in the same month. They also had bank accounts at the same bank, accounts that were receiving deposits from the same Brussels bank. And they share something that seems to connect them with some of your killings, as well. They were both killed by a knife that made similar, unusually large entry wounds."

Koniotis whistled softly. "Well, your investigation support might be less sophisticated than ours, but you found connections before we did. And my gut feeling is that our cases might, indeed, be connected to yours. Our victims had similar knife wounds; we'll have to check on how and when they arrived here and what their banking arrangements are. Thank you, Ms. Ziya. This is too good of a lead to wait for this afternoon. I have to check this out right away."

As he turned to depart the room, Ziya put her hand on his arm to detain him briefly.

"The name is Safa. Please call me Safa," she said quietly.

Koniotis responded with a smile that was, if anything, even warmer than the one she had given him and turned once more toward the door. "I'll let you know what we find," Koniotis called over his shoulder—almost as an afterthought.

Safa Ziya smiled again. She couldn't remember having done so twice in the same day for years—or to have had the incentive to have done so for some time.

From across the room, Dunsford had been watching this conversation as closely as he was able to while still trying to respond to—and somehow gracefully get away from—the two participants who had intercepted his movement earlier. He moved slightly, as if he might attempt to head Koniotis off at the outer door, but he ended up giving in to the inevitable and returning his attention to the conversation. The expression on his face, however, was withdrawn, and the next question that was presented to him had to be repeated twice before he heard it.

* * * *

The early-morning atmosphere was also gloomy in the basement of the Cyprus Museum. This did not have much to do with the temporary disappearance of the sun, however. The overhead slits of windows in the museum's laboratory area didn't let in much light even on the brightest days.

On this particular morning, the heavy atmosphere was being enhanced by the clouding of Caitlyn Koniotis's usually sunny disposition. Her department head, Professor Andriko Visiliou, had descended on her lab and was storming at her about the activities of her college friend and countryman, Justin Chamberlain. Below the surface of the diatribe, Visiliou was commiserating with Caitlyn more than lecturing her, as he was not much less concerned for Chamberlain than Caitlyn was. Visiliou had also been enrolled in archaeological studies at the University of Michigan when Caitlyn and Chamberlain had been there, so he, too, felt some share of responsibility for the flamboyant art dealer.

"I'm truly sorry to have to pass this information to you, Caitlyn, but I've heard even more damaging news about Justin's activities here."

"I guess I'd better hear it," Caitlyn said heavily, as she gently lowered a delicate terra cotta perfume jar to the cotton batting that topped her work desk.

"I'm afraid Justin has been implicated in a case in the States—in St. Louis—where an art broker paid over $1.2 million for four fourth-century Christian-era mosaics that had been stolen from an old basilica in Paphos four years ago. When the broker tried to get them authenticated, the municipal museum in Dallas, which is working closely with our own antiquities department, sent pictures and a description on to our embassy. We're suing now for the return of the mosaics, and the broker is naming names of her connections in an attempt to get her money back. I'm sorry, but Justin's name was one of them."

"This certainly sounds like a messy case all around," Caitlyn responded. In loyalty to her friend, however, she went on, "But, like the other rumors you passed on, this is not exactly conclusive evidence that Justin really is involved. Justin is a highly memorable figure in the Cypriot art export world. This broker might just be throwing up as much chaff as possible to hide the extent of her own involvement."

Visiliou looked skeptical, but he answered, "Yes, of course that might be the explanation. As far as we know at this point, we might find she came over here and pried the mosaics up herself. She might also have dummied up the payment receipt, which carried the signature of a known go-between of questionable character who operates out of Bruges. But please do talk to Justin again and tell him that the authorities are beginning to zero in on him whether or not his activities have been completely aboveboard. He has brought enough suspicion and bad publicity to our university's program already with other activities of his."

"I agree that one of us has to do that. And I think Justin will take it better from me. The two of you didn't leave Michigan as friends, did you, Andriko?"

"No. I know he was very close to you then. But he always did come across to me as just a bit too smooth and always ready to take the shortcuts. I can't dispute his brilliance, however. He would have made a great researcher. There just was never enough money in that end of the business to satisfy his expensive tastes. Or there wasn't enough daring and intrigue, perhaps, which is why I find it so easy to believe he may be involved in illicit activities."

The discussion turned to more professional matters, and just before he left, Visiliou broached a new topic. "Oh, I've forgotten to ask you what I really stopped to ask, Caitlyn. I have been invited by the American embassy to take a group on a sponsored outing across the buffer zone to visit Engomi, Salamis, and Famagusta. Would you be interested in going?"

"Oh, would I!" responded Caitlyn exuberantly. "Assuming, of course, that the Cypriot Government is cooperating with plans. I've been here several months already and have yet to be able to visit the one area of the island I had set my heart to see. And now that I've married Takis, I don't think I could go over to the occupied side without government sanction even if that would be politically wise."

The ancient Greco-Roman city state of Salamis; its even more ancient predecessor, Engomi; and the medieval walled city of Famagusta were located on the east coast in the Turkish-controlled zone and just north of the UN-patrolled buffer zone. Salamis was one of the most ancient and most historically important sites in the eastern Mediterranean. It had been settled as a city state around 1200 BC by one of the Greek heroes of the Trojan war. But the settlement history of the site went further back in time. The first settlers had been the earthquake survivors of an even older Early Bronze Age civilization in Engomi, which was located just a few miles inland from Salamis. Famagusta, just to the south of the Salamis ruins, was a still-existing walled port city that had come into prominence in the twelfth century AD. When the Turks took the Levant coastal city of Acre, the Christian inhabitants of that city had moved almost en masse to Famagusta.

The mere thought of being able to visit the east coast, with its rich history and impressive ruins of civilizations stretching from the Bronze Age to the Ottoman Turk period, brought sunshine back to Caitlyn's face. This was an improvement in the atmosphere within the lab that was matched by an increase in light filtering through the window slits overhead. The clouds had passed, and Nicosia's sunshine had returned.

This rise in spirits, however, did not erase from Caitlyn's mind the early part of the conversation she had had with Professor Visiliou, who had just left her office to make an inspection trip to the Kaliana excavations in the Solean Valley of the Troodos. She sighed and reached for the phone.

"I'm sorry," the voice said on the other end of the line. "Mr. Chamberlain is out of the country. We don't expect him back for several days."

Caitlyn sighed again as she returned the receiver to its cradle. She was worried about Justin, certainly, but there wasn't much she could do about that now. So, she felt no guilt as she turned her thoughts to the coming trip to Engomi, Salamis, and Famagusta. There were so many archaeological points she wanted to check out at these sites. She prayed that the Greek Cypriot government would let her join Professor Visiliou's group.

* * * *

Just a little later and not more than a mile away from the Cyprus Museum, across the walls and in the old city's restored walking street area of Laiki Yitonia, Paul Conte, Alec Stuart, and John Dunsford rendezvoused for lunch. By regular appointment, the diplomats of the three Western allied countries of the United States, Great Britain, and Canada were meeting, as inconspicuously as possible, to compare notes. Their point of intersection was the Piazza Tavern, an open-air restaurant that was nestled in a triangle that had been created by a fork in the road of a major, but narrow street in the oldest section of the walled city.

Stuart, the rugged Britisher, arrived first and thus determined that the luncheon meeting would be outside. The sun had mercifully reappeared and was warming the little square. Even though it was mid November, it was quite warm enough for an Englishman who had been raised to embrace the cold and to worship the sun. The American, Conte, arrived soon thereafter, wrapped in a sweater that wasn't needed by his British colleague from a more northerly country. Dunsford was the last to arrive, having hurried from his seminar at the nearby Ledra Palace. He looked sourly at his two colleagues, who were already swigging their Keo beer. Seemingly almost reluctant to meet, Dunsford dropped into a vacant seat, hunching down into the light raincoat he had worn today because of the gloomy weather that had greeted him when he left for the seminar earlier in the morning.

"I think we agreed this meeting would be about the Russian mafia problem," Stuart opened. The other two nodded their heads.

Stuart continued. "This is a real sticky problem."

The movement of criminal Russian elements into Cyprus posed a dilemma for the Western diplomats. The Cypriots had always been on good terms with the Russians and they also had very liberal laws on money importation and corporate registration. They were only now beginning to see the influx of all these Russians as a problem— and then only to the extent that violent crimes were being perpetrated here by the Russian mafia thugs. The Cypriots wanted to be careful in their response to the issue, because these criminals were only a very small segment of the Russians who are coming here now. Ever since the Iron Curtain lifted and the former Soviet Union began to break up, an increasing number of Russian vacationers had been coming to sunny, exotic Cyprus rather than to the Black Sea coast, which was not, in any event, part of Russia anymore.

The frequency of direct charter flights had increased. With the increase in transport, the influx of Russians who just wanted to get out of Russia for good had also increased. Interspersed in this group were Russian nationals who had gotten hold of some money and who wanted to set up off-shore companies in Cyprus, because it was relatively easy both to get money into the island and to set up a foreign-owned company. And then the Cypriots started to see the arrival of Russians who had a lot of money in tow, money that could only have been accumulated through government corruption or street crime. These were the new crime czars of Russia, the element the world was calling the Russian mafia.

"Speaking of Russian mafia," Conte got down to particulars. "I saw Sergey Stepanov at the airport again yesterday. He was meeting three men on a charter flight from Moscow who looked very much like muscle."

"Stepanov worries me more than just about any of the other Russians we've targeted for investigation," Stuart said.

"Why?" Dunsford entered the conversation for the first time. "Is it because he has money to burn, or because he also controls charter planes and a shipping company—and thus has transport for whatever else he might be doing? Or is it just because he's bringing in thugs?"

"A shipping company?" Conte asked sharply.

"Yes," Dunsford answered dryly. "He only has one, relatively small freighter as yet. It's registered in Limassol."

"Good God," Conte exclaimed.

"No," Stuart said. "What really worries me about Stepanov is this connection with Eleni Piccard. She's so powerful here that we can't get any cooperation from the Cypriots to investigate her affairs. You know that both Paul and I were buttoned up just a few years ago for investigating something Piccard was involved in even though it turned out she herself wasn't doing anything illegal. The closer Stepanov gets to Piccard, the more invulnerable he becomes to us."

"Eleni Piccard," Dunsford mulled, a strange look on his face. "Ah, yes . . ." But he said no more, as Conte was continuing.

"If Stepanov and his cohorts are moving into and expanding the casual drugs and call girl operations on the island in an organized way, innocent little Cyprus is about to meet the big bad world big time," said Conte.

"Yes, I agree—if I've translated what you just said correctly," responded Stuart with a broad smile. Dunsford inclined his head in assent, as well, although he didn't double the smile.

As the trio was getting up to leave the table, Dunsford added: "Actually, what scares me the most about Stepanov is that he was Russian intelligence—KGB—before the breakup of the Soviet Union."

Both Stuart and Conte snapped to attention.

"How do you know that?" Stuart queried, his voice sharp and his words clipped.

"Oh, I know because I know," Dunsford smiled enigmatically.

"Well that explains that," said Conte.

"That explains what?" Stuart now rounded on Conte.

"The airport yesterday. It wasn't just Stepanov and his thugs that I saw. I also saw the Russian embassy's Mikhail Lukenov. He was watching Stepanov's little scene from afar, as well. If Stepanov was KGB, he probably still has connections to the embassy, and Lukenov probably was watching to make sure Stepanov's thugs were getting cleared into the country without problem."

The three of them stood there, each developing their own thoughts on the complexity of the situation. None of them seeming to realize—or to care—that it had grown dark and was beginning to sprinkle again.

"Look at them. Just like a bunch of junior Jedi knights, prancing around with their light swords and declaring, 'My beam is longer than yours,'" Sarah Bristow said at a nearby table.

"Yes, they rather do appear to be enjoying their game," her luncheon partner, Caitlyn Spencer, said. "But John Dunsford doesn't look quite up to snuff. He seems to look more careworn every time I see him. I think he's out of their league."

"If you only knew the John Dunsford I knew, you wouldn't say that," Sarah retorted. "He once was so stylish and had such a rapier wit that all the women in Europe were crawling all over him. I know I was. And believe me, he was well worth crawling over."

"You knew John before you both came to Cyprus?" For some reason this possibility took Caitlyn very much by surprise.

"But, of course. More than a decade ago, when I was a young, impressionable assistant army attaché specializing in NATO-force artillery, John was a dashing, very secretive Canadian diplomat. I was swept off my feet. And then when I returned to the States to work at the Pentagon, there he was again at his embassy in Washington."

Sarah sighed. "But everything was different then. It seems like his light had gone out. I know the light certainly went out of our relationship. I did what I could to keep the flame burning, but he became so standoffish. I kept catching him looking at me suspiciously, and I never could get him to talk to me about his work—not beyond the information we shared, with the approval of our governments, of course, during our Europe years.

"And then, when it appeared like he had followed me to Cyprus, as well, I gave it another go. That's what our date the other night at the Famagusta Gate concert was all about. Seeing if there was anything left of the old attraction. There was, at least enough for us to be close friends, but nothing as torrid as Brussels."

The mention of the concert gave Caitlyn her opening to change the subject. Learning of Sarah's former—and possibly current—affair with John was just a little more information than Caitlyn had wanted—or had been prepared—to hear.

"Well, if they've been meeting over there today to help clear up that poor women's death at the concert, I'd be the last to deny them their game. That's the third death of a foreign resident in a little more than a week. I don't think I'll feel safe until these killings have been stopped." Caitlyn felt a shiver go up her spine that had no relationship to the sudden chill in the air.

Sarah Bristow was just then experiencing a chill, as well. But her chill had more to do with the thoughts accompanying her view of John Dunsford's sloped-shouldered walk as he slowly trudged out of the tavern square than either Caitlyn's perception of a physical threat or the late-fall drizzle.

Chapter Seven

Takis Koniotis and Maria Solonos almost collided in the police department's small graveled parking lot that afternoon. Takis had been waylaid by the police chief when he was returning to police headquarters early from the Thursday morning session of the police investigations seminar and was forced to accompany him on a visit to the president's office. He was only now getting back to the office and only had a few minutes to spare, because Caitlyn was dragging him off to a cocktail party at the Cyprus Museum in less than an hour. Marriage was making an already-busy life very complicated, he thought—although he had no intention of complaining about his changed status. He found that Maria was on her way out of the office to talk with the family of the Belgian soprano.

"Does the minister know you are cutting the seminar?" Maria jibed. "Getting too dull for you?"

"On the contrary. It's turning quite interesting—and, as I've just been to see the president, I don't think the minister will make a peep about my truancy. Come back upstairs before going out. I don't have much time to talk. Caitlyn's dragging me off to the museum for some sort of archaeology exhibit and cocktail party. But I needed to come back here to make myself more presentable, and I also need you to set your research miracle workers on a couple of trails. Where are you going, anyway?"

As both hurried back to their office suite, Maria's heels echoing down the cold stone hallway in an insistent staccato beat, she filled him in. "I'm off to visit the family of the Christos woman. Her husband started settling her affairs and found that none of the relatives she said she had in Europe really exist. He also found that she had quite a bundle of money hidden in her closet. The man seems half afraid we're going to try to connect her—and him—to some dirty work. I thought while he was in the frame of mind, it would be a good idea for me to find out what, if anything, he knows about why someone would want to kill his wife."

"If his wife was the target, of course." They had reached Takis's office, and he motioned her in. After raising the blinds on the window and taking one look at the Turkish flag displayed on the side of the Kyrenia Ridge, he dropped the blinds again and sank into the old lopsided swivel chair behind his desk.

Maria swept a pizza box off the side chair and sat. "Why, what do you know about that?"

"Nothing that you don't know, of course, but she was a highly unlikely target, and the choir was strung out behind her on risers. It's more likely that someone like Stuart or Conte, with their intelligence background, were the targets. They were both in the choir, as well."

"But Stuart wasn't on stage. Didn't you catch that at the time? He was outside smoking a cigarette, or so he says."

"He was? No, I didn't know that. Well, that takes one person off the possible victim list and adds him to the possible assailant list.

I'm just glad this wasn't another knifing. We'd really be under a lot of pressure if these foreigners were dying the same way." With that, Takis ducked his head under his desk and started changing his shoes.

"It would have been a little hard to knife someone on stage and in the spotlight in a filled concert hall," Maria said.

"Ouch!" Takis had bumped his head on the desk in reaction to this comment. "Point taken. I guess we'd better get to work double time, then. I learned at the seminar that there had been a couple of similar knifing murders in the north."

"The Turkish Cypriots shared information with you on crime in the north?" Maria asked in disbelief. "I thought their line was that there was no crime in the north."

"Yes, I told you I was beginning to find this seminar quite useful. The senior investigator in the Turkish zone—who turns out to be Safa Ziya—I'm sure I've told you about the reputation she had for brilliance at my university in America—has already found some connections. For instance, both of the victims had accounts in the same bank in the north, and the same Brussels bank was making deposits into both accounts."

"That should be easy enough to cross-check for the victims on this side," said Maria, as she made a note. "Were there any other similarities?"

Takis took a moment to respond. He was having trouble buttoning the top button on his shirt so that he could start struggling with his tie. Semiformal attire for Cyprus usually consisted of a clean sports shirt and any form of long pants. "Yes, there were other matches. They both arrived by ferry from Izmir in May 1987, although they didn't arrive together or on the same day. Ziya thought this was strange, as foreigners rarely arrive by boat in the north."

"Yes, that fits," Maria interjected.

"What do you mean 'that fits'?" Takis had won the fight with the button and took the opportunity to give Maria a quizzical look.

"All of our recent foreign victims on this side of the Green Line—except the Cypriot boatman—arrived under similar, unusual circumstances."

Takis cut in with an explicative. Maria wasn't sure whether he was commenting on the information matchups or the difficulty he was having with his tie.

"You can exclude the boatman from the pattern," Maria continued. "Except for establishing the probability that he was killed by the same knife that was used on the Russian priest, his death does not need to fit the pattern. He was probably killed because of what he knew—and perhaps threatened to tell—about the Alvarez death."

Maria forged on. "Nearly everyone, especially foreigners who will live here semipermanently, arrive by air at Larnaca airport. The Spanish diplomat, after he retired; the Russian monk; and the Belgian singer all arrived here by boat. And the point of entry in our passport control records for all three was Limassol. The only entry point there is at the boat terminal. They also all arrived about a year apart— Alvarez in 1986, Father Nikolay in 1987, and Christos in 1988. That's all we have for the moment."

Koniotis stopped knotting and reknotting his tie and considered this information before responding. "Are you sure that's all you have? Don't the passport control records also give the point of origin and a vessel name?"

"Yes, of course. I must be slipping." Maria rifled through the slips of paper in a file that had been sitting on Takis's desk. "Yes, here it is. The point of origin for all is Marseilles, France."

"And the vessels?" asked Koniotis.

"Either the *Arsinoe* or the *Pierre Piccard*," responded Maria. The two looked at each other and smiled broadly in unison.

"The Ledra Shipping Company," whispered Maria.

"Eleni Piccard," said Takis almost simultaneously.

"What's this about Eleni?" asked Caitlyn Spencer Koniotis, as she swept into the office and tied Takis's tie in four deft movements.

"Nothing you'd want to hear about Eleni, I'm afraid."

"You're always after her," Caitlyn said. "You haven't forgiven her yet for playing the police for chumps in that smuggling case a couple of years ago, have you?" And then, without waiting for an answer, she turned to Maria. "I'm sorry, Maria, I've got to take this handsome man away from you. He is badly in need of a little culture."

"That's quite all right," Maria laughed. "I have to see a man about a pile of cash, anyway."

It was an unusually cold walk—unusual for balmy Cyprus, at least—during the two-block scurry from police headquarters to the Cyprus Museum. Caitlyn pulled her collar up around her ears and dug her hands deep into her pockets. One of her hands came into contact with the business cards she had picked up at Kykko Monastery.

"Takis, I found—" she started to say. But just then, her husband pulled her back onto the sidewalk as a Mercedes sports car swooped past them at considerable speed.

"What the—? Isn't that your spoiled college friend?" Takis exclaimed.

"Couldn't be," she said. "I called Justin's office just this morning, and they said he was out of the country." Caitlyn took the cards out of her pocket and pushed them into her purse. She'd tell Takis about her find. But he was so irrational about Justin. Although she had to admit that the driver of the car had looked very much like Justin. Maybe Justin was just avoiding her. If he did show up at the cocktail party, she was determined that she would ask him about the cards before getting into the matters Professor Visiliou wanted her to broach. She wouldn't even allow herself to get sidetracked again by asking why his office was saying he was abroad.

And Justin most certainly was at the cocktail party, making quite a spectacle of himself, and ask him Caitlyn did the first time she was able to corner him alone.

"Justin! Don't touch that. Can't you see the sign that says the frames for that exhibit are being regilded? You'll get gold paint all over yourself. Must you be such a child about everything? 'Wet paint' is a warning, not an invitation, you know. No, don't turn away from me, take a look at this and tell me why I found it at a murder scene at the Kykko monastery."

Justin looked at the card with his name on it. "This old thing? I haven't used this style for several years. You found it where? Well, I'm sure I don't know how it got there. Next you'll be mimicking Professor Visiliou and suggesting I was trying to rob the Kykko Monastery of its golden mosaics. Not a bad idea, of course."

"Can't you be serious just this once, Justin? I found these at the scene of a crime. I'm going to have to give these to Takis. It will be much better if I can also give him a plausible explanation of why your card was found there. And do you know anything about this other card? Mehmet Tosun. What kind of name is that? And what street is that? It claims to be in Nicosia, but it doesn't look Greek to me. Is it on the Turkish side?"

"Here, let me see that." Justin's devil-may-care tone had vanished. "No, I don't think that's on the Turkish side. The name sounds Romanian to me. Oh, look, there's Sarah Bristow. I've got a little marble statue of Aphrodite that is just screaming to perch on Sarah's buffet. Catch you later, darling."

He was gone in a flurry. And, to Caitlyn's dismay, both business cards were gone, as well. Also, Sarah Bristow didn't seem the least bit happy to see him. Justin had swept up to Sarah and John Dunsford, who had just arrived at the museum together. Justin was being very animated in his sales pitch, whereas Dunsford was quite bemused and Bristow seemed highly irritated.

Before Caitlyn could break into this unhappy group and try to reclaim her evidence, Eleni Piccard and Sergey Stepanov had arrived at her side from different directions. Stepanov had obviously been here for some time and had taken full advantage of the open bar. Eleni had just come in from the street door, where she had briefly talked with Takis before intersecting with Sergey at Caitlyn's side. Caitlyn thought Eleni was looking very pale this evening, and she definitely was preoccupied by something. As soon as they came together, she latched tightly onto Sergey's hand and occasionally looked plaintively into his face, but she spent just as much time scanning the room, included long gazes at Justin's performance over in the corner.

This isn't at all like Eleni, Caitlyn thought. She usually commands the room at such gatherings. Caitlyn was particularly put off by Stepanov's behavior. Whenever Eleni wasn't paying direct attention to him, he was trying to chat up Caitlyn. Caitlyn wasn't a bit amused. She had no idea why Eleni put up with this self-important thug at all.

As soon as she could—and despite the perceived need to find out what was wrong with Eleni—Caitlyn drifted away from the two. Not too long after that Eleni was alone in a side exhibit hall with the one she had wanted to see.

"I was just stopped by Takis Koniotis. He has asked me to set up an appointment to come down to police headquarters and talk with him. I'm very afraid. I don't know what he wants. Surely he hasn't connected me with Alvarez, the monk, and the Belgian file clerk. What is going on here? I'm not being sold out, am I?"

"You must remain calm. I'm sure he doesn't suspect anything. You did a very good job of covering up your involvement."

Eleni's gaze darted back to the swirling crowd in the other hall. No one was approaching. "This must have something to do with those murders. This can't be a coincidence. And it can't be a coincidence you are here. We were doing so well. I'm so torn. I'm so glad you've come, but everything seems to have fallen apart now."

"Yes, I am equally disturbed by these killings," her companion answered soothingly. "I agree that something unfortunate must be happening. Someone must have found out they are all here and is, for some reason, rolling them up. It might be any of several countries. Someone might have found the records of the operation. Our people may be seen as just a dead liability. But I guess under the circumstances, 'dead' isn't the best adjective to be using, is it, my dear?"

"How can you be so flippant about this?"

"Sometimes it helps to be flippant about such things. I'm doing what I can."

"If . . ." Eleni stammered. "If they are seen as a liability, what are you and I seen as?"

"Now, don't panic. It's not time for that as yet. We must continue as we are for now."

"I don't know if I can just continue. Especially if there are to be more of these killings." Eleni's nearness to breakdown was evident in her voice.

"Then you must leave town. That restaurant hotel up in Kakopetria, up near Troodos. You have an apartment there, don't you?"

"Yes," Eleni whispered.

"Go there. Go there now. Don't contact Koniotis first; just go on up to Kakopetria. I will come up there this weekend, and we will make plans."

"Yes. Yes, . . . My Love." The endearment was tentative, as if Eleni was unsure of being allowed to dredge up the closeness the two had known. But, when this sentiment was not rejected, she continued.

"I long to hold you. You will come? You will take care of me?"

"Yes, you can count on me taking care of you. But we have to get back. Look, that ass is coming our way. Get a hold of yourself and be the ruthless business executive the world sees in you."

* * * *

Safa Ziya had just returned to her own office in Nicosia and was busy putting her coat on. She wasn't doing this to prepare to leave

107

again but because it was actually colder in her dim, damp office than it had been outside.

"That's the one good thing about the seminar," she said brightly to her office mate. "At least they have heaters at the Ledra Palace, even if they don't work all that well."

The only response Safa received was an outraged sneeze. She had never tried to conduct a conversation with the other official before.

"No," she continued. "That's not the only good thing. It really does seem that some valuable collaboration will be possible with the Greek side on these murder cases."

She thought back on the uncensored gratitude Takis Koniotis had shown after she had shared information on her investigations and, for the third time that day, she smiled, ignoring the snort of disapproval from the other side of the room when she had had the gall to say something nice about the Greeks.

Ziya never got depressed by gloomy weather as many of her colleagues did. On such days, her office mate rarely showed up for work from fear that his perpetual cold would quickly turn into pneumonia. With the onset of the rainy, cooler season, Ziya could pretty much count on having her room to herself most of the time between now and April.

She, in fact, very much wanted to have the room to herself now, and just as she cleared her throat to speak again, the man disappeared through the doorway and down the hall in panic.

I wonder just what it is that he does for the department? Safa thought. When he's gone, the paperwork just continues to pile on his desk, and no one seems to be concerned. Out of curiosity, she started for the other side of the room with the intention of taking a look at the papers in his desk.

The creaking of the wheels of a small cart and the shuffling of Tansul's approaching feet, however, arrested Ziya's exploration of her office mate's papers, and she returned hurriedly to her own desk, sat in her chair, and pretended to be studying a report. Slipping into the door and leaning conspiratorially down toward Safa, Tansul handed over several folders in a manner that indicated she really shouldn't be sharing this information with the investigator.

"The chief's office continues to be in an uproar over these murder cases," Tansul confided. "He spent all morning yelling for you and asking everyone in sight why the cases hadn't been wrapped up."

"He knows very well where I was," Ziya snapped, eyes flashing. "And he knows very well why these cases haven't been wrapped up. He hasn't given me the time or facilities to wrap them up!"

"This folder won't help all that much," the thick-skinned Tansul giggled as she pointed to the first file she had handed over. "This doesn't provide any answers, just more questions." The cart began to creak again, and Tansul was starting off for the door when Safa laid a restraining hand on her arm.

"No, please, Tansul. If I'm going to get anywhere with all of this paperwork, I'll need your assistance. Please stay until I've read through this."

Tansul looked delighted, folded herself into the unoccupied desk chair on the other side of the room, and leaned forward, her elbows on her well-rounded knees and her eyes wide with anticipation of adventure.

As Tansul had intimated, the top folder opened up a new inquiry altogether. It was marked with the case number of the Kleist murder investigation, but she could not see how it necessarily fit into the case. Still, it was intriguing in its own right. Because of Kleist's history as an antiquities forger, Ziya had ordered that the Nicosia shop of his cohort, Mehmet Tosun, be kept under surveillance.

The file Ziya was reading described an incident at his shop the previous afternoon. An obviously angry and formidable woman, carrying several suitcases, had accosted Tosun at his shop. She had a volatile and apparently unsatisfied discussion with the merchant who had successfully posed throughout Europe as a mainland Turk for many years but who, Ziya had recently found out, was a Lebanese outcast with a very shady past. The woman then had been taken to the Serail Hotel, very near to Ziya's office. She was still registered there, although Tosun's nephew had taken her off to Kyrenia for dinner the previous evening. A passport check at the hotel had revealed the woman was an American, Peggy Bingham. She had come straight from Boston through Istanbul and had given her occupation on immigration forms as "art collector." She had declared nearly $100,000 in cash when she entered northern Cyprus—which was enough to make any investigator sit up and take notice.

"I wonder how—and if—this fits in with the murders," Ziya said. "Well, we have to start someplace."

"Tansul, I need a full background check on Bertelli and Kleist through Interpol as soon as possible. I know you've been trying to get Istanbul to make some queries, but we need to think of other ways to get international cooperation on this. We need to try to discover what brought them here, whether they were associated with each other before they relocated here, and what they could have been involved in that was significant enough to result in their deaths. It's beginning to look like artifact smuggling might be the answer to the last question. That being the case, I need background traces on Mehmet Tosun and this Bingham woman, as well. Can you manage that for me in half the time the research pool normally takes?"

"But, of course, Safa. Leave everything to me. I have a friend at the British mission here who owes me a big favor. I've just been waiting for the right need to arise." And Tansul, her eyes dancing, took a firm grip on her cart and squeaked off in the pursuit of truth.

Safa sighed and looked up to see that the sun had come out from behind the clouds that only appeared in Cyprus in this season, and that its beams were fighting to pierce through the slats of the window shutters. She rose and threw the shutters back in an attempt to bring some warmth into the room. She suddenly felt very cold, although at the same time she felt she was further down the path toward the resolution of the murder cases.

"If my hunches are correct, the Bingham woman will need some protection. I'd best try to get someone to watch over her." Ziya shuddered from the thought and rubbed her arms vigorously.

* * * *

After walking back to police headquarters with Takis, who had insisted that he had just a little more work to do before he could come home, Caitlyn had driven back to their house. She stopped to admire her garden as she closed the garage door and began to ascend the marble steps to the front door. She had had no idea during her recent whirlwind courtship by Takis that she would be moving into such a comfortable house. Somehow she had envisioned her husband as living in a small apartment with rumpled clothes and old pizza boxes covering every surface.

However, Takis, an only child, had inherited his parents' home when they had both been killed in an auto accident in Germany where his father had been assigned to the Cypriot embassy a decade previously. The house was located about a mile from the old city walls and just two blocks off the Makarios Avenue commercial street that linked the main entrance into the old city with the superhighway to Larnaca and Limassol. The neighborhood was urban, which, thanks to the lack of zoning, bundled together high-rise apartments, commercial buildings, shops, and single-family homes. The Koniotis house, hidden like most of its neighbors behind a five-foot wall, was located on a corner where thankfully streets of minimal traffic and wider-than-normal pavement intersected. The corner was just under the shadow of the steep slope of a hill that was assumed to have been an important acropolis area in ancient times but that the antiquities-rich Cypriots had yet to get around to excavating.

As with many Cypriot houses of its era, the bedroom wing of the Koniotis residence was built over an open space, where the dowry apartment had been projected to be built. As Takis had no sisters, this space had never been filled. Caitlyn had instantly fallen in love with the house, and especially so with the open, concrete-floored area under the bedroom wing. This hideaway was surrounded on three sides by rich plantings of freesias, hibiscus, and bougainvillea, carpeted by the thick matting of succulents, and barricaded against the busy roads on two sides by a hedge of pine trees and the high wall. At the same time, she was both delighted and disturbed by the marble columns, pedestals, and capitals that dotted the naturalized garden. She could tell at an experienced glance that these were ancient and thus thought they must be turned over to the museum for preservation.

Takis had laughed. Such artifacts, he said, were churned up in abundance throughout the neighborhood whenever a house was being built. If everyone turned over everything that was uncovered over to the museum, he had asserted, there would be no place to store it. No, these pieces had come up out of the ground when his parents had built the house, and they jolly well would stay right here where they had come from unless and until the museum showed enough interest to send someone to cart them away. Caitlyn had had to admit that she could see his point. Now each time she passed through the garden on the way to the house, she felt she was in her own little museum garden.

However, she also experienced an unexplainable tugging at her memory, as well as a sharp sense of fear that she could not quite grasp. At those times she thought inexplicably of Eleni Piccard and found her gaze lifting anxiously to the hillside across the road.

On this Thursday afternoon, as she tripped up the front stairs and past the swirls of sweet-smelling jasmine, another thought quickly displaced this inexplicable tinge of foreboding she had about the garden. She was contemplating the only disadvantage she had thus far discerned to such an older home in Nicosia. Takis's parents had been with the Cypriot foreign service. They apparently had been impressed enough with American styles that they had built their home in a split-level configuration. But they must have taken Great Britain rather than the States as the model for their heating system. Now that it was beginning to grow colder, Caitlyn was beginning to see why most of the neighbors didn't surround their houses with pine trees and didn't leave large open areas under their bedrooms. The large overhangs over the windows certainly helped keep the sun out in the hot summer months, but they were equally effective in keeping the sun out in the cooler, windier winter months. And with no enclosure below or above the bedroom wing, these unheated rooms were fully exposed to the chilling winds of winter.

Caitlyn was, in fact, contemplating the challenge that her first full winter in Cyprus would pose for her physical constitution and her disposition when she heard the phone ringing inside the house. It was still ringing when she had managed to get the door open. But she was to be sorry she hadn't just let it ring.

On the other end was a muffled, indistinguishable voice.

"If you value your lives, tell him to beg off the murder investigations. We know where you work, we know where you live, and we know the automobiles you drive." The phone went dead.

She was still standing there, gripping the receiver tightly in her hand, when Takis arrived home soon thereafter.

It was only in the retelling of the story, however, that she was to remember the strangest aspect of the telephone message. The caller, although Caitlyn could not even begin to guess whether it was a man or a woman, had spoken to her in clear, precise . . . French.

Chapter Eight

The peace and quiet that normally graced the central square of the village of Strovolos was anything but peaceful and quiet on the following Friday morning. Now just another suburb of the capital, Strovolos had fought hard to preserve the separate identity of its village square and surrounding narrow streets. And it had been generally successful in maintaining its village-life integrity and tranquillity except for the times, like now, when the Hamiltons were in residence.

Major William Hamilton and his first, now deceased, wife had lived nearly twenty quiet, refined years in their Strovolos apartment. That couple had been warmly welcomed in the neighborhood. Major Hamilton and his second wife were warmly welcomed by the neighborhood too—welcomed, that is, to spend as much time as possible in their Lefkara home.

On this Friday morning, the Strovolos village center was being entertained by a loud, brandy-inspired commentary from Willie on the failings and inadequacies of the famous Greek actor Antonis Demetriou. The second theme Willie was offering was the long-playing litany of Ginger Hamilton's multiple infidelities. Ginger was equal to the challenge and was sharing, in great detail, her very graphic views on the extent and explicit nature of the major's own inadequacies, especially those that had a connection with bedroom maneuvers.

The way in which this argument was fading in and out, depending on which side of the apartment the various neighbors were trapped, indicated that the two were skirmishing back and forth through the apartment's five rooms. As a matter of fact, Ginger Hamilton, master campaigner that she was, was only thrusting and parrying with the right side of her brain. She was using the left side to plan her packing, compose a note to the cleaning lady, settle on a recipe to serve that night to that handsome Cypriot laborer working on that house across the alleyway in Lefkara, and review her cosmetics stocks.

In mid diatribe, the front door slammed and Ginger lugged two heavy suitcases down two flights of stairs. She tossed them into the back of her baby blue BMW convertible and roared off toward the mountains.

The silence in the square was deafening. Everyone's breath for several streets around had been inhaled. Everyone was waiting—anxious and hopeful to hear the Hamilton's door slam again rather than the rattling of the bottles. The latter sound generally marked several more hours of harangued monologue followed by heavy snoring and the ever-present danger that the building would be burned to the ground by a carelessly dropped cigarette. A door slammed. There was a collective exhalation of breath. A Morris Mini backfired and clanked toward downtown Nicosia. And the Strovolos village square was returned to being an oasis of peace and quiet in the center of a bustling national capital. The Hamiltons were no longer at home.

Within twenty minutes, Strovolos' gain was turned into old city Nicosia's loss. The red Morris Mini puffed up in front of the Famagusta Gate cultural center and (sort of) parked once more right in front of the tall central gates. However, this time Major Hamilton did not enter the Famagusta Gate complex but, rather, scooted across the street between moving cars, running around the inner perimeter of the old city wall.

The diminutive journalist made a beeline for the Nicosia municipality's professional experimental theater, Theatro Ena. He walked purposefully through the double main doors, straight ahead and up six steps. Here he stopped at the top row of seats of the main theater to permit his eyes to become accustomed to the dim lights and to spy his quarry.

The small stage was inventively set for Arthur Miller's *Death of a Salesman*, which was opening the following Saturday night with Antonis Demetriou in the lead. The theater's permanent director, Andreas Christodoulides, was sitting in the second row.

Hamilton heard the director speak in an authoritative voice: "Willy! Stage center, please, for act two. Start with the line 'Wonderful coffee. Meal in itself'," and was temporarily taken aback. And then there he was, center stage; in his shirt sleeves, healthy head of graying hair shining, toned muscles well defined within his thin shirt, teeth gleaming in the spotlights. Antonis Demetriou, dressed for his part as Willy Loman.

The fire in Hamilton's eyes flared. He let out a screech of "Lecher. You are a dead man," and lurched down the short aisle and toward the stage. His chosen battle mace was an empty Anglaias brandy bottle—which he had been using as a mock microphone during his recent "discussion" with his wife.

The unarmed and disadvantaged Demetriou, in keeping with the experienced Greek army officer and attaché he had been before he retired to the professional stage, retreated in good form behind the set. Andreas Christodoulides, in keeping with the unflappable director he had become, intercepted the unsteady Willie Hamilton as he wobbled by. In one deft movement, the director had divested Hamilton of the brandy bottle and moved the little Britisher back up the aisle.

"It was so nice of you to come by to preview the play, Mr. Hamilton. Are you doing the review for the *Cyprus Mail*? If so, we will have two good seats waiting for you on Sunday evening. But you'll have to excuse us right now. We still have a lot of work to do on . . ."

And the pair were gone through the passage in the middle of the top row of seats and back down to the front lobby.

The other Willy, Antonis Demetriou, stepped prettily around a stage flat. Returning to center stage, he produced a little self-satisfied smile and sat down at a shabby kitchen table, his best profile turned exactly one-quarter toward the empty theater. Fixing the upper left rear corner of the room in his gaze, he smoothly and steadily started reciting: "Wonderful coffee. Meal in—"

* * * *

Maria Solonos had met Takis Koniotis in the municipal park, located half way between police headquarters and the Ledra Palace Hotel when the latter was returning from the morning session of the bicommunal police seminar. She had wanted him to learn of the results on the research on the attacks on the foreign nationals as soon as possible, but as she caught sight of Takis, she could see that her news would have to wait.

"What's wrong, Takis? You look very disturbed. Has the seminar taken a turn for the worse?"

"No," he said, as he drew Maria over to a bench under a line of majestic royal palms that lined the main path. "Caitlyn received a disturbing telephone call at home last evening threatening dire consequences if I didn't drop the case on the murders of foreigners. I'm thinking of bowing out of the investigation."

"That's not like you. You've never been upset by a threatening phone call before. What's different now?"

"What's different now is that now I'm married. And it was Caitlyn, not me, who received the phone call. I've never before had to consider the danger this work posed on others."

"I can't believe that Caitlyn went into shock over a phone call. She's proven she's tough. She married you, didn't she?"

Maria's jab had the intended effect on Takis. He laughed dryly, and answered, "You're right about Caitlyn. It shook her up a bit at first, but then she started analyzing what happened while I was still blustering about it being just another crank call. Caitlyn pointed out that the caller had our unlisted telephone number and was quite explicit about the reason for the call. The caller also knew that whoever answered the phone would be fluent in French—which both of us are. Otherwise, there wouldn't have been any reason to have used that language. We figured the foreign language was used to put us off guard, which it did. Caitlyn was so rattled, she didn't even focus on whether it was a man's or woman's voice. But we obviously were meant to understand the message being given."

"So, it was someone who knew Caitlyn spoke French. Given her profession, just about anyone could have surmised she spoke French."

"That's true enough, Maria," Takis answered, as they rose and started back to the office. "But there are just a handful of people who know that my family lived in France for several years when my father was a diplomat and that I would be able to speak French. And that small group consists of people I have thought were my closest friends and colleagues." Both were lost in their own thoughts until they had entered the police department and were nearing Takis's office.

"I guess you're right, though, Maria. I didn't go to the trouble to work myself into this job to abandon my cases at the first sign of danger. How did you come to meet me in the park, by the way?"

"I have lots of news on the case front," said Maria. Now that they were back in the office, she had become more cheerful and animated. "I was on my way to drag you out of the seminar, if necessary. The team is anxious to get into the next phase of work on this. I think you'll be pleased with what we found, and I think you'll want to go out and buy a bottle of Johnnie Walker Red for Safa Ziya for giving you these leads."

"OK, I'm ready," sighed Koniotis, as he sank into his chair.

"First, Ziya's lead on the bank. Alvarez, Father Nikolay, and Christos all had accounts at the Engomi National Bank. And, as with the victims in the north, all of these accounts were being fed by a bank in Brussels."

Koniotis grunted. "Now we have a place to start from. I should try to let Safa Ziya know right away that we're working the same case."

"Hold it. Back in your seat," Solonos directed. "You haven't heard the really interesting part yet."

"Which is?"

"Ziya's lead was interesting as far as it went, but our background reports on our three foreign victims are in and there's an even more intriguing common denominator now."

Koniotis lifted an eyebrow, but he didn't interrupt the flow of Maria's report.

"The key word here is 'Brussels.' All our foreign victims were working for their separate governments either at the NATO headquarters in Brussels or for their embassies in Brussels in the late 1970s and early 1980s. Alvarez de Toledo was Spain's representative to NATO. Father Nikolay was the Russian Orthodox representative to a religious organization opposing activities then targeted against the Soviet Union and the East European bloc. The Belgian, Erica Christos—and this was before she came to Cyprus and married a Cypriot—had been a high-level secretary in the NATO headquarters secretariat."

"Interesting," said Takis. "But there's still a long distance between sharing a NATO connection and sharing a death. There must be a more direct connection."

"And I think that connection must have been some sort of major event happening around the 1983 to 1985 period," Maria said. "As we have learned already, all of these people arrived in Cyprus between 1985 and 1988. However, much more significant, the files we have received from Interpol on each victim, without exception, end abruptly in the summer of 1983."

"They all stop in 1983?" Koniotis repeated, his voice trailing off with an emphasized question mark.

"I think I can answer why that is so," she said. But, rather than Maria Solonos, the she in this case was Sarah Bristow, who was entering the office, followed by Alec Stuart and John Dunsford.

"Uh, oh, Maria," Koniotis said. "I think we've just trod on someone's favorite corn." With that he rose from his chair—not having any chairs to offer his "guests," he had no polite alternative to rising to their levels.

"Quite so," responded Bristow briskly, very clearly the delegation leader. Stuart and Dunsford, in fact, looked like this frontal attack maneuver had not been to their liking at all.

Sarah Bristow continued, "We do not, of course, want to seem to be intruding in your murder investigation, and we certainly want you to bring these cases to a successful conclusion. However, we feel we need to help you a bit by noting some parameters you will have to work within. We wouldn't want you to waste time following clues that won't lead anywhere."

"Set parameters for my investigations? Closing off avenues of investigation?" Koniotis's voice was developing a steely edge.

Bristow didn't blink. "Yes. It's not that the three of us will try to establish barriers. In fact, we've come here today to tell you more than you will be able to get out of Interpol, or any entity in Brussels, or the governments of any of the murder victims."

"OK, let's hear it," said Koniotis, crossing his arms tightly.

"The short version—the only version we can provide," Bristow began, "is that a spy ring of unknown sponsorship was uncovered in the Brussels headquarters of NATO in 1983.

Unfortunately, it was not uncovered in time by the active measures being taken by NATO and some of its members. It was only belatedly discovered when a cast of characters—including your three foreign victims—simply vanished from their NATO-related jobs. Quite apparently they were part of an extensive spy operation. We have no idea whether they knew of each other's existence, and there still is no evidence who was the mastermind—or masterminds. They probably scattered because we were starting to receive bits and pieces of the NATO defense secrets back from our own operations behind the Iron Curtain and our various security forces had begun nosing around in Brussels.

"You won't receive even that much information from any other source. I doubt you need any more information than that about the previous lives of your victims to pursue your investigation. We are concerned—and you should be, as well—that if you try to pursue the issue further internationally, you will have agents of most of the secret services of the Western world in your knickers. They will be trying to track down their own traitors in this mess or trying to keep any more of their own governments' secrets from getting out. On the other hand, the three of us, representing major players in NATO, stand ready to help you and your government close this issue out as quietly and as effectively as possible."

"You are too kind," Koniotis responded mildly but not without irony. "You seem to know quite a bit about this issue, Colonel Bristow. That would be because . . . ?"

"Yes, I was in Brussels at the time of the defections. As was, I should add, John Dunsford."

Koniotis gave Dunsford a withering look but said only, "How coincidental." Dunsford looked like he wanted to be anywhere but where he was.

"And you too?" Koniotis's query bored into Alec Stuart, who had literally shrunk into a corner.

"No, not me too," Stuart replied meekly. "I was in Singapore during that period."

"And how, may I ask, were you able to latch so quickly onto your chosen role of 'helpers'?" Koniotis directed the question at Bristow. "The ink is hardly dry on this Interpol report. I find it very hard to believe that your governments can move this fast on a case that has been on ice for nearly two decades."

"Fair question," Bristow answered levelly. "John and I recognized the woman you know as Erica Christos at the concert the other night. At least I did, and John eventually remembered her. She was one of the principal NATO secretariat employees, and her identification photo was emblazoned in the brains of all of us who were trying to do damage control. After she was murdered, John and I started working on the case through our own separate channels, and we met your own research in the middle at Interpol last evening.

"Well, that's all we can say. We'll leave now. Our ambassadors will be talking with your minister. We'll have to arrive at some sort of arrangement to share—and to contain—information." The trio shuffled toward the door.

"Excuse me," Koniotis stopped them in their tracks in a tone that could not be ignored, "but you have not told me everything that you know and that I need to know."

"Meaning?" responded Bristow testily.

"If you and Dunsford were working the investigation in Brussels—"

"I said I was working the investigation," Bristow cut in. "I did not say John was working the investigation."

"All right, if you were working the investigation in Brussels, you have some idea how many spies were involved. We've already seen at least five of them killed on this island in the last couple of weeks."

"Five?" Bristow asked sharply.

"Yes," Koniotis answered. "The three on this side of the Green Line—the three that we know about; there may have been others, of course—plus a German and an Italian on the other side."

"Ackerman and Gianni?" Sarah blurted the names out—and immediately looked mortified.

"If so, not by those names," Koniotis responded after a pause and then continued. "As I said, we know of at least five probable members of this spy ring who have been killed here in recent days. It is imperative for you to let us know just how many more could be here and in danger. We have to try to get to them before any more are killed. For our part, we're not all that pleased to have foreigners being murdered left and right. For your part, surely you want to catch some of these people alive."

Bristow looked hard at Koniotis. Her jaw started to work, and she appeared about ready to respond when Dunsford broke in.

"We're very sorry, but that really is beyond our brief. Our own people will have to be consulted and we'll have to work that one out through your ministry."

Koniotis was about to explode when Dunsford went on, "I do think it would be useful for all of us to keep an eye on the Russian,

Sergey Stepanov, however, which could provide an answer to your concern."

Now Bristow looked uncomfortable, as a confused Koniotis, his anger dissipated, asked, "Stepanov? What are you implying?"

"As far as I know," Dunsford went on, "he was not implicated at the time in the NATO spy case—was he, Sarah?"

But the colonel just pursed her lips without responding, so Dunsford continued, "I do know from my own end of the business, however, that he was in Brussels during this period and quite obviously was not up to any activities that would have been helpful to NATO or to any of NATO's constituent members. As Stepanov is here now, and spies are dropping like flies, it's fairly probable that our best combined activity for the moment would be to watch him to see if he pops off the occasional foreigner here and there. This is developing all of the markings of a classic spy ring sponsor cleanup."

"You mean a 'retired with prejudice' operation?" Stuart blurted out. "If so, what a brilliant scheme. Cyprus is the ideal place for a spy salting operation."

Both Koniotis and Solonos registered confusion, but then Koniotis's face showed the dawning of understanding.

"Ah, yes. I heard those terms just the other day from one of your colleagues." The three gave Takis a questioning look, but he did not tell them of his conversation with Paul Conte the previous week at the Troodos mountain resort. "I guess that term is more prophetic than I thought—and more relevant to peace and order in Cyprus than I ever thought would be possible."

"Yes," Sarah Bristow picked up the thread, "it looks like it is quite possible that the Eastern Bloc sponsor of this spy ring first

126

relocated all of the agents involved to Cyprus—probably without telling them that the others had been hidden here as well—the spies probably had never known about each other even in Brussels. Then, after their authoritarian system had broken up along with that of the rest of the bloc, they felt it prudent to silence any and all who could eventually lead Western investigators back to the specific Eastern Bloc intelligence activities."

"Under the circumstances, then, I would appreciate all the help your embassies can give my unit on this case," Takis said. He had no intention of letting the three either bog down or take over his investigation, but if these killings did reflect a massive intelligence operation, he fully realized that he would need their assistance. When the three had gone, he turned to Maria and told her to ignore, to the extent possible, any barriers the Western embassies might try to throw into her research path until they had received a formal restraining order from the interior minister.

He then picked up the phone and moved his finger toward the dial. But his movement was arrested in midair and he looked perplexed.

"What's the matter?" Maria asked.

"That's strange," Koniotis said in a wistful tone. "I've never done that before. I picked up the telephone because I need to consult with Safa Ziya, and I suddenly realized that I can't telephone Safa Ziya. We have no telephone connections with the Turkish zone. I had never before realized—or cared—just how totally we have cut ourselves off from the Turkish Cypriots. Now I can't talk to her until the seminar resumes on Monday. And if it were not for the seminar, I couldn't consult with her at all. Well . . ."

He stood in deep contemplation for a moment. Then he shook his head, sighed quietly, reached once more for the telephone, and dialed a number. The voice at the other end of the line said, "I'm sorry, Mrs. Piccard is out of town until at least Monday."

Then, in response to his follow-up question: "No, I'm sorry, I don't know where she went."

"Damn," Koniotis exclaimed as he replaced the receiver. "Piccard and her company's travel accommodations seem to be an angle those three haven't latched onto yet. I only hope we can keep that one to ourselves until Piccard returns to town. I can't wait to schedule an appointment now. I'm going to have to camp out on her doorstep until she returns. Better yet, Maria, could you please have a surveillance team put on her house and ask them to let me know as soon as she returns?"

"Will do," answered Solonos, as she moved to the door.

"Oh, and she has a flat up at her hotel restaurant in Kakopetria as well. Could you arrange for someone to go up there tomorrow to see if she's there?"

"I'll go up there myself tomorrow afternoon," Maria answered.

She stepped out of the door but was stopped as she entered the hallway. There was a murmur of voices and Maria returned, looking perplexed.

"A development?" Koniotis asked.

"More of a wrinkle. I'm afraid the cases aren't necessarily focusing. Now a new connection is developing with the Cypriot boatman."

Koniotis held off the question, and Maria continued—but he could tell there was something unsaid that was bothering her.

"The boatman was just helping that weekend. He came down to the pier with Alvarez. His real job, however, was as driver for Justin Chamberlain, the art dealer, and both he and Chamberlain had been under scrutiny for possible involvement in antiquities smuggling."

"And?" prompted Koniotis, trying to draw the concealed concern from his associate.

"Well, that strengthens another possible common denominator. Chamberlain, the boatman, and Kleist in the north—they all have possible connections to antiquities smuggling. Alvarez was an avid art collector. Who knows what others among the victims might also have had such connections. If so, maybe they are linked by some sort of connection with the Brussels spy ring. But maybe the victims were actually killed because of their connection to smuggling—not because of anything they did in Brussels."

"Yes, of course, I accept that remains a line of inquiry. But, Maria, you still seem to be upset about something else."

"Yes, I'm sorry, Takis . . . but I was also told that before the Cypriot boatman worked for Chamberlain, he was a laborer at the Kaliana dig. He was a favorite of—and was recommended to Chamberlain by . . . your wife. Caitlyn recommended him."

Chapter Nine

Shortly after bidding good-bye to Takis Koniotis on the Ledra Palace Hotel steps, Safa Ziya walked as briskly as her crippled leg permitted from the Friday morning session of the police seminar to her office off Ataturk Square in the center of the walled Turkish sector of Nicosia. She felt she and Takis had been making a connection that could eventually benefit the communities of both sides, but Takis had been more withdrawn into his own thoughts today than in any previous session.

He had, of course, not been rude to her. In fact, after the first seminar session, he had henceforth been flatteringly attentive to her views. But throughout today's session, he had seemed entirely preoccupied. Conversely, John Dunsford had been particularly pesky about asking her for her views and experience on anything and everything that was brought up. She had had no time whatsoever to consult with Koniotis on the foreign murder cases or to try to find out what was disturbing him. And now they were totally cut off from each other by the impervious Green Line curtain until Monday morning's session.

Funny, she thought. Until this seminar I saw the buffer zone as my protection from my enemies. Now I'm not so sure. At least at the moment it clearly is a barrier between me and a quicker solution to these murder cases—murders that endanger all Cypriots of both communities. Who knows if the killing has stopped? I feel like I am running out of time before the next murder.

Ziya's slow march had brought her to the street that crossed over the Venetian wall and into the old city. She hadn't taken more than a couple of steps when she was snapped out of her reverie by brushing hard between a couple of northern European tourists. This caused her to look up. Although somewhat dazed, she found herself looking straight into the eyes of Mehmet Tosun, whose bulk was stuffing the door of his shop.

Both hunted and hunter took in a sharp breath. Tosun had never formally met the Turkish Cypriot police inspector. But he had every reason to know who Ziya was, what she did for a living, and just how well she did her job. In response to the unexpected encounter, Tosun gave a little snort and retreated a half step. This, unfortunately for him, served only to bang his head on hanging copperware and wedge him more tightly in his doorway. Ever the optimistic salesman, however, he quickly covered his surprised expression with a jolly countenance, raised his arms in a welcoming gesture, and started to speak. But Safa Ziya had recovered her own wits even more quickly and had hurried on.

She paused near the Venetian Column in Ataturk Square to look up at the Serail Hotel—the current resting place of Peggy Bingham. She almost could imagine that she saw Bingham there in one of the windows, boldly looking down her hawklike beak at Safa. The police investigator tore her attention away from the hotel façade, and she quickened her pace across the square.

Mehmet Tosun and Peggy Bingham. She did not have to wait for further results on the murder cases from the more sophisticated research facilities of Takis Koniotis to have constructive work to do. Tosun and Bingham gave her investigation possibilities concerning some crime, she was sure, even though it remained to be seen if they were connected to the same crime. Her pace picked up along with her resolve to plunge her energies into the question of Tosun's activities for the rest of the afternoon.

Ziya crossed the square and into the old British administrative building that had replaced the original Venetian governors' palace in 1904. She then exited this building through a passageway off the back and into her own far less grand office block at a more determined pace than before she had encountered Tosun and thought of Peggy Bingham. No, it would not do to start to depend too heavily on help from the Greek Cypriot police, she thought. There was work available to her with her own meager resources, as it always had been available to her. It was foolish to dream that the effort would get any easier.

* * * *

"Mr. Tosun!" Peggy Bingham shouted down the crackling telephone line in a booming voice that would have carried the six blocks to Mehmet Tosun's shop without the aid of science. "Have you ever managed to keep down a meal you ate at the Serail Hotel?"

The severe Bostonian was standing in the window of her third-floor hotel room and looking down into Ataturk Square. A ball of a woman, stuffed in a chain-stitched, drab-beige woolen sweater, had come to a precipitous stop next to the Venetian Column below and was looking piercingly up at the façade of the early Stalinist-style Serail Hotel. Bingham involuntarily drew back into the room and then moved aggressively back to the window, chin out, in an irritated move that even she didn't understand. Why had such a tired old Turkish housewife given her a fright? The woman in the square below resumed her fast waddle toward the British colonial-style building to the north of the square.

"But of course, Dear Lady," Mehmet Tosun answered in a smooth voice that completely ignored the imagery Bingham had created. "The Serail is, indeed, the finest hotel in Nicosia."

"I sincerely hope not," Bingham snapped.

"I am so sorry to break into your fine vacation, Your Grace, but I have heard from Mr. Roentgen."

"Well, why didn't you say so sooner? Where is that little shit?" Peggy asked acidly, revealing that she was only a Bingham by marriage. She had, in real life, been billed in her youth as Madeleine LaRue of the Rockefeller Center Rockettes chorus line. "I'll be damned if I'll sit in this sewer one more day. I want my icons or my money, and I want them before I'm served up one more plate of slop in this dive."

"Yes, yes, Pretty Lady," Tosun said. "I knew you'd be pleased about Mr. Roentgen's return. His business keeps him at the port. But he has told me he can meet with you early Sunday afternoon at Othello's tower in Famagusta to present you with the icons. He is happy to report that there will be just one more small bill for just a little more money he had to pay to obtain the authentication papers."

"More money? Now you listen and you listen good, you slimy toad. I have no intention—"

"Yes, very good, my assistant will pick you up after your lunch at the Serail on Sunday and will convey you to Famagusta. In the meantime, I'm arranging some wonderful activities for you."

Something like a death rattle was forming on Peggy Bingham's foam-flaked lips, but Mehmet Tosun had already rung off.

* * * *

By seeming coincidence, but really by intricately preplanned design, Tansul was creaking her cart past the door to Safa Ziya's office as the investigator was huffing up the last set of stairs. Tansul smiled a conspiratorial smile. She looked meaningfully up and down the hallway, which, in fact, was cluttered with people, all with their eyes glued with fascination on Tansul. Being thus assured she had an audience, she slipped several folders to Ziya as conspicuously as possible and rolled noisily on down the hallway.

Ziya managed to look both shy and embarrassed, as she struggled into her office to the sound of snuffling from across the room. It figured. It was warm today, so her office mate was back in full sneeze. He was shuffling through the paperwork in the tray on the right front corner of his desk. He looked up at Ziya as she entered the room, gave her a short, somewhat accusatory stare, and opened his mouth as if to inform her that he had counted his folders and was one folder short. But, instead, he snapped his mouth shut. This led to another coughing fit and subsequently to another accusatory stare at Safa.

Ziya settled in her chair. She opened the top folder, and, after a short sideways glance to note that her office mate was actually just slowly transferring his files from the tray on the right front corner of his desk to the tray in the left front corner of his desk, started to read.

The first folder Tansul had given her provided background on Gina Bertelli, also known as—aka—Sophie Gianni. Safa's review of this material was followed by that of the folder marked Detrich Kleist, aka Hans Ackerman, followed by that of Mehmet Tosun, aka Nabil Jallud. The third, last, and thinnest folder was that of Peggy Bingham, aka the richest and meanest old patrician in the American city of Boston.

There wasn't much information in any of the records arrayed before her, but there was enough to tell that only Bingham didn't fit a pattern. Bertelli and Kleist, under other names—and even Tosun, under his current name—had been living in Brussels in the late 1970s and early 1980s. Bertelli had been the maid of record, but mistress by fact, of the Italian representative to NATO. Kleist had been a code clerk in the German embassy. Tosun had been, well, whatever Tosun was anywhere. But at that time he was being Tosun in Belgium. The Interpol chronology of the records she had been given on all three ended abruptly in the summer of 1983.

Only Peggy Bingham had no connection to Belgium during the period in question. The records on her came from a Boston newspaper clipping file rather than from Interpol, which had claimed it had no file on the woman. According to the Boston papers, Bingham's major crimes seemed to follow normal business magnate schemes. The gossip columns indicated Bingham spent many of the early years of the 1980s not in Brussels but in trying to dry out at various alcohol treatment centers in the far West of the United States.

Ziya was beginning to organize all of this information in her mind when the phone on her desk rang. Her office mate looked at her accusingly, threw his papers on the desk in disgust, rose indignantly from his chair, produced two small hacking coughs, and flounced out of the door.

Ziya rose from her chair as she picked up the receiver and side-shuffled over to the other desk. She could bear the suspense no longer concerning whatever function her office mate performed in the department.

The sound produced on the line was mainly static, which meant this was a local call—if the call had come in from Antarctica, there would have been no static.

"Hello, Safa, this is John Dunsford. I'm calling from the Turkish checkpoint. I tried to talk to you directly after the seminar session, but you left before I could catch up to you. I must come over to see you immediately. It's about some name checks you ran with Interpol."

With only half attention to Dunsford, Ziya agreed to see him as soon as he could get to the office. As she replaced the receiver, she was digging through the papers on her office mate's desk. They were promotion recommendations. She sifted through the piles. They were all unprocessed promotion recommendations. Several years worth of recommendations, judging by the date stamps.

There was a knock at the door, and Tansul's head appeared around the corner at a disconcerting ninety-degree angle.

"Excuse me, Miss Ziya, there's a woman downstairs who says she must see you. She's very determined; says she's from the American embassy."

The door yawned wider, bringing into the room both Tansul, struggling mightily to maintain her footing, and Colonel Sarah Bristow, stance wide and jaw firmly set.

136

"I understand you've been sharing information on murder cases with Takis Koniotis of the Greek Cypriot police," she said.

"Why, yes, I have," Safa answered. "And he has been quite forthcoming himself."

"Oh, you think so? In that case, it's a good thing I came to see you. I think there are some things you need to know about the quality of Mr. Koniotis's cooperation with your efforts."

"I guess you had better sit down," Safa responded with a sigh. Somehow she had known that the possibility of cooperation with the Greeks was too good to be true.

Chapter Ten

The police seminar was not in session on Saturday, and Safa Ziya was at her office, shuffling her file folders around as if this in itself would help her to move her case toward resolution. She had never felt such a sense of isolation before. Maybe it had actually been better for her before the bicommunal seminar had begun and before she had been teased into believing that a helpful connection with her colleagues on the other side of the Green Line was possible or desirable.

She had been a fool—convincing herself that the Greek Cypriots wanted to work with her on this case and that the two communities could actually put their differences aside to fight such serious crimes. Takis Koniotis had played her for a fool. Her visits from the American and Canadian diplomats had opened her eyes to what was really happening. She now knew the Greek Cypriots had no intention of doing anything that helped the Turkish side of the investigation.

"Think, Safa." She sat at her desk and beat her brow with her fist. "What would you have done a week ago to move forward? You no longer can count on just waiting until Monday morning to see how they are doing with this on the other side of the buffer zone."

She reached for the telephone directory to find the number for Mehmet Tosun's shop. Maybe it's time to start making him sweat a bit, she thought.

The man who answered the telephone declared he was the shop assistant, Tosun's nephew, rather than the 'honorable proprietor'.

"I'm sorry. He has taken a client on an outing. May I tell him who has called?"

"No, thank you. I'll try again later," she said and rang off quickly.

She chewed on the side of a pencil momentarily. Once again it was colder in the office than it had been outside during her walk to work. She shivered and rewound her long, dingy woolen scarf around her neck and shoulders.

She reached for the telephone again and called the Serail Hotel, thinking there was no reason she shouldn't see what the Bingham woman had to say about what she was doing in northern Cyprus.

"No, I'm sorry, Inspector Ziya, but the woman is not in her room. Disagreeable, demanding sort. I'm not surprised you have called. Please give me a minute. Perhaps someone here knows where she is."

The clerk was back in a moment. "Well, I almost lost my head when I'd asked when the dining room staff had last seen her—something about having pushed her supper away untouched and having made very rude remarks as she swept out of the dining room.

The doorman says she went off early this morning with that Lebanese tourist gouger who has that junk shop over by the checkpoint."

"Thank you, Leyla," Ziya responded. "Could you please let me know when she returns?"

"Certainly, I'll try to call you if she returns and will leave a note to that effect with my relief. As far as we are concerned, Safa," Ziya's old schoolmate giggled down the line, "he can push her down a well."

"Thank you," Ziya answered dryly, "but we've had quite enough of that lately already. And then she'd still be my worry and you'd still have to call me."

* * * *

Eleni Piccard stood looking out over the railing of the balcony of her hotel near the upper reaches of the mountain village of Kakopetria and drank in the clear, cool mountain air. She looked up the slope at the snow-covered, radar-domed summit of Mount Olympus—the highest point in Cyprus. She then turned to look down the Solea Valley, across the reaches of the lower portion of Kakopetria. On this clear day she could see to and beyond Galata, the next village down the slope, which had merged into the lower levels of Kakopetria. She could even see past the archaeological digs around Kaliana, a project her own philanthropic Ledra Foundation was funding, and out toward the central plain and the Bay of Morphou in the distance.

It was late afternoon, the lull time in restaurant business between the lunch and the dinner crowds. The mill complex itself was in the shadows of the western slope behind it, but the afternoon sunshine still spilled into the valley below.

"I haven't done badly for myself. Our dream is just about fulfilled, Guy," she whispered into the breezes swirling up from the valley. She sighed contentedly. A return to her girlhood village and to the apartment she had set up at the top of the old mill in memory of her lost family always seemed to have a calming and centering effect on her.

Kakopetria for many long years had been a favorite mountain retreat for the inhabitants of the central plain. Its primary attraction was that two small rivers running off Mount Olympus forked in the middle of this village. They provided flowing water—and, more important, the sound of flowing water—year round to a water-starved central plains populace that could not hear running water in all seasons in any more accessible location.

Eleni Piccard had been born in this village and had later gone down the mountain and even to Europe where she had met and married the scion of a French shipping empire. The two had eventually returned to Cyprus to help extend and prosper the Piccard holdings here. To these holdings, Eleni had contributed her own inheritance, a seventeenth-century flour mill located near the fork of the Solea Valley river. The property also included a gigantic, six-story nineteenth-century storage building that was constructed against the steep western slope of the valley. It had been Eleni and Guy's dream to establish a restaurant, hotel, and folk art gallery in this warehouse.

However, their dream had been crushed with the Turkish invasion of the north in 1974. The couple and their son, Pierre, had been caught by the invasion in their northern coast vacation home in the mountain village of Bellapais on the seaward face of the Kyrenia ridge and high above the harbor town of Kyrenia. When they had received clearance, thanks to their French passports, to travel back across the newly established buffer zone to Nicosia, Eleni had gone ahead to Nicosia and Guy had taken Pierre down to Kyrenia for an important business appointment before motoring to Nicosia. However, the two had never joined Eleni. They had been listed as missing for twenty years until remains unearthed recently in a remote section of the huge Byzantine Kyrenia harbor castle had been identified as theirs.

Eleni had restored this Kakopetria restaurant and inn in the memory of her lost family, and they had both become successes. She was in the process of resolving to move forward immediately in filling out her husband's plan for this complex by opening the folk art gallery when she saw a familiar SUV pulling into the riverside parking lot far below.

She waved happily, pointed to herself and then to the small elevator shaft that brought diners from the ground level to the restaurant, and headed for the north end of the restaurant balcony. She would be the perfect hostess and provide the welcome at the ground-level entrance. Although the exterior stone staircase was a safer way to get down than the cramped, temperamental elevator, she couldn't wait another minute to greet her guest.

But when she got to the elevator door, the car had already started its wheezing journey up the building. As the indicator light made its claim that the elevator had arrived at the restaurant level, Eleni pulled the door open in great anticipation of her lover's arrival. Quite unexpectedly, however, she was pulled into the elevator, losing her balance and slumping painfully into the back corner. The door was jammed shut, and the elevator started screeching and groaning back down the building.

* * * *

Caitlyn Koniotis was standing next to the smoldering fireplace in the family's tiny study ladling out a small portion of neat scotch to her tired and weary husband, who was stretched out on a lounge chair and ottoman. One of the only changes she had as yet tried to make in her new husband's habits was to take the edge off of his participation in the Cypriot men's love affair with Johnny Walker red label.

He took the slug of scotch in one gulp and handed his glass out for more medicine.

Although she did refill the glass, Caitlyn sank down in the adjacent chair and took a pronounced, critical look at her husband.

"These murder cases are getting to you, aren't they?"

Takis needed someone to talk to about the cases. He had sent Maria Solonos up to Kakopetria in search of Eleni Piccard, and access to Safa Ziya was cut off to the extent that she might as well have been on another planet. His wife was lending him a willing ear—far more, he fully realized, than he had done for her in her own demanding job—and he both loved her all the more for it and proceeded to fully review the cases he was investigating.

As he was ending a general wrap-up of the connections between the victims that Maria and her research team were uncovering, he noted that he was trying to interview Eleni Piccard.

"Why do you think Eleni is involved in all this?" Caitlyn asked. "Just because she owns the shipping line many of the victims used to come to the island doesn't come close to proving she's involved in any of this."

"It's very unusual for foreigners to come here by ship at all. Eleni is involved with Sergey Stepanov. And John Dunsford has warned us that it's likely that Stepanov is a key player in whatever is going on with this case. John told us Stepanov has had Russian KGB links. I wonder about Dunsford. He always seems to know far more than he's telling."

"You know," Caitlyn said, breaking into the monologue. "It's funny, but I think I've heard something about that NATO case. I had a friend whose father was involved in something like that. The father was the commanding general of the NATO forces headquartered in Brussels at the time. He had been a World War II hero, but he came home from Brussels under a dark cloud, because something had been going on under his nose that somehow damaged NATO."

"What a coincidence," Takis agreed, his mind not fully focused on what Caitlyn had said.

"Yes, an even bigger coincidence is that he is here," Caitlyn went on.

"The father is here?" Takis's attention was now completely focused on what his wife was saying.

"No, silly," Caitlyn laughed. "Not the father. The son. I'm talking about Justin Chamberlain."

"Justin Chamberlain? That provides a link I hadn't known about." Takis pulled himself up in his chair and winced as his glass fell to the floor. It didn't break, but a few drops of expensive scotch had been wasted. And then he remembered what he had been meaning to ask Caitlyn since the previous afternoon.

"Oh, I'd forgotten to ask you something, Caitlyn. Maria's research into the Spanish diplomat's death surfaced the report that you had recommended one of the laborers at the Kaliana dig, Lambos Tsangaris, to Justin Chamberlain."

"Yes. Well, sort of," Caitlyn answered. "Why do you ask?"

"Well, Chamberlain, in turn, moved Tsangaris on to Alvarez. And Tsangaris was the boatman who was murdered after Alvarez was killed in the parasailing incident."

"Lambos?" Caitlyn exclaimed. "I had no idea. I hadn't paid any attention to the names in the newspaper accounts. Oh, how awful!"

"What did you mean when you said you 'sort of' recommended him to Chamberlain?" Takis asked.

"I'm not exactly proud of the story, particularly now that Lambos has been killed," Caitlyn responded, "But Andriko Visiliou is the one who really suggested it."

Takis looked quizzical.

"Well, Professor Visiliou thought that Lambos was stealing small artifacts and pottery shards from the dig, but he couldn't catch him at it. Andriko told me he had decided to fire Lambos anyway. I liked Lambos and thought it unfair to fire him without proof. Andriko just laughed and suggested that I get Lambos a job with Justin and then we'd have a matched set of artifact thieves. This has been an old argument between Andriko and me, and I was irritated. So, I'm afraid I did just that. I recommended Lambos to Justin, and Justin hired him. Since then, Andriko has shown me enough evidence for me to be worried about Justin's activities. If Lambos was mixed up with something illegal with either Justin or Alvarez, it looks like I put him in that spot."

"Now, that's not true," Takis said as he took her hand and led her over to snuggle with him in his chair. "Andriko Visiliou was probably absolutely right about Lambos. And if Lambos got into any dirty work, it was of his own doing, not yours."

"All the same," Caitlyn said in a low voice, "I'm even more worried about Justin now. Just yesterday I heard he may be involved in smuggling activities on the Turkish side, as well. Oh, and I just remembered. You know when we were up at Kykko monastery the day the Russian priest was found? I found one of Justin's business cards on the ground below where the priest fell."

"His business card? We were looking for whatever might have fallen out of the assailant's pocket when he was struggling with the priest. Where is it? Why didn't you give it to me sooner?"

"I'm sorry, Takis. It's gone. I put it in my coat pocket that day when you sent me out to mobilize the investigation team, and I didn't remember it again until I saw Justin at the cocktail party at the museum. I tried to ask him about the card then, but he was evasive. And when he left me, the card was missing."

"But, why did you say you thought Justin was involved in shady dealings on the Turkish side of the island?"

"I found another card at the same time. Some Middle Eastern name I can't remember, but there was an address, which, when I asked him about it, Justin said was Romanian. I'm sure he wasn't telling me the truth, and he seemed to recognize the name."

"I guess it's time for me to have a talk with Justin, then."

"And it's time I started to forage for something to eat."

"Something to eat?" Takis yelped, forgetting entirely that he'd intended to admonish his wife for tampering with evidence. He'd been hoping for more than a cuddle before dinner. "It isn't even dark yet."

"I know," Caitlyn responded wistfully, as she extricated herself and headed for the kitchen. "You Cypriots don't eat dinner before my normal bedtime. But if I don't have something to eat soon, I'm going to double over with hunger."

Not more than a few minutes later, however, Caitlyn found herself doubled up on the kitchen floor, and it wasn't from hunger. While taking stock of what was hiding in the refrigerator, she had felt a stabbing pain in her abdomen, which had knocked the breath out of her. The pain was so intense she wanted to scream, but all she could do was sink to the floor.

The vision was back, and this time it was passing before her eyes in broad daylight.

She was standing outside the pillared room. Phyllis again was singing her siren song and the earth had begun to move. But this time Phyllis's lover did not remain in the shadows. As the pillars began to sway, he rushed into Phyllis's outstretched arms. She could see the flash of steel, and a circle of red stain blossoming on Phyllis's chiton. Then Acamas dashed back to safety as the earth trembled and then buckled, and the columns fell inward, in swirling dust.

As Caitlyn's breath started to return, she heard herself moaning, "Oh, Eleni," over and over again, calling Eleni's name in whispered, mournful tones. She wasn't calling for Takis, and he could not hear her from the other room. It disturbed her that she wasn't calling for Takis. She dragged herself up by grasping the refrigerator handle. When she was on her feet, she leaned heavily into the counter. The pain in her abdomen was subsiding, but the pain in her heart was acute.

She started toward the hall to find Takis, but then she stopped. Takis wouldn't understand. She didn't understand herself. She only knew on some primal level that something was terribly wrong, something she couldn't explain to Takis or anyone else—much less to herself. But no matter how inexplicable it seemed, it was real and it involved Eleni Piccard.

Somehow Caitlyn managed to get to the bedroom without disturbing Takis in the study. Her hand was trembling so badly that she dropped her address book twice before she found the page she needed and had to abort the dialing of the long distance number several times. When the call to Kakopetria did go through, it rang and rang until she thought she'd scream in frustration, but she waited it out and she was eventually rewarded by a completion of the connection.

"Eleni, Eleni? Is that you. It's Caitlyn. Oh, Eleni, I just had that vision again, except this time it was much worse."

No response.

"Eleni! Can you hear me?"

Silence. No, not silence. Ragged breathing. And then a decisive click.

* * * *

Maria Solonos pulled off the road from Nicosia up to Troodos at the Kakopetria exit. As she dipped down and under the mountain highway on her way into the village, she was practically forced off the road by an SUV that was moving out of the village at a high speed. The near accident barely registered in her mind, however.

She was arriving in Kakopetria several hours later than she'd intended. She'd met Antonis Demetriou for an early lunch, the menu of which had broadened out considerably at his apartment afterward into the "forbidden fruit" food group. He'd told her he couldn't go on stage without having first satisfied his libido. Well, he was quite a hunk, and Maria's libido could stand some satisfaction just now, as well, so she wished *Death of a Salesman* a very long run.

Maria neatly maneuvered through the town square and across the stone river bridge and turned left into the parking area for the Old Mill Restaurant, which loomed overhead on her right. She'd meant to take the stairs, which she almost always used when she came to the restaurant because she did not fully trust the elevator. But the noontime games had been just too tiring, and she found herself moving toward the elevator at the north side of the building.

As she approached the elevator, she could see that the door was propped open.

Now who would have left a pile of laundry in the lift doorway? Maria asked herself.

But it was not a pile of laundry. And Eleni Piccard hadn't been wearing a red dress when she'd been pulled into the elevator at the restaurant level.

Chapter Eleven

In the quiet village of Lefkara in the Troodos foothills, Ginger Hamilton sallied forth into the courtyard of her rustic mountain home, scotch bottle and crystal glass in hand, to review her strategic position. She had spent most of the previous day on campaign. The first battle had promised victory but had been spoiled by the untimely retreat of the quarry.

After having watched the sexy, dark laborer sensuously working on the neighboring roof most of the previous afternoon following her flight from Strovolos and Willie's tiresome jealousies, Ginger had very much been in the mood for love. Luckily, she had been able to clearly see her Apollo at work from her vanity table. She had thus had hours to work her cosmetic magic on herself.

She had little trouble enticing him in for an intimate dinner when she approached him at dusk. And she could clearly tell that he had no illusions or objections concerning what was on the menu. The candlelight dinner itself and the preliminary skirmishes had gone quite well. The forces had even gotten into close hand-to-hand contact and were getting the feel and measure of each other's weapons. Suddenly and quite unexpectedly, however, the Apollo broke off the engagement and fled the field on the excuse of being urgently needed on some other front.

Oh, well, thought Ginger philosophically, as she set at the table in her little courtyard and swigged at her glass of scotch. There are always other battles. There were even other Apollos. She had spent a good part of the afternoon in the village reconnoitering just that possibility.

She sighed and tossed off a slug of scotch. During this maneuver, she noticed Apollo had returned to the neighboring roof and turned her position in the chair so that she could offer up the most uplifting frontal visage. But, as Ginger was at least subconsciously beginning to realize, not all of the building cranes in Cyprus now could have lifted her frontal visage sufficiently to sustain the interest of the Apollos of this world.

She filled her glass again, took a sip, and, almost to avoid thinking about any more painful topic, turned her thoughts to having found her front gate lock forced and the door slightly open this afternoon when she had returned from the village center.

It was strange, she thought, that her house was the only one in the alley that even had a lock on the front door, and someone chose her place to break in. She supposed that the whole village must know how meticulously they had restored the village house and must have assumed—falsely, of course—that they kept valuables here. She once more reviewed the inventory she had taken. For the life of her, however, she could not account for anything having been stolen. She couldn't even say anything was touched, she thought in frustration and confusion.

The frustration caused her to start gazing about the courtyard one more time for signs of tampering. Why had the big olive oil jar arrested her inspection this time? Was it perhaps just a bit off the precise spot Willie had established for it? And was there a shadow of something behind it?

Ginger had just started to rise to inspect the jar . . . when the bomb went off.

The clamor from over the wall knocked Apollo off his perch and onto his godly behind in the alleyway below and automatically prompted all of the neighbors to say to themselves in unison: "The Hamiltons must be at home again."

* * * *

Helmut Roentgen managed to clear the arrivals hall at the Turkish zone's Ercan Airport without having been challenged. Security here was so lax, he thought. This was an ideal location for his operations.

Upon exiting the terminal, he was happy to see that Tosun had left the inconspicuous, but still quite comfortable, old Mercedes in the parking lot for him. This service belied the impression Roentgen was forming that the thieving merchant couldn't approach any activity straight on or fully fulfill any assignment.

"Ah, yes, typical," he observed as he climbed into the driver's seat. The car was here, where it was supposed to be, but the gas gauge registered nearly empty. For some reason there was no petrol station near the airport, but Roentgen decided to trust his luck that he could get to Bogaz before the Mercedes had exhausted its resources.

The village of Bogaz, sheltered in the east coast cavity where the Karpas Peninsula jutted out toward the Turkish coast, had long been famous as a smugglers' port. It also had given succor to a long line of revolutionaries against the various manifestations of authority on the island. The village knew Roentgen well, and when his luck held out and he managed to reach the town without incident, he was able to fill his gas tank, and one of its fishing gear shops supplied him with a parcel that he had ordered there several days earlier.

After exchanging macho adventure stories with a couple of the local blockade runners long enough to keep them satisfied that he was just one of the boys, Roentgen hid the parcel he had acquired in a special compartment in the car's trunk, climbed back into the Mercedes, and motored down the coast to the Salamis Bay Hotel.

The Salamis Bay was an incongruous high-rise resort hotel located on the beach just to the north of the ancient ruins at Salamis and halfway between the village of Bogaz in the north and Famagusta in the south. The hotel was nearly deserted this November, the end of the normal tourist season in the north now several weeks in the past.

Roentgen returned for a drink in the lower lobby after retrieving his package from the Mercedes, checking in, and going up to his sixth-floor room, which overlooked the ruins of Salamis, backdropped by the city skyline of the former tourist area to the south of Famagusta. That area was called Varosha and had been locked in time in the buffer zone since 1974. The lower lobby consisted of a sunken conversation area surrounding an open fire pit. There was a roaring fire in the pit, which put Roentgen into a better frame of mind than he had been in all day.

His mood was brightened even further by the friendly smile of the waiter who had brought him his drink. Roentgen returned the smile, with interest. His slender artist's fingers strayed through his curly hair and ended up scratching an itch behind his ear. When he brought his hand away, he discovered that his finger was smudged. He looked closely at the finger. It was smudged with gold gilt. Roentgen pondered. Where could that have come from? Then he remembered the last time he had come in contact with gold gilt and smiled. He then laughed out loud and called the waiter over for a refill of his drink and some follow-up conversation and negotiation.

Later, when his new friend had departed and he was at last alone in his room, Roentgen unwrapped his parcel. He picked up a leather strap and began to strop his purchase, a mean-looking hooked fish-cleaning knife. As he stropped, a rhythmical line repeated itself in his mind--- It's time to cut loses.

* * * *

The modern Western theater had its origins in the Greek and Roman dramas. These dominated the Mediterranean basin and gave rise to the creation of many open-air amphitheaters that were prominently located in the cities of these eras and were often the best preserved of the Greek and Roman constructions that survive to today. The Greeks had maintained their love for all forms of drama. One Cypriot company, in particular, the Theatro Ena national experimental theater in old town Nicosia, was known for its daring choices of plays and it creative and imaginative staging.

This was a season in which the Theatro Ena was highlighting American plays, and it had chosen to intermix standard classics with works by new playwrights and avant-garde productions. While it was currently running an avant-garde play in its side auditorium, it was providing balance by presenting a Greek-language version of Arthur Miller's Pulitzer Prize–winning classic *Death of a Salesman* in the main theater. The set was inventive and jutted out into the audience. The stage had no curtain.

Tonight was opening night and the small theater was packed with the cream of the city's theater patrons. The atmosphere was electric with anticipation.

The action of the Saturday night opening performance of *Death of a Salesman* was about twenty minutes into the play. Demetriou, as Willy Loman, had gone out into what was being depicted as a yard beside the house set to try to see the stars. As the actress playing his wife, Linda, was talking to him, the lighting was set so that the audience could see Willy. The character's son, Biff, entered the scene to have a discussion with his mother. The lighting on Willy then slowly faded out as he was settling on a chair in the yard to wait for the stars to come out.

Not more than five minutes later, the lights on the exterior started coming up again, as Willy was supposed to interrupt one of the mother's lines with a call to his son: "Hey, hey, Biffo!"

But Willy didn't interrupt his wife's line, and the wife helplessly continued rambling and trying to feed Demetriou his cue for his own line.

But Demetriou wasn't interested in the actress's line or even in his own. As was becoming increasingly obvious as the exterior house lighting brightened, neither Demetriou nor Willy were in any condition to continue with the play. The actor was sprawled on the chair, covered in blood.

A hubbub of frantic calls and comments arose from the audience, Linda gave a curdling scream that projected, expert actress that she was, to several buildings away, and the stage lights were doused. Unfortunately, there was no comforting curtain to close on the tragedy at the Theatro Ena.

Arthur Miller was so right. The salesman was indeed dead.

Chapter Twelve

Sunday morning or no Sunday morning, Takis Koniotis had summoned all of his troops to the office. That, unfortunately, had to include Maria Solonos as well. She had not been dating the Greek actor very long. But her reaction to his death told Takis that their relationship had been very close. However, Maria was absolutely necessary to the operations. When he strode into the central squad room, he was in high dungeon and ready to tear the country apart. When everyone was gathered, he didn't see his deputy and was just as happy that she wasn't there yet to endure the instructions he had to give.

"All right, Ladies and Gentlemen," announced Koniotis, as he gathered his detectives about him, "I've just visited the minister, and he has agreed we are to pull the stops. Enough is enough. We have bodies piling up in the corners, and our separate cases are expanding geometrically. From this moment on, everyone works double time until we wrap up at least one of these murders. We're losing foreigners so fast I'm not even sure we have an accounting of all who've been murdered—and I don't even have any idea how many villains we have to track down."

"Theo," Koniotis said, "I need to have Sergey Stepanov located and brought in immediately. We've suspected he was mixed up in the murder of the foreigners, and now the woman he's been dating is dead—Eleni Piccard. The politicians, business community, and press will all be on our necks about her death."

"I'm so sorry," said Maria Solonos from the far corner of the room. "If I'd only gotten to Kakopetria sooner, maybe I'd have gotten to her while she was still alive."

"And maybe you'd have gotten there just in time to get murdered yourself," Koniotis shot back, and then he softened instantly. He'd been so shocked when he realized Maria was here that he had answered on reflex. This was no time, however, to engage in his usual banter with Maria.

Maria looked terrible. She'd obviously been crying and she was trembling. But she was on the job and, as Koniotis instinctively had known would be the case, she had gotten the office machinery running in all the right directions while he'd been consulting with the minister.

"I didn't mean that to be critical, Maria," Koniotis said gently. "You're worth a hundred Eleni Piccards, regardless of her wealth and influence. You said you'd check out the restaurant on Saturday afternoon and you did. I thank God you didn't get there earlier. I only regret we lost our closest link to the spy ring murders. The murderer—assuming there's only one—is staying one step ahead of us. We've got to think of a way to get ahead of him."

"I'm also sorry you've had to come in to the office," Koniotis went on. "But I'm not sorry you did. The truth of the matter is that I can't let you go home now. You are the heart of this operation. We need to get out there and put a stop to this, and I need you to get that done."

"It's all right, Takis," Maria responded as she squared her shoulders. "There's no place else I could be right now."

Koniotis turned back to Theo. "Now, about Sergey Stepanov . . ."

"That's already been checked out," Maria responded for Theo. "Andreas and Lena went up to his house in Makedonitissa this morning. He was gone. Somebody had been there and had obviously left unexpectedly."

"What do you mean?" Koniotis asked.

"The front door was open; a suitcase with a few men's clothes was overturned in the foyer near the door. The lights were still on, and there were four place settings of a partially eaten breakfast on the kitchen table."

"Sounds like Stepanov got some sort of warning and he and his goons took off on short notice," said Koniotis. "We'll have to put out a police call for his car."

"It's not that easy, Takis," Solonos answered. "Stepanov's Land Rover was sitting out front of the house. Strange, though. There was a fresh bouquet of flowers on the front seat." Then, after a brief pause. "For Eleni Piccard, do you suppose?"

"I guess we'll only know when we've found him," Koniotis responded.

Then Koniotis asked: "Has Hamilton been found?"

"Yes," Maria answered. "Theo found him passed out in his Strovolos flat this morning. He's in your office. Do you want to talk with him now?"

"Yes, I guess I'd better get that over with. Although, I hardly have time to get involved in a domestic war in the middle of all this other crap."

"Do you want me to sit in?" Solonos asked.

"No, you need to stick with the knifer. We need a full background on Demetriou."

"Androulla is on it."

"Good. His death looks like the result of jealousy, but he was knifed in the same way all the others other than the Spanish diplomat and the Belgian singer were. We need to quickly discount his connection with the spy ring case. Also, get in touch with Dunsford, Stuart, and Bristow. They wanted to be kept informed. Well, I want more information and cooperation out of them, as well. Tell Dunsford I want to meet separately with the three of them and Safa Ziya at the Ledra Palace's Treaty Room tomorrow morning. Dunsford can have his seminar continue without us—and somewhere else, if need be—for a few hours."

"The Canadians probably won't like that," Maria said. But for the first time that morning she was revealing the hint of a smile.

"Tough," answered Koniotis, getting her drift and returning her smile. "They wanted bicommunal police cooperation. Now they've got it. I agree that Dunsford will be upset and won't even get the point that he has succeeded in his assignment."

Then, as he started toward his office, he said, "And it's time we got ahead of this maniac. Get the records of Limassol port passport control for 1985 to 1990 opened. Get a list of all foreigners entering from France on a Piccard vessel. And then start checking for people with a Brussels or NATO connection."

"Naturally," Solonos flipped over her shoulder, as she passed through the squad room door. "I was saving that for myself." And she was gone.

The worst moments of Maria's ordeal over, Koniotis took a deep breath and entered the battle zone.

* * * *

The calm demeanor of Caitlyn Koniotis covered a highly distressed woman as she closed the door of the house behind her and slowly descended the marble staircase toward the garage, which was located under the balconied living and dining rooms. She had been deeply disturbed by Eleni Piccard's murder—not least because she had foreseen it, although she had not attempted to tell Takis about her vision.

Caitlyn hadn't seen much of Eleni since the two had been swept up in a complex international intrigue case a couple of years earlier. That did not mean, however, that Eleni, with her strange emotional hold on Caitlyn, had ever been far from the younger woman's thoughts. They had maintained their distance not only because they had both been too traumatized by the events and Eleni's part in them to be fully comfortable in each others' company, but also because Caitlyn had married the investigating officer in the case.

Caitlyn knew that Eleni had both hidden and manipulated evidence to wreak her own vengeance. But she had done so to revenge the murder of her own husband and son more than twenty years earlier. Caitlyn could fully understand and appreciate the familial instincts that had led Eleni to act as she did. Both Eleni and Caitlyn had very strong personalities, and Caitlyn knew that she herself could very easily have acted just as Eleni had done under similar circumstances.

Besides, before the unfortunate events that had brought Eleni, Caitlyn, and Takis together in an international quagmire, Eleni—as the head of the foundation sponsoring Caitlyn's research project—had been very helpful. It had been Eleni who had done the most to introduce Caitlyn to the history and archaeology of Cyprus. Caitlyn had heard Eleni expound on her pride in the island and her activities in unearthing and preserving its heritage. And Caitlyn could not deny that the two had become kindred spirits.

Thus, after Takis had been told of the previous day's events and had rushed into the office, Caitlyn had decided to continue with their plan for the morning. There could not, she thought, be any place better for her to be just now than in church.

Caitlyn reached the garage. Takis must have opened the garage door for her as he left, Caitlyn observed absentmindedly. He let her park in the single-car garage, and he usually parked on the street or in front of the garage.

But something in the back of Caitlyn's mind was disturbed. She had a sense that she was not alone. She felt a presence, the presence of Eleni. Tears came to Caitlyn's eyes. Was this what deep mourning or mild shock were like? She took another step toward the garage, but there was the presence of Eleni again. A much stronger presence, and Eleni seemed to be calling to her.

But no, it wasn't the Eleni she knew, the Eleni of the present. It was Phyllis. Caitlyn felt she was slipping into the daydream of the earth shaking and collapsing pillars again, except this time Phyllis was focused on her, not on Phyllis's lover. Phyllis seemed to be gesturing

162

for Caitlyn not to enter the room beyond the pillars. Caitlyn sensed that she was stepping back, and as she did so, the earth began to tremble.

"No, not again," Caitlyn shouted aloud as she shook her head and her body went rigid. "No, I can't keep drifting into this nightmare. Takis will take care of this. Takis will find Eleni's killer."

With determination, Caitlyn entered the garage. She got in the car and was driving it out of the garage when she heard the telephone ringing insistently inside the house. Her first response was to ignore it, just as she had chosen to shake off the return of the vision. Then she thought perhaps Takis was trying to call her. Too many strange things had been happening for her to just ignore the telephone. She got out of the car, leaving it running, and climbed the front stairs, digging in her purse for her door key.

The bomb blast from inside her garage dug up many of the pretty flowers in the Koniotis's intimate garden. It hurled assorted metal and glass shards from Caitlyn's car as well as several ancient stone carvings against the front of the house. The four plate glass windows that stretched across the living and dining room walls shattered.

In an SUV parked a hundred feet down the street, the Knife smiled, disconnected a cellular telephone, and drove slowly away.

The telephone in the Koniotis residence had stopped ringing. Caitlyn sat, like a pile of used rags, legs askew, against the front door—staring wide-eyed at nothing in particular.

* * * *

If Takis Koniotis had expected Willie Hamilton to be pugnacious, he was quite disappointed. The journalist looked defeated.

163

He looked like he had the world's worst hangover on top of which he seemed to be suffering from shell shock.

Koniotis's heart really wasn't in this interview. He had known that Ginger Hamilton tormented Willie mercilessly with her infidelities. He was also aware that Demetriou had flaunted his conquests. And he had always liked the little Brit in spite of—or perhaps, more accurately, because of—his bulldog pursuit of his newspaper stories. Koniotis respected Hamilton's careful research and his balanced, yet incisive reporting. He also admired the reporter's courage in the face of threats he had received for his exposés. Besides, Koniotis did not for a minute think Hamilton was involved in the spy ring murders. And, while not denigrating the seriousness of a crime of passion, Koniotis could not put the Hamilton-Demetriou case in the same league as the expanding NATO spy murders.

Koniotis looked briefly through the file on his desk and then turned to Hamilton, who sat in the only other chair, staring blankly at the window, oblivious to the investigator's presence.

"Mr. Hamilton. Willie," Koniotis began gently.

Hamilton turned his dull gaze toward the sound of Koniotis's voice.

"Takis?"

"Willie. You know what happened to your wife and to Antonis Demetriou?"

Willie stared for a moment, then covered his face with his hands, and blurted out, "I didn't do anything."

"Willie. Our people found you at your flat this morning. Obviously you'd been on a binge. Do you remember anything about yesterday?"

"I went to the mountains."

"Lefkara is in the mountains, Willie."

Hamilton was quiet for a bit longer, and then said, "I went to the Troodos. I needed to be alone. . . with a bottle of brandy. No, that's wrong. I wanted to be alone with several bottles of brandy. I wanted to walk up near the Calladian Falls. That's many miles away from Lefkara. I often walk in the mountains when I have to cool off."

"And why did you have to cool off, Willie?"

"You know," Hamilton shot back, beginning to regain his famous pugnacity. "It's probably in your file there. I went looking for that Greek actor on Friday. And, yes, I'm sure there are many people who will tell you I threatened him. I said I'd kill him, I know, but I don't kill people."

"You never killed anyone in your long distinguished military career, Major?"

The look Hamilton turned on Koniotis was, itself, sufficient to kill.

"And your wife, Willie?" said Koniotis. "Why was your wife in Lefkara while you were in Strovolos—or perhaps in the Troodos Mountains?"

"We had a fight," Hamilton answered tightly.

"And when was that fight?"

"It was Friday also. And, yes, the fight was about Demetriou. The whole village of Strovolos could probably tell you that. But I didn't do anything wrong. I was walking in the Troodos Saturday afternoon. I got drunk. I went back to my car to sleep it off. It was too cold in the car in the mountains, and I somehow got back to the Strovolos flat during the night on Saturday. And that's the truth."

165

"You were walking in the Troodos all afternoon and evening on Saturday?" Koniotis let the question drift in the air for a few moments and then he changed gears.

"Do you own a hunting knife, Willie?"

"Yes, of course. Don't you? Doesn't every Cypriot?"

"And what was your personal specialty in the British army, Major?"

Hamilton gave Koniotis a venomous stare, started to speak, snapped his jaw shut, and then began again. Now much of the fight he had briefly regained was gone. He answered wearily, "Demolitions. I suppose that's in the file as well."

"Yes, I'm afraid it is. Did anyone see you while you were walking in the Troodos on Saturday?"

"Not as far as I know. But, then, after the first bottle of brandy, I suppose I could have encountered a whole tribe of Mongolian nomads up there and not have remembered."

"I'm sorry, Willie. I really am, but we're going to have to hold you on suspicion. You know enough about the system and evidence to know we have to hold you."

Hamilton sank into his chair. "Ginger. I've got to know about Ginger. Is she going to be all right? Can I see her? Not as a free man, of course. I understand that. But I've got to see her. See that she's going to be all right. I've got to talk with her. There's so much I have to say to her."

"Yes," Koniotis answered. "She's bruised and shaken up and still unconscious from the concussion. But I'm told she should be all right. The bomb blast flipped a table up in front of her. And although the table caused all her injuries, it also saved her from the effects of the bomb. It may be several days before she's conscious, however. I'll see what I can do about getting you over to see her when she's conscious." Koniotis rose and pulled Hamilton up out of the chair.

Tears were flowing freely down Willie's face.

"I know it looks bad for me, Takis, but I love my wife. I didn't kill the Greek actor. And I couldn't do anything to hurt Ginger. She's my world. Without her, I couldn't go on."

Strangely enough, Koniotis believed him.

He was deep in thought after Hamilton had been taken away for processing, and Maria had to nudge him twice when she entered the office.

"Yes, Maria, what is it?"

"Androulla has just reported. Antonis Demetriou was a Greek colonel assigned to NATO in the early 1980s. He meets the arrival profile, as well."

Koniotis processed this information, and then said, "Maria, get a team of detectives up to the Calladian Falls area. Have them ask every trekker they can find up there whether and when they saw Hamilton's red Mini. I don't think he did it—either of the attacks. In fact, I wouldn't be surprised if the bomb in Lefkara had been meant for him because of his newspaper articles. If we can, I'd like to have him cleared before his wife regains consciousness. If he's innocent, we owe them that much."

For some reason Takis felt a lot better after Maria had gone. He kept returning to the phrase, "She's my world."

And then a very distressed Maria rushed back into the office, and Takis's own world came crashing down on his head.

167

Chapter Thirteen

Just down the road from Koniotis's office, near the Cyprus Museum and across the street from the Parliament building, stood the rambling old Nicosia General Hospital. This was the only place in Cyprus to go for the treatment of special maladies and the last hospital anyone would go to who was conscious and able to defend themselves.

Ginger Hamilton, now resting in the third-floor intensive care unit, was not conscious and had not been able to defend herself from admittance.

She had also not been able to defend herself from the effects of the bombing in Lefkara the previous evening, or from the unstylish indignity of the hospital gown she now wore, or from the life-sustaining tubes attached to her arms and her nose. And she was now totally defenseless against anyone who might wish her further harm.

She looked like hell. If she'd been conscious and had access to a mirror, she'd probably willingly have given up the ghost.

Somewhere out in the hall, a furtive figure was hovering about, fully willing to help her do just that. But, as chaotic and unorganized as the ward was, the figure could not get close enough to Ginger's bed unseen to finish the job.

A nurse looked up and said brightly, "Yes, may I—"

But the figure had melted away into the shadows.

Meanwhile, Takis Koniotis had steamed into the first-floor emergency room, having run all the way from his office. Maria Solonos, her high heels tucked under her arm, was close behind. She arrived to find Takis covering a dazed, but otherwise unmarked, Caitlyn with kisses.

Fortuitously, Caitlyn had reached the front door inset before the car bomb had gone off. She had been blown against the door and down onto the doormat. Although the front of their living room area now looked like a war zone, all of the sharp glass, metal, and marble shards that had reached the door inset had gone over Caitlyn's head. Much of her shock had resulted from looking up to see the assortment of objects the force of the bomb had deeply embedded in their wooden front door mere inches above her head. She had wound up with a lap full of cyclamens that had been thrown up from the garden below. These had merely caused her to laugh hysterically until the first concerned neighbors had arrived on the scene.

Takis was devastated. "That's it," he declared. "I'll get off this case, and we'll go on a trip somewhere."

"You will do nothing of the sort, and you know you won't," Caitlyn snorted. Takis's statement had been just what she needed to pull herself back to reality. "That's exactly what someone wants you to do. And, if for no other reason than that, you can't—and won't—do it."

"But you can't go back to the house, and I can't investigate these cases when I don't know if you are safe."

"Yes, I've already made arrangements along that line," Caitlyn responded.

"What do you mean 'arrangements?'" Takis queried.

"Sarah Bristow has already been here. I know you'll be at the office day and night until you break this case. And we both now know that we're under siege ourselves until you track this killer down. So, Sarah has offered to take me in and I've accepted. Her place is perfectly safe—it was specially selected to be safe—and Sarah is perfectly capable of protecting me and herself, as well."

Takis hadn't processed much of this information. He was still struck on Sarah Bristow having already been to the hospital.

"Slow down, Caitlyn. How did Sarah Bristow get here?"

"Simple—and completely innocent, Takis," Caitlyn answered. "Sarah was the duty officer at the American embassy. She was already here when I was brought in."

"You've lost me." Takis's voice was getting a little on edge.

"There's no mystery," Caitlyn said calmly. "Some of the embassy's off-duty marine guards had gotten into a barroom brawl, and one of them was brought in here for treatment. As duty officer, Sarah had to come check on him."

"Sorry, Honey. You're right. This has me rattled. I'd still prefer that you left for a while. You could go back to the States to see your folks for a few weeks."

"Maybe later, Dear, but not for a few days at least." Caitlyn ruffled Takis's hair. "I'm being included in an archaeology group tour to Salamis tomorrow. Salamis was on the top of my sightseeing agenda when I came here years ago, and I have never gotten there. My only other opportunity to go there was disrupted by one of your murder cases, and now that I'm married to a Greek Cypriot, there won't be many opportunities for me to be able to go over to the Turkish zone. I have no intention of letting another one of your cases keep me away from tomorrow's tour."

Takis looked skeptical.

"Anyway," Caitlyn plunged on, "your murderer is on this side of the Green Line, isn't he? The safest place I could be is on the other side of the line."

Takis seemed mollified. Caitlyn, of course, wasn't all that concerned whether or not Takis was mollified. She had already made up her mind.

As they were getting checked out of the hospital, Caitlyn developed a pensive look. When Takis looked at her with an unspoken question on his lips, she said, "You know, I was saved by a ringing telephone. If I'd stayed in the car, rather than leaving to answer the phone, I wouldn't be standing here talking to you now. I bless whoever made that call. They are a life saver."

This was not, of course, one of Caitlyn's most accurate assumptions. If she had driven off to church rather than having gotten out of the car to answer the ringing telephone, she would have been well away from the blast when the bomb detonated.

It wasn't until hours later, after Caitlyn had packed her bags and Takis had deposited her with Sarah Bristow, that the fallacy of Caitlyn's earlier argumentation occurred to him.

"Wait a minute," Takis said angrily to himself as he pulled into the office parking lot. "There have been related murders on the other side of the Green Line . . . Oh, my God. Why haven't I focused on that before? That limits the number of suspects." And he rushed up the stairs, no room for thought about anything now but the spinning threads of his investigation.

* * * *

Standing at the battlements of the Famagusta citadel, where the arm of the fortress jutting out into the harbor joined the main keep, Peggy Bingham was looking out toward sea. She gazed toward the Syrian coast some sixty miles in the distance and then directly down into the small, but busy port immediately below. Then she turned her gaze back across the citadel ruins to take in the many spires of crumbling churches in the walled city. The unusually large number of churches in Famagusta—reputedly one for every day in the year—had been built by the French crusader Lusignans in the twelfth century and refurbished by the Venetians in the sixteen century. From where she stood, Bingham could clearly see the current Mosque of Lala Mustafa Pasha in the center of the old city. This dominating structure had been built in the fourteenth century as the imposing Gothic-styled cathedral of St. Nicholas in which for two hundred years the Lusignans had been crowned as kings of Jerusalem.

She was glad to be free of that chatterbox, Mehmet Tosun's nephew and assistant Ahmad, for even a few minutes. She had to gather her thoughts for the appointed meeting here with Helmut Roentgen. She and Ahmad had been walking around in the lower courtyard and she had managed to distract the youth's attention long enough to slip up an isolated staircase, which had led her to this perch. She really should use the moments before Ahmad found her to review her intended verbal assault on the antiquities broker, but the charm of Othello's tower had gotten to her.

Who would have known that Shakespeare could have drawn the characters and setting of his classic play *Othello* from real life and that these could have been located right here where she stood, in the ancient east coast Cypriot harbor city of Famagusta? Peggy Bingham was a simple woman at heart, and she had no trouble both believing in the Othello legend and being totally swept up in the mysterious and melancholy mood of the citadel.

She looked down into the now-roofless rooms in the circular tower just below her perch. It required very little effort for her to permit her imagination to take over. She was conjuring up the figures of Othello and Desdemona in the large chamber just off to her left. Desdemona was sleeping peacefully and vulnerably on her heavily curtained bed. Othello was slowly and fatefully approaching the bier, tears streaming down his face. And here, at her own level, off in the shadows, sharing her vision, was the triumphant Iago. Watching. And then moving. Moving out of the dream and into an all too genuine reality. Peggy Bingham did not even have time to scream. She went over the parapet and landed amid a carpet of early-season anemones and assorted, ragged rubble on the floor of the circular tower. She looked up accusingly and ever so briefly at her assailant, the Othello to her Desdemona, and then her eyes glazed over.

Moments later, standing outside the citadel's entry gate, the detective Safa Ziya had assigned to keep an eye on Peggy Bingham had just decided he would have to enter the citadel to see what Bingham and Tosun's assistant were doing. As he rose from the bench by the pathway, the assistant raced out of the gateway, almost knocking the policeman aside. His eyes were wide, and his mouth was gaping as if in a silent scream. By instinct, the detective gave chase as soon as he could recover. But the youth had escaped through the opening in the wall that had been made to connect the walled city with the modern-day port. In no time at all, he had disappeared among the busy laborers loading and unloading the three small vessels that were tied up at the quay.

As the detective returned to the citadel, he was passed by a tall, slender, elegantly dressed West European gentleman. The man was whistling happily to himself as he walked down the pathway from the citadel entrance. The policeman hurried through the gate and guardroom areas and into the central courtyard of the citadel. Othello's tower was quiet as death. The detective turned in circles, panic setting in. It was too quiet. She had not had time to leave without him having seen her. The retreat of the youth had clarioned that Othello's tower had written another horrific tale. The shocked departure of the youth had also knocked from the detective's memory the encounter with the other person on the pathway to the citadel. Where to begin the gruesome search?

* * * *

Mikhail Lukenov's displeasure was viscerally evident as he brought the mortar shell casing, which served as a grim memento of his service in Afghanistan, crashing down on his desktop. As he did so, three of the four men arrayed in front of his desk at least flinched. But this was not good enough for Lukenov. Sergey Stepanov was tough— possibly too tough for Lukenov to control. And the Russian spy chief knew he could push this agent only so far.

"I told you to find out if the Piccard woman had told anyone about the resettlement of the NATO incident spies. I did not tell you to kill her."

"Nor did I," Stepanov snapped back. His three thugs were scared speechless and just sat rigidly, looking from one official to the other, their eyes wide as saucers. "It took me some time to find out she had gone up to Kakopetria. I was going to go up there today to start trying to find out if she had kept written records and who she might be working for now. I'd even bought flowers for her to put her in a good mood for talking. And then you sent the car for us, and here we are."

"And I suppose you did not murder the retired Spanish diplomat or Father Nikolay either," Lukenov interjected. His sarcasm cut like a knife.

There was a moment of silence from Stepanov. His goons squirmed uncomfortably in their chairs. Then he said, "No, as a matter of fact, I did not."

Lukenov gave the younger man a hard look. If Moscow wanted to close out any opportunity for embarrassment over that old Brussels operation, and they had sent Stepanov to handle it, there was no reason why Stepanov would admit this to him. Truth be known, Russia's official intelligence chief in Cyprus was all too willing to see such wet work done by others and only too grateful that he would be kept officially in the dark about the operation. He therefore decided to change the subject.

"When I approved your use of business enterprises as a cover for your operation, I did not say that you should become openly involved in Russian mafia dealings. I also didn't tell you to take such a prominent woman as Eleni Piccard as your mistress that you attracted the active attention of the Cypriot authorities. You do understand, don't you, where you would be this minute if we had not found out and warned you that the police were about to pick you up?"

More silence from Stepanov.

"I don't think, Comrade Sergey, that we can afford to have you here anymore."

"I don't think, Comrade Mikhail, that such a decision is within your authority to make."

The two agents squared off like a couple of wrestlers.

Then, after a brief pause, Lukenov took on the air of a busy bureaucrat shuffling from one troublesome transaction to another.

"There is an unmarked delivery van waiting down in the courtyard to take you and your men to the Larnaca marina. From there you can take your motor launch out to the *Chechnoya*. I cannot afford to have you identified with the Russian embassy. If you are arrested before you can clear Cyprus, you will have to stick with your Russian businessman cover. I cannot help you. I will have to say that the embassy does not support Russian mafia activity inside Cyprus any more than it would support it in Moscow. You should remain outside Cypriot territorial waters at least until the effect of all these murders cools down. I actually suggest you turn the *Chechnoya* toward the Black Sea and go home, Sergey. You cannot do any more good for Russia here. Your, shall we say, inappropriate behavior . . . your, yes, inappropriate behavior has ended your usefulness here."

"If the authorities pick me up, you will notify Moscow immediately and will do everything you can to obtain my release. And I would not suggest," Sergey leaned across the desk menacingly, "that any reports you might send to Moscow use any phrase like 'inappropriate behavior,' Mikhail. As for leaving the vicinity of Cyprus—"

But the Russian official had risen from his desk. "Good-bye, Sergey, and good luck," he choked out and left the room.

Later, as he watched the departure of the van from his office window, which overlooked the American embassy across an empty field nearly directly opposite, Lukenov's consternation broke through his previously cool demeanor.

"Stepanov is dangerous," he thought. "He is a dangerous man to both himself and to Russia now. Why wasn't I given full control over this operation? What is the extent of the orders and authorities Moscow has given him? Is he here to clean up from the NATO incident? In fact, what are Moscow's interests and sensitivities in this matter? Could he. . . . Hell, could he be here to investigate me?"

This thought was accompanied by a ripping noise. Lukenov discovered that he had gripped the curtain so hard he'd ripped the material from the rod.

An hour later the van arrived at the large marina at the eastern end of the café- and hotel-bordered pebbly beach and wide promenade that extended down the southern coast Larnaca seafront. Stepanov's vessel, the *Chechnoya*, lay at anchor just off the newly refurbished European-style seafront promenade, and his motor launch was berthed at the Larnaca marina.

As he and his three companions chugged out to the ship, Stepanov eyed the line of beachside hotels, which ended in the stone fortress at the eastern end of the beach. This ancient Mediterranean seaport—so old that legend held it had been settled by the son of

Noah and that, more probably, it was the final resting place of Lazarus—was one of Stepanov's favorite locations on the island. Taking one last sweeping look at the promenade, the Russian thought bitterly to himself, "I have no intention of abandoning Cyprus, Mikhail. Nor have you seen the last of me."

And then, as he turned his gaze out to sea, toward the rusting hulk of his trawler, he found himself thinking: "The NATO spies. The Knife. When should be—will be—the next encounter?"

* * * *

Safa Ziya was hobbling as quickly as her legs and her seething anger could carry her from her Nicosia apartment to her office. By the time she reached the police department, however, her anger had dissipated and only her calm, analytical professionalism remained. She had been called at home by the detective she had assigned to watch Peggy Bingham. In frightened, breathless tones, he had told her of his discovery of the body of Bingham in the Famagusta citadel. The woman had been stabbed and flung from the ramparts into one of the roofless, stone-littered rooms in the ruins. He also told her of the flight of Mehmet Tosun's assistant.

"He must have been ordered to kill her and then went into shock over what he had done."

"It sounds much more likely," retorted a chief inspector, who was trying her best not to reach down the telephone line and grab her subordinate by the throat, "that the boy saw the murder and fled in total fright. Come back to the office immediately. There is nothing we can do for Bingham now. Let the Famagusta police initiate notifications and start their own investigation. That will give me a couple of days to prepare before the case is dropped on my desk."

Before leaving the apartment, Ziya had called ahead to the department to have several junior police officers brought in to help her. She had also directed that arrest and detention orders be issued for Mehmet Tosun's nephew. She had done so more to protect the youth than with any thought he had been involved in murder. Her last order had been for someone to try to track down Tosun at his Nicosia shop.

Two detectives met her at the police department door. Mehmet Tosun had not been found at his shop, they said, but the shop's door had been forced and his office had been ransacked. There was no telling what, if anything, had been taken until they could find Tosun.

Ziya was no longer angry at the detective she had assigned to Bingham by the time he arrived at the office. He could not have helped Bingham, Ziya knew, unless he had gotten so close that Bingham and Ahmad would know they were being followed. And those had not been the detective's orders. As it turned out, it was a good thing she did not dress the detective down after he arrived, because his fears for his job and for Ziya's continued respect for his work had dissipated enough by that time for him to remember the other person he had seen on the citadel pathway and to convey this information to his superior.

"Hmm, that sounds like the description of Helmut Roentgen, Tosun's confederate, who has been slipping in and out of the island." Ziya picked up the telephone and called the passport control section at Ercan Airport. Her hunch confirmed, she immediately put out an arrest and detention order on the German antiquities dealer.

As she plugged her electric tea kettle in and eased herself into her desk chair, she thought that it was going to be a long night. But she was determined not to miss the seminar the next day. No matter what she had been told about how Takis Koniotis was just toying with her, there were a few pieces of vital information she was going to force out of him even if she had to crash the Greek checkpoint to get to him.

* * * *

Ahmad was madly driving around northern Cyprus, trying to find his uncle, Mehmet—to warn him. What he had seen in the citadel brought the whole world down on his head. He knew that his uncle had to know about this right away. He was in so much danger. Mehmet was not at the resort complex near Bogaz that he usually used when he was coming to the east coast. The youth had also gotten to the shop in Nicosia just after the police had reached it. He saw the broken door and he heard them talking about the ransacked office. All of this only added to the boy's fright. But they obviously had not found his uncle, so there was still time. The trip over the mountain to Kyrenia also failed to flush out the shopkeeper in any of his usual haunts there.

It was an exhausted and very scared Ahmad who eventually rolled up to the doors of the Salamis Bay Hotel. Luckily his adrenaline was still pumping away, however. Just as he was entering the lobby, Ahmad saw the last person he wanted to encounter sitting in front of the fire pit in the lower lobby. His long legs were stretched out and his feet were propped up on the fireplace ledge. He was talking with the waiter who had brought him a brandy, and both were laughing. He tossed off the brandy as the waiter returned, briefly, to the bar, and then the two of them walked toward the elevators arm in arm. Ahmad backed into the gift shop so that he would not be seen, and, when the elevator had come and gone, the youth ran out of the hotel.

Well, if he could not find his uncle tonight, he knew where he would be in the morning. It did not look like he was in further danger tonight.

Mehmet Tosun was, at the moment, not more than a half mile away from the Salamis Bay Hotel. In fact, as Helmut Roentgen was standing in his altogether on the hotel balcony and gazing down toward the ruins of the ancient Greco-Roman city of Salamis, he was unknowingly looking directly at Tosun.

Tosun had no sensation of being watched, however. It was so dark he knew he could not be seen. He was digging near the foundations of the fourth-century Christian basilica of St. Epiphanius, the largest excavated early Christian church on the island.

Chapter Fourteen

After a busy night's work at the Salamis ruins, Mehmet Tosun went down to a shed on the beach to catch a few hours of sleep in preparation for the following day's work. "With luck," he had thought as he turned out the lantern and rolled himself in his old friend's blankets, "this could be the making of my antiquities business."

The shed had belonged to an old Frenchman who'd spent most of the closing years of his life beachcombing the verge of the sea at the Salamis site. In his younger days, he'd been attached to the excavation at the even more ancient copper-producing city state of Engomi and had just stayed on in the area after the rest of the archaeologists had departed. Beachcombing here, however, was such as could not be found and enjoyed anywhere else. Although the Greco-Roman ruins on the land above the beach were extensive, most of the ancient city state of Salamis was actually under water, having been submerged by earthquakes in the fourth century. This made the subterranean portion of Salamis a favorite area for snorkeling and scuba diving. It also made an early morning walk along the tidal area very interesting and often very profitable.

The old Frenchman had staked his informal claim to the beach and had lived a simple existence there for decades. Unknown to most, who thought he was just a crazy layabout, he had also pulled a wealth of Roman glass, coins, pottery, and even the occasional golden trinket, from the surf. Thus he'd died a very rich man. Actually, he was only potentially a very rich man when he died. His "craziness" had prevented him from placing worldly value on what he found and from capitalizing on his treasure. The Frenchman, however, really had felt enriched by his findings. Each newly discovered artifact delighted him, as did each and every morning walk down the beach. He probably wouldn't have valued the profit from selling what he'd found half as much.

Tosun had been the one who'd capitalized in worldly terms from the Frenchman's morning walks. As a young man, a refugee from Lebanon, where he'd become too well known in police circles to anticipate a long life, Tosun had wound up in Famagusta. There he'd scratched out a living by scavenging in the Salamis ruins at night for the odd artifact he could sell. After the Turkish troops arrived in 1974, Tosun became a Turk.

The Frenchman had befriended him, which, for Tosun, was a sensation he'd rarely experienced before—or since. It had been a struggle for the young man when he'd seen the treasures the Frenchman had collected in his shed. Which was to be the strongest pull—friendship or greed? To his credit, greed only won by a hair— and then with mitigating circumstances. Tosun initially took only what he needed to sustain life—and, yes, maybe to embellish life a good bit too, if the truth be known. He also ensured that the old man's declining years were more comfortable than they would have been otherwise. For his part, the old man never seemed to miss what Tosun took. Or, perhaps, he simply never begrudged sharing his pretty trinkets with his friend Mehmet.

When the Frenchman died, Tosun took it all and was able to set up his antiquities business, but he also ensured that the Frenchman's body was returned to his family in Marseilles for burial—smuggled across the buffer zone and delivered aboard a Piccard vessel. That was how Tosun had met Eleni Piccard and had gotten involved in the affair that had had him constantly looking over his shoulder for more than a decade.

Tosun rose the next morning, thoroughly rested. There was no place on earth as comforting as this little shack near the monotonous but calm sound of the rising and falling surf and the memories of the simple yet complex Frenchman. Occasionally, Tosun came down to the shed just to sleep and to think—and to contemplate the simple, satisfied life of the old beachcomber. But Tosun knew that life could never be that simple for him.

As he drove away from the Salamis dig toward his appointment at the checkpoint in Nicosia, Tosun looked up at the Salamis Bay Hotel tower. Roentgen was there. And now that Mehmet's thoughts had been pulled back to reality, he remembered that he was supposed to have met Roentgen in the hotel for breakfast more than an hour ago. He turned north out of the entrance to Salamis and toward the hotel. But, as he was about to park in the hotel lot, he looked at his watch and decided he didn't have time now to check in with Roentgen and still make his appointment in Nicosia. He didn't even have time now to stop at his shop before he met the bus.

He decided that Roentgen and the Bingham woman issue would just have to wait. There was a reputation and money to be made, and it was beginning to look like Peggy Bingham was more trouble than her money was worth. Roentgen would be furious he didn't show up, of course, but he'd hardly shoot Tosun for it.

* * * *

The rains of the previous week had completely cleared that Monday morning when Takis Koniotis strode up to the front door of the Ledra Palace Hotel. The sun was out and the atmosphere was crystal clear. He'd left his investigations early enough the previous evening to help board up the windows across the front of his house. Afterward he'd sat alone in the tiny study—missing Caitlyn badly but glad that she was safely stowed away with the formidable Sarah Bristow. He'd spent an hour organizing his investigations in his mind and then had gotten the first good night's sleep he'd enjoyed in a week. He'd left the house and, after checking his car carefully for the chance bomb or two, had pointed the vehicle's nose toward the old town.

As he drove toward the city, the clearness of the morning made the Kyrenia mountain range stand out invitingly across the horizon to the north of the city. The sight gave his heartstrings a tug, as it invariably does for all Greek Cypriots who could almost reach out and touch the mountains on a morning such as this. The painful thrust to the heart, however, was that he couldn't get any closer to them in reality than the Green Line that split Nicosia down the center. His mind filled, first, with wistful memories of family picnics in St. Hilarion, Buffavento, and Kantara, the three crusader castles straddling the top of the Kyrenia ridgeline. Then the anger flooded in as his gaze was arrested once again by the huge, offending Turkish flag that had been fashioned in painted concrete just below the peak, immediately opposite the capital city.

Koniotis had very nearly turned his car away from the checkpoint and toward his own office at the sight of the flag. Why was he even trying to work with the Turkish Cypriot police, he thought bitterly. Then he'd thought of Safa Ziya. Who could consider such a woman as the enemy?

John Dunsford was waiting for Koniotis at the door to the hotel. He did not look pleased, and he was not pleased.

"Alec Stuart and Sarah Bristow are inside, as you requested, Takis. But this is highly irregular, and it is disrupting the seminar. If you insist on this meeting, I must ask that we keep it short and get back to business as soon as possible."

"I thought the 'business' of this seminar was to enhance bicommunal contact in police investigations, John," Koniotis said pointedly. "That is exactly what you have achieved with Safa Ziya and me. You should be proud of what you have accomplished."

Dunsford started to retort, but Koniotis cut in.

"However, I don't particularly care if you don't see it that way. I have an important investigation to pursue here, and Ziya appears to be pursuing the same investigation on her side. We're going to meet on this issue with Stuart and Bristow this morning. You can meet with us, if you wish. And you can decide not to meet with us, if that is your wish."

"You do realize, don't you, that both you and Ziya are here under the auspices of the Canadian high commission's program?" Dunsford pronounced stiffly. "If you want to withdraw from the

186

seminar, the high commission has no responsibility to bring you and Ziya together."

"True," Koniotis shot back. "In that case, however, I'm sure that either Alec Stuart or Paul Conte would be happy to sponsor our meetings. I don't know what Ziya might have to share with me, but I have quite a bit to tell her, and I will do so if I have to go through Ankara to get to her. Is that what you want, Dunsford?"

"No, of course not," Dunsford replied wearily. "I'm sorry. It's just that when you and Ziya are off in discussion, no one else seems to pay any attention to what is going on in the seminar. You are, of course, right that the seminar is a success if you and Ziya are comparing notes. Come inside and let's get this meeting over with, so we can get back to the main business of the seminar."

Koniotis disappeared into the hotel's ornate front doors. Dunsford remained at the entrance, however, as he had now been joined from inside by a fretful Sarah Bristow. As the two whispered in urgent and obviously concerned discussion, they failed to notice the presence of Safa Ziya in the shadows just below the entrance porch.

Ziya had actually been there for several moments, and she'd heard Koniotis's declaration that he intended to work with her. This was quite different from what she'd been told when the American and Canadian diplomats had visited her separately a few days earlier. Hesitating to put in an appearance just yet, she observed the intense conversation between Dunsford and Bristow. When they were finished and had moved into the hotel, Ziya squared her shoulders and followed them. Her spirits were much higher now than they had been for several days. And the possibilities of what might be happening behind the scenes were becoming clearer, as well.

As it turned out, the meeting did not last all that long. Both Koniotis and Ziya quickly reviewed the status of the investigations. And they just as quickly concluded that the violent rolling up of members of the NATO spy ring was the main event, if not the only event, facing them. At one point during the discussion, Koniotis asked whether any of the three diplomats had been able to discover anything helpful to the investigation since he'd last talked with them. But they were uniformly as informative as clams. Bristow went as far as to try to suggest again that a more important, international security issue was at stake than the investigations. She declared that it might be time for the Cypriots just to step out and let the embassies handle the situation.

This was clearly not the best approach to take with Koniotis and Ziya. The two Cypriot investigators graphically closed out on this possibility in terms that drew laughter from the seminar room just beyond a folding door.

Safa Ziya followed up with the bald statement, "The crimes are here. We have jurisdiction here. And you can cooperate with us or butt out."

Koniotis nodded his head vigorously in agreement and added, "But you can only walk away from helping us with this investigation if the walk ends at an airplane door. I'll be going straight to the minister from here, and he is not in a pretty mood. You can count on formal representations to your embassies to require cooperation by midafternoon."

Stuart and Dunsford looked a little shaken by this declaration. Bristow remained serene.

Upon returning to the thread of the case review, Koniotis became quite animated when he was told of the murder the afternoon before of Peggy Bingham by the same type of weapon that had been used weeks before on Bertelli and Kleist.

"This may be just the break we need," said Koniotis loud enough to cause the seminar discussion on the other side of the folding door to be reduced to silence. This won a sour look from Dunsford, who had been sitting there with a stunned look on his face before the laughter from the seminar area had brought his attention back to the discussion.

"What do you mean?" demanded Bristow.

"How closely did you indicate you could isolate the time of the Bingham murder, Safa?" Koniotis asked.

"Within minutes with reasonable certainty. Within three-quarters of an hour with complete certainty," answered Ziya. "My detective saw her go into the Famagusta citadel with her guide. Within thirty minutes, he saw the guide leave in panic—which quite possibly marks the time of death within minutes. Within ten minutes of that time, he found the body. Which means, Takis?"

"Which means that we might now be able to locate the killer in the Turkish zone at a precise time. This is something we could not have done in the case of Bertelli and Kleist, both of whom had been found several hours, or in Kleist's case, several days after they had been murdered."

"So?" asked Stuart.

"So, if we can assume there is a single killer, we seem to be looking for a killer who can go back and forth between the south and the north—which, in itself, limits the number of suspects. In addition, we know the killer must be based in the south if he is murdering people in the south as well as the north. The border gate only swings in one direction, and it only opens for foreigners. If you can cross the boundary at all—meaning if you are not of Greek extraction—you can go to the north from the south and return. But you can't live in the north and come to the south. And the best news is that we have very good information on who has gone from the south to the north and when. There's a slight chance they moved back and forth by boat, but the waters are just too well monitored for that to be likely. Still, I have my people checking with the coastal patrols, and I'm sure Ms. Ziya can do the same from the northern side. Chances are best that it was someone who could go through the checkpoint here, though."

Bristow and Dunsford looked quizzical. Stuart, who'd been in Cyprus far longer, caught on immediately and looked sharply at Koniotis.

"Safa," Koniotis said. "I think the next order of business is for you to get the list of all people who crossed the Turkish checkpoint yesterday. I can get most of the registration numbers of diplomatic cars and names of the walk-in day tourists from the Greek checkpoint. But your border guards keep the best records, I'm told— all logged in by name, vehicle license number, as appropriate, and time. We can concentrate on those people from the south who were in the north during the time covering the Bingham murder."

"I fail to see what that will prove," Sarah Bristow sniffed. "A lot of people were probably in the Turkish zone yesterday. Why, I was over there myself yesterday afternoon. And so were you, Alec and John, weren't you? There was a reception in Kyrenia. A lot of diplomats were . . ."

Bristow's voice trailed off. Dunsford looked mortified. Stuart's angry eyes bored into the American defense attaché.

"Well, that certainly gives us a place to start," Ziya inserted cheerily into the void. She was still smarting from the diplomatic effort to drive a wedge between Koniotis and her on this investigation.

Bristow no longer looked quite so serene.

Laughter floated through the folding doors once more. The seminar seemed to be going well, even in the absence of the moderator and the two senior investigators.

* * * *

Caitlyn was gliding around the eastern coast of the island like a school girl on her first outing. Wherever they stopped, she was the first one off and the last one back on the bus. They went from Engomi, the site of one of the oldest trading civilizations on the island to the church of St. Barnabus, reputed final resting place of Cyprus's own apostle and now a fine little museum of icons and archaeological artifacts. Then they proceeded to the royal tombs of Salamis, where the fossilized skeletons of the horses used to pull the funeral coaches still lay in front of the tomb entrances where they had been sacrificed. She could not thank Professor Visiliou enough for having included her in this excursion. All thoughts of the previous day's bombing incident were blocked from her inquisitive mind.

Only the talkative, obsequious, sweaty tour guide Visiliou had picked up at the Turkish checkpoint was an impediment to Caitlyn's full enjoyment of the day. He'd singled her out as someone who needed to be followed closely and given a full explanation of all she was seeing. She needed no explanations. She'd studied the Salamis area in her graduate college courses so fully that she could've given the lie to nearly every silly legend and archaeological "fact" the roly-poly guide prattled. She could've done so, that is, if she'd dared risk even closer attention by engaging him in conversation at all. Whenever they were alone, Professor Visiliou apologized profusely for the irritant, explaining that the presence of this particular guide had been a Turkish Cypriot condition for the excursion—which invariably meant some official had been bought off.

Salamis itself was all that Caitlyn dreamed it would be. The large gymnasium area, with its multicolored mosaic floors and columns, was magnificent. The Roman amphitheater, one of the most impressive sights in Cyprus, was in itself worth the trip. And once the bus had reached the main section of the Salamis ruins, Caitlyn savored every moment of the experience. She refused to be hurried, even though the guide seemed anxious to move the group on to the area of the fourth-century St. Epiphanius basilica.

Once having been herded to that large ruin, however, Caitlyn had to admit that it was breathtaking. Although originally located far inland, it now, thanks to a couple of earthquakes that had submerged most of the ancient city, jutted out on a promontory toward the dark blue Mediterranean.

The tour guide was skipping ahead toward the triple apse area near the sea and beckoning Caitlyn to follow him. But Caitlyn's attention was arrested by beautiful mosaics in the floor of one of the aisles. Even if the mosaics hadn't been worth the stop, she would've tried to find an excuse to shake the guide.

When she looked up and out toward the sea, she could see the guide standing near the foundation of the apse and flapping his arms excitedly in an apparent effort to catch her attention. But then, out of the corner of her eye, she saw what immediately registered as a familiar figure incongruously saunter out of the undergrowth.

"Surely that's. . . . What's he doing here?" Caitlyn said to Professor Visiliou. But the professor had left her side, and Caitlyn found she had only been talking to herself. She looked back toward the elegantly garbed figure, who'd stopped abruptly. Caitlyn followed his gaze to see that he was looking fixedly beyond the tour guide and seemed to be hesitating in his intended movement.

The tour guide was no longer alone, and he was no longer flapping his arms at Caitlyn. There was a young man with the guide, who was tugging at his arm and drawing him toward one of the pathways down to the beach. The guide and youth stumbled toward the path, picking up speed.

It looked like the tall figure who'd been watching this tableau had now made up his mind and was beginning to move rapidly toward the departing pair.

Caitlyn found herself calling out after him: "Justin. Justin, over here!"

Caitlyn's voice seemed to stop the figure in mid movement. He paused for what seemed to be an eternity, but for what must have only been a moment. Then, without even looking in Caitlyn's direction, he plunged back into the undergrowth.

When she looked around, Caitlyn saw that Professor Visiliou was returning to her side. "Strange," she said. "I could've sworn that was Justin Chamberlain. But it couldn't have been. I understood from our meeting at the museum the other day that he was leaving the country again. How would he have gotten over here?"

"Who knows why Justin does whatever he does?" Visiliou answered. "I don't think I've ever known anyone so self-destructive.

But I can't see him thrashing around in the underbrush out here. Anyway, whoever it was, he's gone now. And we must go, as well."

The rest of the tour of the Salamis area and of the walled Venetian city of Famagusta went much smoother for Caitlyn than the first half of the tour had gone. Although the bus waited for some time at the basilica and honked for a good ten minutes, the tour guide never reappeared. Not least because of the absence of the tour guide, Caitlyn found Famagusta, and particularly Othello's tower, so interesting that she only thought of the strange appearance of Justin—or of his double—in short, troubling snatches.

* * * *

Just returned to the office from the Ledra Palace meeting and intent on picking up the threads of the NATO spy ring investigation, Koniotis was, instead, immediately sidetracked by the Hamilton case.

"We've found an alibi for Willie Hamilton on Saturday," the assistant Androulla reported to Koniotis as he was entering his office.

"Good," answered Koniotis, disappointed to have to spend time on the Hamilton case. At the same time, he was pleased that his team had followed up so quickly on Willie's claim to have been in the Troodos during the attempt on his wife's life and the murder of the Greek actor. "OK, who says he was where?"

"We found a couple of men who placed Willie in the mountains when he said he was there. They are reluctant witnesses at best, because it seems they had been illegally hunting in the Troodos. But, when we let them know we had no intention of following up on the poaching issue if they could help us with establishing Hamilton's whereabouts, they gave him a full alibi. They say they ran across him on one of the footpaths near the Calladian Falls during the late

194

afternoon. They reported he was stumbling about, quite drunk, and swinging a nearly empty brandy bottle. Late that night, when they were returning, they saw Hamilton's red Mini parked near the entrance to the path and investigated. They say they saw him curled up in the car but were afraid he'd freeze, so they pulled him out and tried to talk with him. He apparently took a couple of drunken swings at them, jumped into his car, and roared off down toward Kakopetria and Nicosia. They say this happened at about 8:00 PM. Nicosia is more than an hour away, and Demetriou was murdered in Nicosia just before 9:00 PM."

"Good work, Androulla," Koniotis said with a broad smile. "Get their statements signed before they have second thoughts about compromising themselves for illegal hunting. And get Willie released and over to the hospital. Where's Maria?"

"Right here," Maria said, as she appeared on the scene, "and have I got news."

Koniotis didn't have time to ask.

"We've been compiling the lists you asked for on foreign travelers entering at Limassol from France on Piccard vessels in the late 1980s, and the name just popped out at us."

"Whose?" asked Koniotis.

"Ginger Remington. She is now known as Ginger Remington Hamilton. She fits the profile. It wasn't a mistake. Mrs. Hamilton must have been the target all along."

"Oh, my God, and she's the only live one we have at the moment," Koniotis exclaimed. "Maria, get a guard on her hospital door immediately!"

"I put out the order as I was coming up with the news."

* * * *

Late that evening, as the sun was setting over the smuggler's fishing village at Bogaz, a fishing boat was putting out to sea. This would be an uncommon occurrence in most fishing villages, as most deep-sea fishing was conducted during the daylight hours. But Bogaz was not a common fishing village, and its boats put out at all hours of the day and night. Its major source of income was not, and never had been, fish.

Standing in the center of the little vessel, oblivious to the scurrying about of the two deck hands who were striving to get the unlit boat safely away from the coast as soon as possible, stood Nabil Jallud—or Mehmet Tosun or whoever he would soon choose to be. His nephew, Ahmad, was standing beside him. Ahmad was staring back at the disappearing island that was the only country he'd ever known. His eyes were wide and tear stained. Nabil/Mehmet, however, was staring out to sea in the direction of the Turkish mainland, a bare fifty miles to the northeast. He loved Cyprus no less than Ahmad did. But he knew better than Ahmad the necessity of bending with the wind. He'd be back when it was safe. Also, he had grown used to having to leave the lands that he loved.

Tosun might not have waxed so philosophically at that moment if he'd known that just then another small fishing vessel was also dashing for the Turkish mainland. The second boat, also taking advantage of the protecting darkness and not projecting running lights, was putting out of the new harbor of the northern town of Kyrenia.

In the stern of this boat sat a grim, yet somewhat satisfied Helmut Roentgen. This was not the way he'd wanted to leave Turkish Cyprus. He was irritated whenever he had to travel in anything less than first class, accompanied by a brass band. But under the circumstances, a quiet exit seemed best. He hadn't finished all of his business, certainly. But that could wait. He had found the Bingham woman's icon miniatures in Tosun's office, however.

Roentgen felt the parcel strapped to his chest beneath the cashmere sweater. Well worth the risk, he chuckled to himself. Ah, but, on second thought, the risk alone was its own reward. And he laughed lustily at both the diminishing Cypriot shoreline and the handsome young Turkish boat hand who was arching so prettily over the tiller, black curls falling over his eyes, straining every chiseled muscle in the effort to keep the vessel on a steady northeast course. All for his benefit.

Chapter Fifteen

Although the morning air was cold in the upper Solea Valley, the sun had risen above the ridge running down from the Mt. Olympus peak and had begun to take the edge off the chill. It could not, however, take the chill off Caitlyn's heart as she watched the casket being lowered into the ground. The bright blue, cloudless sky inexplicably seemed to dim as the casket descended. Caitlyn leaned into Takis and looked up into his face to see if he was as perplexed as she was by the gathering gloom, but she could see that he was completely unaffected by the phenomenon. And then, as the Orthodox priest, followed by the surrounding villagers, began to drop handfuls of earth into the grave, Caitlyn started to choke and clutch at her husband.

"Caitlyn! What's the matter?"

"I don't know, Takis, it suddenly got so dark and I feel like I'm suffocating. No, not now," she began to moan, as Takis led her off to the side and helped her to sink onto a stone wall around an olive tree. "Not until it's finished. I can't see them. They should be here. Where are they?" Then the she felt as if she was floating and all the panic and concern she'd felt was melted away.

"Caitlyn! What's happening? Here, lean on me. What's wrong? What do you mean 'dark'? The sun's shining brightly."

But Caitlyn couldn't answer because she had blacked out.

Just steps away, the internment ceremony for Eleni Piccard continued. The funeral had attracted a large gathering of friends and associates from all points of the Greek sector of the island even though the ceremony had required a trip up to Kakopetria on an early Tuesday morning.

The all-knowing, ever-watchful Mt. Olympus peak, snow clad and gleaming in the morning sun, jutted out above the valley wall, bearing silent witness to the second Piccard family burial in less than four months. Caitlyn and Takis had also attended the earlier funeral, more than twenty-five years delayed, of Guy and Pierre Piccard, Eleni's husband and young son. The remains of the two—presumably murdered during the confusion of the 1974 invasion, their bodies left hidden in an isolated chamber of the harbor castle at Kyrenia—had been interred here in the courtyard. Fittingly, this just-completed Orthodox church at Kakopetria had been constructed largely with the financial help of Eleni Piccard in memory of her missing family.

Now it was Eleni Piccard's turn to be consigned to the earth. Such a small coffin for such a powerful woman. It was with a feeling of great sadness that Caitlyn had approached the place of internment and caught sight of the casket. She'd still been in shock over the violent manner of Eleni's death. Her intellect had told her that only now would Eleni be at peace—now that she would be reunited at long last with the family she'd mourned for more than a quarter century. But Caitlyn's emotions were in turmoil; she couldn't get over the feeling that Eleni was trying to get through to her—if anything, more strongly in death than in life—and that for some strange reason Caitlyn herself was in danger.

Caitlyn quickly recovered under the concerned ministrations of Takis and a village woman, who miraculously appeared with a clay flask of water and a tipple of brandy.

"I'm all right now, thanks," she said, as the woman patted her hands and admonished her for not wearing a scarf, as all blonde women should do in the Cypriot sun, never mind doing so in respect for the dead.

"But I was wearing a scarf," Caitlyn objected. "It was one Eleni had given me. One she said she'd gotten from an old friend in Belgium. Where did it go?"

Just then the priest beside the grave exclaimed, stooped down, and pulled a square of material from the excavation.

Takis pointed to it and said, "That's it, isn't it? Isn't that your scarf?"

Caitlyn shuddered. For some reason the scarf was suddenly an object of revulsion. "No let it stay with Eleni," she whispered. "I don't want it."

The service over, Takis gently guided Caitlyn down to their car. He could feel her shivering beneath her coat and sweater and knew that this was only partially in reaction to the temperature. Caitlyn was very quiet the entire trip back down to Nicosia on the central plain, and Takis carefully avoided breaking into her thoughts. But there were no thoughts, really. She no longer felt either panicked or suffocated. She just felt empty.

Once back in Nicosia at Sarah Bristow's house, Takis delayed getting back to the office and his investigation long enough to linger over a cup of coffee with his wife. Bristow was in her room getting ready to attend an embassy cocktail party with John Dunsford, after which she said she had to drive down to the southern coast for a hush-hush meeting at one of the British sovereign bases. She hadn't gone to the funeral. She said she hadn't known Eleni Piccard very well and had had no professional dealings with the businesswoman in the few short months she'd been in Cyprus.

As they sat at the breakfast room table, avoiding discussion of their divergent memories of Eleni, Caitlyn described her previous day's outing to the Salamis and Famagusta areas. As she spoke, she became increasingly animated. The further removed she became from the funeral, the more she returned to the enthusiastic, yet intellectual, archaeologist Takis loved.

"We really are well matched," Takis thought happily to himself. "She is as much the tireless investigator as I am, but she has her own field of work. Neither of us has to deal with living in the shadow of the other."

When Caitlyn mentioned the two strange incidents near the end of the day, she captured Takis's complete attention.

She had mentioned the tour guide's name, Mehmet Tosun, describing how he had irritated her and had then left abruptly. She said that his name had been familiar to her, but she couldn't quite place why. Takis remarked on having seen Tosun's name mentioned in connection with the murdered German artist, Detrich Kleist. He was about to delve further into the question of the Turkish merchant, when Caitlyn rushed on to say that she also thought she'd seen Justin Chamberlain at the Salamis ruins.

Takis was digesting this information when Caitlyn broke off the conversation and headed for the telephone. "If that was Justin, then he must be back in the country and he must have gone over to the other side on a day pass. I really must reach him to find out about these rumors of illegal smuggling before this goes any further."

She phoned his office but once again was told that Justin was still out of the country.

"How peculiar," she murmured as she replaced the receiver, ". . . Now I remember."

"Remember what?" Takis asked.

"Now I remember where I'd seen the name 'Mehmet Tosun' before. That was the name on the other business card I found near where the Russian priest had been killed. Justin's name was on one card, and Mehmet Tosun's name was on the other card. Now I wonder what those two have in common?"

The combined references to Tosun, Chamberlain, and a day pass to the Turkish side had already mobilized Takis. With a quick kiss and a hug, and he was out of the door and steaming back to his world of loose threads and intrigue.

* * * *

"Now I've got you, you bastard—doubly!"

Safa Ziya had just hung up the telephone from a call that had topped off her morning and had given occasion for her first smile in days. But, as she looked up, she was caught by the disapproving scowl of her office mate, the sight of whom turned her own smile sour.

"Speaking of bastards," Safa whispered just loud enough for the man to try to strain to hear her, "I wonder how many of my promotions are languishing in that pile in front of you?" She'd done some checking since she'd found all of those promotion recommendations on her office mate's desk and had learned that he was the bottleneck through which all such transactions must navigate. She now understood why the department kept such a sluggard. By just sitting on his work, this man saved the government considerable money.

But even her resident hypochondriac could not put a dint in her euphoria.

Although neither Tosun nor his nephew had surfaced following an intensive search of the small Turkish sector, this news was not all bad. It was bad news that they hadn't turned up alive, but it was good news that they hadn't turned up dead. More disturbing, if only because it was so much harder for a German national to hide in northern Cyprus than Tosun and his nephew, was the fact that Helmut Roentgen had not been found either. By midmorning, however, they had found someone who identified him as a guest at the Salamis Bay Hotel the previous two nights. The witness had also said Roentgen had been on intimate terms with one of the hotel workers. The police had subsequently managed to lift some fingerprints before the hotel room was cleaned up. The hotel bar waiter who'd spent the night with Roentgen was even now being grilled concerning what he could reveal about Roentgen, his activities, and current whereabouts.

Then Ziya decided that, if Roentgen couldn't be located in northern Cyprus, perhaps he had flown off the island again. Thus, she'd just spent a valuable half hour in discussion with various people at Ercan Airport. She had learned from passport control that Roentgen had not cleared the island in the past day. More important, however, she'd just discovered that he was ticketed to take today's last flight to Istanbul.

She slapped on her beret cap and started winding her muffler around her neck as she headed for the door. She also yelled for one of the detectives at the top of her voice as she shuffled out. "Sami, get a car! We're off to Ercan."

This exclamation caused her office mate to let out a hiss of disapproval, which she answered with a leer and a wink that practically propelled him out of his chair and onto the floor.

Both Tansul and Sami met her at the door.

Tansul handed her an envelope, which Safa hardly noticed as she slipped it into her purse. She had a job for the researcher. "Tansul, I'm worried about not being able to trace down Tosun and that nephew of his, who probably witnessed the murder of Peggy Bingham. Neither one of them came back to their Nicosia shop last night. They probably don't even know as yet that it has been ransacked. Could you put out an order for all police stations to check at all of the ports and fishing villages to try to determine if they left that way? Have them show that passport control camera photo of Roentgen around, as well. I want to know if he's been looking for the nephew. Oh, and yes," she added, her voice starting to fade down the hall, "I want that list of the people and cars who crossed over the checkpoint on Sunday ready by the time I get back."

* * * *

No sooner had the elevator door closed on the departing Takis at Sarah's apartment than the ground-level buzzer rang again.

"So, what did you forget? Wasn't one farewell kiss enough, Takis?" Caitlyn murmured into the intercom in a silky voice.

"One's never enough, but since when are you copping kisses from Takis, Sarah?" the intercom squawked back.

"Oh, sorry," Caitlyn quickly replied, glad that her total embarrassment did not register through the intercom. "This is Caitlyn. Come on up, John. I'll buzz you in. I think Sarah should be just about ready."

Sarah entered the room just then. Caitlyn's mouth fell open and she began to tremble. Sarah quickly reached her and had her seated back at the breakfast table and sipping out of her cup of coffee when John Dunsford entered the room.

"What's the matter, Caitlyn?" Sarah asked. "Are you still weak from the funeral this morning? Takis said you blacked out."

"No, it's not that," Caitlyn managed to get out. "That scarf you're wearing, Sarah. Where did you get it? That's the same scarf I had that blew into Eleni's grave this morning."

"This scarf? Why I've had it for years. I bought several myself—or it was a present. I can't remember which. I got it when I was serving in . . ." But she didn't finish the sentence. Dunsford cleared his throat, causing both women to look up at him. He had a very stern expression, one that still lingered in Caitlyn's mind long after the two had left her with a fresh cup of coffee and had clattered off to their embassy function.

* * * *

Hours later, Safa Ziya stood forlornly at the railing of the observation balcony above the small departure and arrival halls of Ercan Airport. The last scheduled departure of the day, the plane on which Helmut Roentgen had a confirmed, but presently empty seat, was lifting into the air and circling toward the east for the short flight to Istanbul.

She shouldn't have counted so much on Roentgen complaisantly showing up for his scheduled flight, she berated herself in disgust. She beat her fists on the railing in frustration. This caused an envelope to flutter out of her purse and onto the ground. She picked it up. Where had it come from? Ah, yes, Tansul had handed it to her as she was leaving her Nicosia office.

Ziya split open the envelope, unfolded the typed letter inside, quickly scanned it. She then reread it with relish, let out a whoop of laughter, ripped the piece of paper into very small bits, and slowly scattered the shreds into the wind over the Tarmac.

"Thank you, Tansul," Ziya declared to the heavens as she turned and headed for the parking area, "I needed that."

And as she walked off, the scraps of the recommendation for her office mate's promotion gently floated down to the ground.

Back in her office—at the moment mercifully hers alone—Ziya was bombarded with the results of the research she'd set in motion in recent days and just before she'd left for the airport.

The check with the Turkish authorities had revealed that, although Roentgen's frequent movements between Istanbul and northern Cyprus could be charted from passport control records, there was no evidence he ever left Turkey for any other foreign destination. At the same time, it was becoming increasingly clear that he must be going somewhere else or that he did not want anyone in authority to know where his base of operations in Turkey was located. The Istanbul address he always listed on his departure and arrival cards had turned out to be a women's public bath house, and he was not listed in the records as a legal foreign resident of Turkey.

Interpol also had no records of any kind for a Helmut Roentgen, and the fingerprints Ziya had provided did not match any of those in Interpol's international criminal files.

Ziya had had to query Interpol through the Turkish police, as northern Cyprus had no international standing with any country except Turkey itself. The Turkish police official she contacted following much delay in telephone connections asked her if she'd like for Interpol to start the laborious process of checking the fingerprints through the files of its member countries. He'd made it sound like the request would be a huge imposition—on him no less than on Interpol.

"Absolutely!" responded Ziya. It had been many years since she'd let herself be bullied.

The initial results she received hours later, however, hardly made the effort worthwhile. The Germans had been adamant that they had no German national named Helmut Roentgen with the fingerprints they had been given. No such Austrian or Belgian national had surfaced either. The Swiss did not answer the query. Instead of providing any information, the Americans countered with a series of questions of their own—which Safa promptly "lost" in her bottom drawer in a fit of exacerbation. The German response declared they had not issued the passport number the Turks claimed was being used by this Helmut Roentgen, and they were also beginning to ask more questions than they were answering.

"You realize a comprehensive fingerprints check through Interpol will take forever, don't you?" jabbed Tansul.

"You're right, Tansul," Safa answered with a sigh. Then after a short, contemplative pause, she added, "Tansul, call the American embassy office on this side and tell them I need to get something to Paul Conte quickly."

Tansul didn't move, the unvoiced question gluing her to the spot.

"Go, go, woman. It's obvious from what we've learned from Turkey that Helmut Roentgen is an assumed identity. If he's our killer, he must have left fingerprints on the Greek side as well. We won't worry about how he gets back and forth at the moment. We'll follow the fingerprints."

"But why Conte?" asked Tansul, stubbornly riveted to the spot. "The other American, the Brit, and the Canadian have all said they would help. Why not one of them?"

"I don't trust any of those three," Ziya shot back. "The only reason any of them volunteered to help was to get their hands on whatever we knew for their own countries' purposes and to impede our efforts. All they have done so far is to try to keep the two sides of the island from linking their investigations. And I'm not bringing Conte himself in on this either. I'm going to give him a sealed envelope to pass directly to the Greek investigator, Takis Koniotis. And I'm going to tell him I'll be checking with Koniotis at Friday's closing session of the bicommunal police seminar—Damn! I wish those sessions hadn't been suspended for the next two days. I'll be checking with Koniotis to ensure that the envelope reached him with the seal intact. Come, come, woman, get moving."

But Tansul remained planted to the floor, this time wide-eyed in shock. "You are going to deal with the Greeks? You trust the Greeks more than the Americans, the Canadians, and the British?"

"At this very moment, yes. I can't answer for tomorrow or for other investigations, but for this case, yes. These are crimes that all Cypriots abhor, and the Americans, Canadians, and British have just been toying with us. Now go!" But then, realizing what a help Tansul was to her, Ziya softened the command. "Please, Tansul. It's important."

As Tansul was sailing off into the hallway, Ziya was receiving yet another report. It had taken a mammoth effort, but a fisherman had finally owned up to having seen Mehmet Tosun and his nephew put out to sea from Bogaz the previous night—not, of course, on his boat or on any other he would identify as belonging to the Bogaz villagers. Ziya was so happy to get that information that she told her detective not to put the screws to the fisherman. Of course he knew precisely who had transported Tosun. But they did not have time to take on side issues and investigations. She was just grateful that the fisherman had revealed as much as he had. All that she asked was that the detective try to make the fisherman comfortable enough that he revealed where in Turkey Tosun had been landed.

More important, her instructions to flash Roentgen's photo had paid off in a way she hadn't imagined. A boatman in the new Kyrenia Harbor had recognized the picture and was more than eager to admit that he'd taken the German to the small Turkish mainland port of Ovacik. He saw no reason not to admit that he had done so. The man had shown him a permanent residence card for Turkey, which made the crossing perfectly legal. The boatman was anxious to discuss the transaction. He was steamed to the gills that he'd had to spend the entire night and much of the next day at Ovacik and was just getting back to Kyrenia, with the result that he had lost a full day's work. He had also lost his best helper, which had made him even more angry than the loss of the day's fishing. The boy had been persuaded to show the German to the hotel and had never returned to the port.

Ziya put out the order to inform the Turkish authorities that Roentgen had returned to the mainland.

"Maybe they can track him down now," she said with an enthusiasm she didn't feel. In her heart she knew they were too late and that Roentgen—or whoever he really was—had slipped out of Turkey already.

Chapter Sixteen

"Nyet, Nyet, you oaf! It's the big leather one over there. Nyet. No! Not to drag it. Where does the hotel find these people?"

As he followed the plush Paphos Amathus Beach seaside resort's weaving driver from the airport baggage claim area to the street, what was really irritating Sergey Stepanov poured back into his mind. This operation was getting out of hand, and he wasn't sure any longer whether it was time to sheath the Knife or to play out the situation a bit longer. He did know for sure that the situation was getting very dicey. But that was exactly why he was in the trade and what made life interesting. The thrill of the game. His superiors might be right, however. It might be time to head his game pieces for home.

The driver was waving at him from the curb in front of the terminal. But Stepanov just waved back, pointed at the wall near him, stepped up to a telephone, inserted his pay card, and dialed. No answer. No matter, he thought. The hunt was on.

* * * *

Halfway across the country, in the center of the capital city of Nicosia, Caitlyn Koniotis was bending as closely as she could over the small gold cylinder she was examining at her workbench. The light was bad in her basement office at the Cyprus Museum whenever winter clouds obscured the sun in the courtyard outside. At such times, these small offices—albeit highly coveted by the researchers precisely because they were located within the confines of the museum proper—took on the characteristics of dreary monks' cells.

The object Caitlyn was examining was covered with scratchings, which the experienced archaeologist was busy attempting to decipher. The cylinder was typical of the name seals that originated in Syria and Egypt and that began to turn up in Cyprus as trade goods in the Early Bronze Age period, stretching from about 2300 to 1850 BC. They were often found in the excavations of ancient grave sites. Gold was resilient. It maintained its properties over the centuries better than most any other substance.

The thrill Caitlyn found in this particular cylinder was twofold. First, the object was gold—and had been dated from an era in which copper predominated in Cyprus. That meant this was probably connected with a very important person of that time. Second, and much more exciting, was that Caitlyn had found the cylinder herself and had done so in her own neighborhood.

One evening, before Takis had been swept up in his current international murder investigation, the couple had been walking in their neighborhood at the base of one of the old mounds. The foundations for a house were being dug virtually into the base of the acropolis mount. Caitlyn had walked over to the excavation to see if any artifacts were being surfaced in the work. This had been when the strange vision of an ancient time where she had come close to being crushed by an earthquake had started to become crystal clear. For some reason the vision had been linked as much to this location as to her friend, Eleni. After the vision had passed, Caitlyn had looked closer at the foundation diggings and quickly discerned the signs of ancient walls and a collapsed chamber roof within the exposed earthen hillside.

Caitlyn didn't feel she could tell, first, Takis and then Dr. Visiliou that her hunch was rooted in a vision. Luckily, however, observable evidence of ancient habitation was readily at hand at the construction site. She thus had managed to get the work stopped immediately—much to the chagrin of her prospective neighbors. They had already sunk considerable money into the lot and were more concerned with their present life and comfort than with their ancient heritage. And there, just where her vision had led her, were the foundations of an ancient principal dwelling, perhaps even the palace for a very early civilization.

Caitlyn was soon being hailed as the divining rod of the Cyprus Antiquities Department. Just a few years previously she'd found a major Chalcolithic period (3900–2600 BC) settlement. Now she'd uncovered a Bronze Age site within the capital city itself. Her reputation in Cyprus was thus assured and her fame was already spreading further afield.

Such was her concentration on her ancient golden object that she did not notice the tall, thin figure separating from the shadows near the door into the corridor.

* * * *

The voice was melodic, amused, and urbane, as he lit a cigarette. "Bravo, Ms. Spencer. I've heard you've worked your magical connection with the ancients once more and are the toast of the Western world."

213

"Justin?" Caitlyn responded to Chamberlain's appearance with genuine pleasure—which she knew she shouldn't feel. She was supposed to be angry with Justin.

"It's Mrs. Koniotis now, and don't you forget it. Why are you always sneaking up on me? And where have you been? I've been frantically calling you. And put that cigarette out. You've been in museum workrooms often enough to know you can't smoke in here." Try as she might to sound peeved, however, Caitlyn just couldn't pull it off. She was always eager to see Justin. He was ever interesting and brilliant.

"Yes, ma'am, Mother Koniotis," Justin responded, although he continued smoking. "And I know you've been trying to call me. I couldn't see the top of the desk for all the phone messages you made my secretary record. Couldn't be helped. I had to go to Vienna for a couple of days in pursuit of a Grecian vase that was so naughty you wouldn't have allowed it in this dowdy museum of yours."

"Perhaps you haven't spent enough time in our Grecian export pottery exhibit just above our heads," Caitlyn said with a laugh. But then she became more serious. "In Vienna? But weren't you over in Salamis on Monday? I was sure I saw you there, although you didn't respond to my call."

"Nein, nicht, not guilty, my dear," Chamberlain countered almost too quickly. "I was indulging in Wiener schnitzel and snow in the Vienna Woods that day. As talented as I am, a person cannot be in two places at one time."

"I could have sworn. . . . But that's not important, Justin. What is important is that Andriko Visiliou told me the authorities were about to pull you in on artifact smuggling charges."

Chamberlain interrupted, angrily snuffing out his cigarette against the silver lighter, "Andriko. Andriko. I'm tired of Andriko trying to poison your mind against me. You know Andriko never did like me. And he was always trying to wedge himself between the two of us."

"I can't understand what happened between you and Andriko at the university, Justin. At the beginning you and he were such friends, almost inseparable. And then suddenly, it was as if you couldn't stand to be in the same room with each other. What happened at the university to set the two of you against each other?"

There was no answer.

"And I'm afraid it's not just Andriko, Justin," Caitlyn persisted in a soft voice. "Other people have told me the same things. Paul Conte of the American embassy among them. Everyone is saying Eleni Piccard was helping you to smuggle Cypriot antiquities out to France on her ships."

"Eleni Piccard?!" Chamberlain blustered. "That's ridiculous! Where's a telephone? We'll call Eleni right now, and you can hear her dismissive laugh at the charge with your own ears. She was charged with that years ago and you yourself helped prove it was someone else who was doing the smuggling."

"Oh, my God. You haven't heard, have you?" Caitlyn turned pale.

"Haven't heard? Haven't heard what?" Justin was on full alert.

"I'm sorry, Justin. Eleni is . . . dead. I don't know how else to tell you this. She was killed last Saturday. Apparently by the same killer who murdered the Russian monk last week and the Spanish ambassador Alvarez the week before. She was buried up in Kakopetria yesterday morning."

Now it was Chamberlain's face that drained of all its color. Caitlyn had gotten the impression that his reaction to her charge that he might've been engaged in illicit activity with Eleni had been a controlled act, but she could see that his shock now was genuine.

"No. That can't be so. Not Eleni. I was told—"

There was a long pause, during which Chamberlain looked more disconcerted than Caitlyn had ever before observed in the born actor. Eventually, Caitlyn looked hard at the elegantly dressed art broker and said: "What were you told? And by whom? Justin, what were you told?"

But Chamberlain was not paying attention. He was stumbling toward the door, stumbling not being a movement Caitlyn had ever before associated with her old university friend. And he was muttering to himself: "No, impossible. Not Eleni. If Eleni, then where does it stop? Who's safe?" And he was gone.

The only evidence left of the just-concluded dramatic scene was a cigarette butt on the floor and a silver lighter on the workbench. Caitlyn picked up the lighter and turned it over and over in her hand as she contemplated the possible meaning of what she had just heard. The scratchings on the surface of the silver lighter brought to mind the scratchings on the gold seal cylinder she'd been examining when Justin first materialized from the shadows of her laboratory. These scratchings were words, as well. They were in French and said simply: "Remember Brussels. All My Love." And then she noticed something written below that. She couldn't quite make it out in this light. It seemed to be a set of initials, but they were so worn from having been repeatedly rubbed that she could not readily read them.

She put the lighter in her purse, knowing that she could encounter Justin again at any time and could then return it to him. She then returned to her workbench, sighed deeply and picked up the gold cylinder. In a very short time she had escaped back into the more inviting and less disturbing world of the Cypriot Bronze Age.

* * * *

Willie Hamilton was enjoying a morning coffee in the lower lobby café of the five-star Paphos Amathus Beach Hotel when he heard the familiar laugh that almost made him spill the hot liquid down the front of his shirt.

Ginger had yet to come out of her coma, and the little Brit had been nearly worn to a frazzle by his ordeal with the police and with his frustrating—and thus far unrewarded—vigil by his wife's bedside. He had thus jumped at the chance to go to the country's third largest city, the ancient political and cultural capital of Paphos on the west coast. Paphos had a picturesque harbor, complete with a fortress dating back to the Byzantine era. In the modern era, large resort hotels had been added along the beaches to the north and to the south of the old city to take advantage of a history and ruins that stretched back to earlier than the Greco-Roman period.

It was the modernization of the harbor itself that had brought Major Hamilton to Paphos. Somehow a group of well-meaning, but culturally blind businessmen had acquired the long-abandoned Turkish- and British-period customs houses at the northern end of the harbor and had received permission to refurbish them. Unfortunately, though, their idea of refurbishment had amounted to constructing an abstract concrete superstructure over the old buildings. The city's conservative citizens and resort hoteliers had successfully screamed bloody murder over what they argued was the visual ruining of the picturesque harbor. Willie Hamilton had subsequently been sent to Paphos to cover the dismantling ceremony for the Cyprus Mail.

Willie enjoyed the good life, and the clout his newspaper connections had gained him free lodging at one of the most luxurious hotels on the beach. He was belly up to the lobby bar when he realized that the distinctive laugh he'd heard wafting down from the reception desk in the upper lobby could only belong to Sergey Stepanov. Hamilton shuddered. What Ginger had told him hadn't meant much to him at the time. He could forgive Ginger anything, and, frankly, he didn't care what she'd done in her earlier life as long as she'd come to him. But now, in the wake of the bombing attack on her and the other deaths and with the sudden appearance of Stepanov, the whole sordid tale was resurfacing in his mind. It was not so much that he was scared, either—although he certainly was scared for Ginger. What he really felt was deep anger and determination.

He wasn't about to tell Takis Koniotis this part of the story. He'd do something about this himself. And there was no time like the present. The intrusion of Stepanov had mobilized the old soldier. The Russian's arrogant laugh had been the catalyst.

First he needed to find out where Stepanov was going to light. Willie walked halfway up the stairs toward the upper lobby and peeked at the reception desk. Stepanov was finished checking in and had moved off toward the elevators in long, confident strides. As the elevator door shut, the bellboy headed toward another elevator with Stepanov's luggage. Willie merely fell in step behind the young man and pushed a button two floors above the one the bellboy had. After the bellboy struggled out of the elevator, his attention on the suitcases, Willie surreptitiously followed him down the corridor until he could see which room Stepanov had been assigned.

Then Hamilton returned to his own room, opened his largest suitcase—the one that was reserved for transporting his brandy bottles—and sat, and sipped, and schemed. Eventually, he picked up the telephone and rang a number. When he finally reached the person he was calling, he swallowed a large slug of brandy and asked, "Is this the Knife?"

There was a deep intake of breath on the other end, then an angry voice asked, "Who is this? What do you want?"

"I think you know who this is. We've met before. I know that you certainly are acquainted with my wife. You know, the woman you tried to blow up to keep her from talking?"

There was a moment of silence on the other end, followed by an intense but controlled query, "I asked what you wanted. Where are you?"

"We'll come to both of those questions, but not just yet," answered Willie, his voice gaining strength and purpose. "First, I want you to leave my wife alone. I know everything she knows, so there's nothing to be gained by doing her any more harm. Do you understand? Leave Ginger alone. I've written the story. It'll be filed the moment any harm comes to her."

"Yes, I understand," said the voice at the other end after a moment of hesitation. "Where are you? We need to talk."

"Yes, that's the other point," Willie answered. "We do need to talk. Walk into Kolossi Castle exactly at 9:15 Friday morning—not before, and not after. I'll meet you in Queen Berengaria's chamber on the second level."

The receiver went dead without further comment. Willie downed the rest of the brandy in his glass and began to murmur, tears rising in his eyes: "It'll be all right, Ginger. Willie will take care of you. Willie will always take care of you."

* * * *

Not more than a half mile away from where Caitlyn Koniotis was engrossed in studying her Bronze Age gold cylinder, senior police inspector Safa Ziya was sitting in her office in the Turkish sector of Nicosia. Safa was just then conducting her own research into antiquities. Tansul had squeaked her cart into Safa's office, once more mercifully devoid of its other occupant, and had slapped two files and a small parcel down on Safa's desk. Instead of leaving the office, though, the researcher settled herself comfortably in the other desk chair and looked at Safa expectantly.

Safa knew Tansul would not go back to work until the files had been inspected and she had been profusely thanked for her effort. The first file indeed proved to be interesting. It reported the interviews that had been conducted with Peggy Bingham's Boston lawyer and with the few people in Boston who'd claimed to have been acquainted with the woman. Those who had claimed to know why Bingham had come to northern Cyprus agreed that she said she was on the hunt for some miniature Orthodox icon paintings she'd paid for but not received. Her housekeeper had said that her mistress had been visited several months previously by an art broker by the name of Helmut Roentgen. The housekeeper said she remembered the name distinctly because Bingham had been invoking the name in vain constantly on the telephone during the past several weeks.

Bingham's lawyer had been even more helpful. He also knew all about the miniature icons. He had nervously tried to establish with the Boston investigators that he'd tried to warn her off of becoming involved in the purchase of what most likely were stolen antiquities.

"But," he had said, "you had to have known Mrs. Bingham to have understood how stubborn and opinionated she was."

"I think we more or less gathered that from our interviews with her in-laws in Boston," the investigator responded with a smile that was designed to put the lawyer at ease and to loosen his tongue.

The ploy had worked. The lawyer had become quite helpful. Most notably, he had come up with the telephone number Mrs. Bingham had left for a contact in the Turkish zone of Nicosia—Mehmet Tosun's store.

"Good work, Tansul," Safa praised the researcher when she had finished the file. "This is all beginning to fit. This independently links Bingham, the buyer, with Roentgen, the art smuggler, and Tosun, the middleman. From the timing, it seems like these might be the miniatures that were stolen from the icon museum in the old Greek church near the Kyrenia harbor late last spring. We thought we had traced them to Brussels, but the ones that surfaced there turned out to be forgeries. Good forgeries, however. Whoever painted them had to have had access to the real ones. This is beginning to add up to an operation in which Tosun arranged to have the icons stolen. Then they were copied by Detrich Kleist for sale—probably by Roentgen—to one buyer. After that they were peddled to Peggy Bingham, as well—probably also by Roentgen."

Ziya was silent for a while. Then she said, "Yes, interesting, but somehow it doesn't fit into the bigger picture. I can conceive of Roentgen killing Bingham because she had started to become a nuisance and he already had her money. And I can understand why he and Tosun would've cleared the island and ended their operations here if they thought the police were on to them. But why would he have killed Kleist weeks before Bingham came here and before the police pressure was beginning to be applied? Surely Kleist was a valuable commodity to the operation? Or was he getting too greedy or scared? And where did the other knifing victim, Bertelli, fit into the operation? In fact, what does this all have to do with the NATO spy ring case?"

The other file contained detailed records of the vehicle licenses and names of those who had crossed from the Greek zone to the Turkish zone via the only public border crossing during the last several weeks. Ziya looked through the list on the off chance that she would find Helmut Roentgen's name there—or even the other name they knew Mehmet Tosun by, Nabil Jallud. But she didn't expect to find either name—and that was the case.

Ziya looked up and noticed that Tansul was still there and still sitting forward in the other desk chair, looking at her expectantly.

"Yes, thank you Tansul. These files have been a big help."

Tansul didn't move, and she didn't change expression, but her eyes went to the other, forgotten parcel that she had placed on Ziya's desk.

Ziya looked at it. It was a rubber stamp. The investigator examined it more closely, only to find that it was a stamp of her office mate's signature. She looked up at Tansul with a questioning gaze. But Tansul was still smiling. Then, as it dawned on her, a wide grin started to form on Safa Ziya's face, as well. She suddenly, for the first time in years, felt empowered.

* * * *

His tie off and his shirt loosened out over his pants, Sergey Stepanov lay back in the hotel suite's overstuffed armchair and sipped at his scotch. He didn't look happy, however, as he slammed the receiver down on his telephone.

"Busy, damn it," he declared.

He ran his beefy free hand through his coarse brown hair and started to unlace his shoes. The shower was already running, and he'd arranged for his favorite Russian cabaret girl from the small Paphos nightclub district to be here soon. He'd hoped to have been able to do some business before fun. And, oh what fun. He rose and started to strip as he moved toward the shower.

But then he was on the phone again. And this time when he'd hung up he was no longer smiling.

He began to pace about the room, castigating himself. Where had the plans gone wrong? How had he been discovered here so quickly? He'd intended to get to him in time, but had wanted it on his terms. Well, no matter. He thought he could outsmart him and escape, but he was wrong. It would be best to close out this part sooner than later.

He quickly started to put his clothes back on and called the desk to come pick up his luggage. He was checking out. He did this so quickly that when a young girl showed up at his room within the hour, the only sign of habitation she found was an open door, a half-full glass of scotch, and a running shower.

* * * *

"Hail, hail, the gang's all here," Alec Stuart called out over the boisterous noise enveloping the Plaka Tavern, an open-air meze restaurant in one of the ancient village squares that had been swallowed by Nicosia's sprawl to the west. Sarah Bristow and John Dunsford hesitated just long enough for it both to be obvious they had heard Stuart's invitation and to be equally obvious that they would've preferred not finding their colleagues at the restaurant. But Takis and Caitlyn Koniotis were already making room at the table, so Sarah and John bowed to the inevitable and joined the group.

"Didn't you see us waving at you?" asked Caitlyn, as everyone settled back into their seats and surveyed the vast collection of small plates of food that made up the traditional Cypriot meze. In response to their expanded group, waiters were descending on them from all quarters of the table-choked village square with more plates of food and bottles of beer and wine.

"I assumed you were waving us off, that you didn't want to consort in public with people who were under suspicion," Sarah responded with an icy tone in her voice. "Or didn't you know that your husband has requested official responses from several of us, including both John and Alec, concerning our whereabouts at the times of the recent killings? That's just a little bit below the belt, Takis."

"Oh, Sarah," growled John Dunsford, as he pulled a pack of cigarettes from his shirt pocket and started patting around his body in search of a match, "Can't you give it a rest? The man's just doing his job. Safa Ziya has intimated that we should be included in the list of suspects, and Takis can't ignore that. Damnation, anybody got a light?"

Both Takis and Alec started exploring their own pockets, with little result.

"Well, that's not what you said on the way over here, John. You were furious about this."

Caitlyn remembered that she had the lighter Justin had left in her office in her purse, wanting to have it with her the next time she saw him, and she took it out just as one of the waiters floated up and lit John's cigarette. Immediately thereafter he also lit the candle in the middle of table. The flame from this flared up, it's light reflecting brilliantly off the engraved surface of the silver lighter Caitlyn was holding over the table.

The attention of everyone at the table was drawn to the lighter, and Takis looked quizzically at his nonsmoking wife. But just then someone abruptly rose from a closely-placed adjacent table and the waiter and his lit match nearly fell into Takis's lap.

In the wake of Sarah's speech of irritation, the impromptu dinner group lost any chance of conviviality, which had little effect on the general party mood of the surrounding tables. No one could enjoy a good late-night meze dinner under the stars on one of the last evenings of the year the outdoor restaurants could be used than a Greek Cypriot. The food, beer, and wine just kept flowing around the little square, and the decibel level quickly reached to a crescendo that made all conversation impossible. No one from the surrounding tables noticed that everyone at this table, except Caitlyn, who was experiencing such an end-of-season Cypriot ritual for the first time, had withdrawn into a blue funk. Some did, however, notice that John Dunsford and Sarah Bristow left even before the fruit platters that crowned the meze whirled out of the kitchens.

Chapter Seventeen

It was Thursday morning, and Caitlyn had been so engrossed in her work on the artifacts found at the acropolis diggings that it was only the shooting pain that started at the center of her back and flashed down into her legs that told her she'd been perched on the stool at the workbench for too long. She'd been working with a gold fertility necklace pendant, a primitive female figure in cruciform that had inexplicably brought her lost friend, Eleni Piccard, to mind. In her senses, it had taken on the form of Eleni herself and seemed almost to be whispering what appeared to be some sort of warning.

Caitlyn wrenched her attention away from the amulet and jumped off the stool, wanting to return the circulation to her legs—but a very real sound caused her to turn toward the door. Was that her name being whispered? And was that what had drawn her attention from her work rather than the cramp in her back and legs?

She walked to the door and poked her head out into the dark corridor, whose only light—from a high, barred and dusty window at the far end of the passage—bounced unevenly off the old plaster walls and brick vaulted ceiling.

She heard it again. "Caitlyn. Come." The voice was muffled and distant, but the storeroom door just down the corridor was open and there was a flicker of light.

"Coming, Eleni," she said, without even realizing she had responded to a dead woman. She moved down the passage. The windowless storeroom was dark, but she really did seem to see a strange glow back in the corner as she looked in the door.

"Yes, I'm here. Who's there?" she asked as she stood dimly silhouetted in the doorway. The only answer was a slight wheezing sound and then the sound of metal clicking on masonry.

"Caitlyn. There you are. I've been calling for you." Dr. Visiliou had descended the stairs from the museum proper and was beckoning to his prize archaeologist. "The delegation from the Athens museum is here. I'm about to start the review of our find at the Kaliana dig, and you're needed."

Caitlyn shook her head, sure now that she had just imagined the other voice, her senses having been dulled from sitting on the stool too long and concentrating closely on her work. She turned and followed Dr. Visiliou up the stairs, grateful at the break from her routine.

Minutes after they had ascended the stairs, a figure emerged from the shadows of the storeroom, dropped a crushed cigarette on the brick floor, and sheathed a rather large-bladed knife inside his coat. He looked into Caitlyn's workroom in frustration, climbed the stairs, and departed the museum. There would be other opportunities, but time was getting short. She knew too much.

* * * *

227

Safa was not at her own desk. The late morning hour had, rather, found her at the other desk in her office, where she was gaily stamping away at the pile of papers that had been suffocating that work area. She reached into the pile, pulled out a piece of paper, looked at it, and either smiled and stamped it or frowned and threw it off to one side. She then folded the stamped papers into envelopes, wrote a name on each envelope, and tossed it into a box at her side.

She was so taken with this activity that she didn't notice the form that appeared at her door and slid slowly toward her own desk.

Blinded momentarily by the sun's rays that were spilling into the small office, the American embassy's Paul Conte hadn't seen at first that Safa was not at her own desk. It was only when he heard her giggle that he looked over at the other desk and that she, in turn, looked up and saw his handsome, athletic visage glowing in the sunlight.

"Mr. Conte," she said with embarrassed surprise, unconsciously concealing the stamp she had been using under the untidy stack in front of her. "May I help you? It's such a surprise for you to drop in so soon."

"Yes, I imagine it is, Mrs. Ziya," Conte answered politely.

"It's Ms. Ziya," Safa said firmly and somewhat wistfully. And then, more business-like, as she moved back toward her desk, she added, "Please have a seat. Here, let me close the shutters a bit, so the light won't blind you. I'm sorry about the sudden cold. All of my American friends only think of Cyprus as a Mediterranean island and conjure up visions of a warm and temperate climate year round. None of them understand that we have seasons just as most of them do, if not as extreme." Safa was plainly put a bit off balance by Conte's appearance and was filling the air with small talk until she could get her bearings.

"That's quite all right," responded Conte to no particular comment. "I've come because Takis Koniotis is so excited that I could only get him to promise not to try to crash through the border to come see you this morning by saying I'd come straight over myself."

"Has Mr. Koniotis managed a breakthrough in the Belgium spy ring case?" Ziya asked with genuine interest.

"No, Ms. Ziya. You have."

"I?" Ziya responded with surprise.

"Yes," Conte continued. "We found a match for the fingerprints you sent over late Tuesday afternoon."

"So soon?" Safa exclaimed.

"Yes. I hope you don't mind. I know the envelope you sent me was sealed. And I assure you it was handed over to Koniotis sealed. But he did let me stay to see what you had sent over, and suddenly several things started to fit."

"I don't understand," Safa said.

"I'm sorry. Let me back up a bit. As you know, as the U.S. Treasury Service's representative on the island, smuggling of various kinds—as the interests of the United States are involved–come under my responsibility."

Ziya nodded. She was beginning to pick up the thread.

"I was following a developing antiquities smuggling case on the Greek side and Takis mentioned that your side of the spy ring murders investigation seemed to have an artifacts smuggling aspect. Let me cover the more straightforward aspect of this first."

"Please proceed as you see fit, Mr. Conte," answered Safa.

"Right. I understand you have connected an antique shopowner by the name of Mehmet Tosun to both the spy ring murders and to art smuggling."

Ziya nodded. "To smuggling, certainly. And we found he was in Belgium during the period the spies were active."

"Well, we've been zeroing in on him for some time. One of my service's agents in Europe came in contact with him there. The agent was dickering with Tosun to pick up some icons that surely had been illegally obtained. This agent came to Cyprus and examined these icons—they were miniatures—in Tosun's shop just a couple of weeks ago. We received copies of the reports you received from Boston on Peggy Bingham, and the description of the icon miniatures she'd thought she'd paid for match the icons my agent was shown and was arranging to buy from Tosun. I think we can help you put together enough evidence to close his operation down and maybe to implicate him in the Bingham murder."

"Thank you for the information and offer of help, Mr. Conte, but it may come a bit too late."

Paul Conte raised a questioning eyebrow.

Ziya continued: "Mehmet Tosun and his nephew have fled the island. And his shop has been ransacked. Our people sifted through what was left."

"And did they find some icon miniatures?" asked Conte.

"No, I'm afraid not. And I would not be at all surprised if that was why the shop had been burgled." Ziya switched gears. "But those weren't Tosun's fingerprints I sent over," she said pointedly.

"No, and that's the most important and exciting news I have," Conte answered. "It was really the description of Helmut Roentgen that you sent over that did the trick. Do you recognize the man in this photo, Ms. Ziya?"

"Certainly," she said immediately and without hesitation. "That is Helmut Roentgen. See, I have a photo of the same man here that was taken at passport control at Ercan Airport a couple of days ago."

"No, his name isn't Helmut Roentgen," Conte continued. "That is an American art broker by the name of Justin Chamberlain."

* * * *

Colonel Sarah Bristow's luxurious apartment in the old acropolis section of Nicosia outside the walls was just about as safe as one could be from possible terrorist attack in Cyprus while still enjoying gorgeous sweeping views of the old walled city and the stretch of the Kyrenia mountain range to the north. The apartment was a two-story penthouse, with the living area windows rising the full two stories, atop one of the city's tallest buildings. The north façade looked out toward the Kyrenia Range. To the south could be seen the ribbon of the Nicosia-Limassol highway snaking around the towering Troodos Mountains and toward the commercial and resort coast.

Although the outer walls of the Bristow residence consisted almost entirely of plate glass windows, the apartment was considered to be very safe from attack. This had been the main requirement in the leasing of quarters for the American embassy's senior military representative. There were no neighboring apartments at Bristow's level, and her dwelling was at the pinnacle of the tallest building for a mile in any direction. There were wide balconies. But these were protected on the outer walls and below the level of vision by nasty-looking spikes intertwined with electrical wiring that had proved to be

231

a last, deadly fascination for the few birds that tried to cavort in this area of the city. The only access to the apartment was via either a private elevator or a locked back staircase that rose from a private, windowless lobby (with guardroom attached, sporting several surveillance cameras) to another windowless foyer at the apartment's door. The only access to the lower lobby was via a double parking garage with an automatic door.

All of this security, of course, was too protective for Sarah Bristow's own needs, but the American embassy had jumped at the opportunity to acquire the property. Ironically, the security devices that now protected one of the embassy's senior officials had, until very recently, served as a Cyprus stronghold for the radical Abu Nidal faction of the Palestinian Liberation Organization. Until Takis Koniotis's investigative unit had uncovered and closed down the operation some four months previously, this faction had been using Cyprus to launder its operational funds and to arrange its international travel. The American embassy had acquired the apartment to keep it out of the hands of another such undesirable organization.

Now, just as ironically, Koniotis was making use of the apartment's tight security to protect his wife, Caitlyn.

On this late Thursday afternoon, the Koniotis couple and Sarah Bristow were sitting in the living room, cocktails in hand, appreciative eyes glued to the sparkling display of sunlight on the foothill villages of the Kyrenia Mountains. Their attention, however, was more narrowly focused on reality, as they were reviewing the status of the NATO spy ring case.

Takis was tired and had taken a break from his methodical sifting through the records of the Limassol passport control office and of the recent border crossings to spend a few hours with Caitlyn. Besides, he felt that he needed to bring the news to her in person concerning Justin Chamberlain's double life and probable implication in at least one—if not many—murders. He wanted to get to her before anyone else did.

Caitlyn was taking the news badly—as badly as any close friend would. Oddly enough, however, Sarah Bristow seemed quite pleased by the revelations. She had, of course, been prickly with Takis at first, still smarting from their encounter at the Plaka Tavern two days previously and by her status on the suspect list that had precipitated her anger that evening. But when she had heard that a case was building against Justin Chamberlain as the killer, her attitude had completely changed. She acted just like a jilted jealous lover would under the circumstances of getting even, Takis observed, with interest. He made a note to look more closely into Sarah Bristow's past.

Sarah was saying that she and John Dunsford had been seeing quite a bit of each other while they were both assigned to Brussels. During this time Justin, whose father was the commanding general of NATO in Brussels, had popped up fairly frequently and had often made himself somewhat of a nuisance by turning the dates into threesomes.

"Well, Justin was brilliant," Sarah said, "and usually quite amusing, although his sarcasm could become old awfully fast. And he could be such a pest about not leaving John and me alone."

Unfortunately, this wasn't the best time to be making such comments in front of a saddened Caitlyn, who uncharacteristically fought back. "Strange," she observed in a carefully even, but still pointed tone, "Justin told me a somewhat different story. He said that you seemed quite flattered by receiving attention from two men at once, and most notably by one whose father was so important in NATO military circles. He indicated that he was the one who was embarrassed by your persistent attentions."

Sarah bristled and started to respond, but, having delivered the jab, Caitlyn turned to her husband and changed the topic.

"Did anything surface in all of the work you've done so far on the Limassol arrivals from France and the border crossings these past three weeks?"

"Nothing much, I'm afraid. But in my business, just as in yours, negating paths of investigation is almost as valuable as finding positive clues. It's possible Chamberlain is the sole murderer. It's also possible that someone other than Chamberlain was using double identities and international flights to go between the Cypriot zones, as well. We haven't been able to find any more people who fit the Limassol debarkation part of the victim profile. That could be good news. It could mean that there are no more victims in wait out there.

"It looks like Eleni Piccard was the broker who got these people into Cyprus—at least the ones who arrived on this side. Mehmet Tosun probably provided this service on the other side. So, we're going over Eleni's background with a fine-tooth comb. There's some evidence that she traveled to Brussels frequently when she went to France to check in with the Piccard family. We're concentrating on that aspect of her travels."

Sarah looked uncomfortable, started to speak, and then clammed up.

"What is it, Sarah?" Koniotis queried. "Do you have an idea about Eleni's movements in the 1980s?"

"Well, perhaps you should know that the Piccard family is involved in defense industries, as well, and that Eleni Piccard did, in fact, show up several times in Brussels in the 1980s to help peddle armaments for her husband's family."

"And you knew Eleni Piccard then?" Takis had to fight hard to control the tone of his query. He needed to keep Sarah talking.

"Well, yes, mostly socially, of course. Both John and I saw her at cocktail parties occasionally. Even Justin Chamberlain socialized with her, for that matter."

"And you hadn't conveniently forgotten this, had you?" Takis said, barely able to contain the sarcasm. "And you only decided to mention it when it looked like we might find it out anyway, right?"

"Right," Sarah answered in a calm, direct tone. "Your minister has not, in fact, coordinated with my ambassador yet to bring about the release of information from our own investigation, Takis. When this happens, I'll be happy to open my government's own records to you. Until then, I can only help you in areas that are not under classified seal. In spite of that, I have given you this information. I could have made you dig it out yourself."

"OK," Takis conceded wearily. "This is a delicate investigation for all of us."

"What about Sergey Stepanov?" Caitlyn adroitly changed the subject again. "Have you found him yet? And what's his involvement?"

"No, we haven't tracked him down yet," answered Takis. "His ship is off Ayia Napa harbor and is being watched. He checks out as having formerly been Russian KGB and to have been working the Western European account. That probably connects him with the spying on NATO, and he is a very good candidate for our killer. It would make sense that he has been sent here to kill off the spies now that the cold war is over to keep them from revealing the details of that operation. They were probably all located here to make them readily available for just such a contingency."

"I don't suppose you ever encountered Stepanov when you where in Brussels, did you, Sarah? I'm sure you would have told me if you had?"

"Yes, we knew about Stepanov in Brussels," Sarah responded, "But I'm not at liberty to talk about that. And I don't think anything I could tell you would make a big difference. It's true that there's every reason to believe that he's in this mess up to his neck and that he may also have done some of the killings."

Sarah looked pensive for a few minutes. Then she asked, "Did Stepanov show up in the border crossing records?"

"Oddly enough, he didn't," Koniotis responded. "He has no diplomatic status here, so he could only have gone over on a day pass. We do know from other sources that he was on the other side a couple of times in the past several weeks, and they both checked out as short luncheon trips in the company of other foreigners to Kyrenia harbor—but for some reason even these trips didn't show up in the border crossing records. That doesn't mean, of course, that no one else in the Russian embassy could've been doing his dirty work for him over there. Also, he has a ship and charter planes available to him. There's no telling how hard it would be for him to leave from the Greek zone, go beyond international waters, and come back in the Turkish zone. That's illegal and we do everything we can to stop it, but it could happen."

"Anything else interesting pop up in the border crossing charts?" Sarah asked.

"Well, we don't have the records from the Turkish side yet, and they keep far better records than those on our side. The Greek guards just try to record diplomatic license plate numbers as they pass through. The Turks make the cars stop and sign in by passenger name. But no, the only names that came up in the border crossing records of people who had a connection with Brussels were such diplomats as you, John, Alec, and Paul, who had regular business on that side. There wasn't any record of a crossing by Justin Chamberlain or by his alter ego, Helmut Roentgen, either. But we now know how he was getting back and forth. He's going out from both sides to some point in Europe and then coming back and using aliases to disrupt the paper trail."

Sarah looked troubled and again acted as if she would speak, but when queried, she just said, "It's probably nothing. Just a loose end I thought of that needs to be taken care of. By the way, has Ginger Hamilton come out of her coma yet?"

"No," Takis answered. "But we have her under heavy guard and we'll be talking with her just as soon as she wakes up."

Caitlyn had looked unhappy again when the conversation had come back around to the topic of Justin Chamberlain. Takis decided not to avoid the subject; she had to come to terms with the situation as it was.

"It is really too much of a coincidence that Justin Chamberlain's father was central to the NATO scandal and went home in disgrace and then Justin conveniently popped up here in

Cyprus along with the NATO spies. His father's disgrace must really have been a blow to Justin when he heard about it at the university."

Caitlyn looked startled: "Oh, Justin wasn't at the university when all of this happened. He was in Brussels interning with his father at NATO and living with his parents."

Koniotis did a double take and looked searchingly at Sarah for verification.

"She's right." And then, she added defensively, "I had no idea you didn't know he was in Brussels full time during much of that period. That wasn't a secret."

Koniotis turned back to his wife. "Do you know when he came to Cyprus, Caitlyn?"

"Certainly. He came here sometime around 1987. He said he had to get away from the situation with his father. The old general had become suicidal, and Justin isn't very good at facing up to other people's problems. He loved Cyprus, though, and it was at least partially his glowing descriptions of the island and of the archaeological opportunities here that brought me to Cyprus, as well. Of course there was the pull of heritage. My mother had Cypriot ancestors."

"Takis," Caitlyn continued. "I really must talk to Justin. Have you brought him in? Or can I still reach him at his apartment?" She started to reach for the telephone receiver.

"I'm sorry, Caitlyn," Koniotis responded gently. "Justin isn't either at police headquarters or his flat. He cleared out after talking with you yesterday. We tracked his movements to the airport, where he took a plane to Europe. He had already arrived and disappeared on the other end before we could catch up with him there."

"His destination?" Sarah asked.

"Brussels."

All three took large gulps of their drinks and turned their gazes back to the now-dark Kyrenia Range. Although there were dancing city lights in the foreground, the Turkish zone was now in total darkness. This was either the result of the periodic electricity shortages imposed on that embargoed zone or of the occasional blackouts the Turkish army ordered to remind all that the island was still officially on a war footing. Either explanation was plausible, and both were very depressing to the three people sitting high above the city, each enveloped in her or his own troubled thoughts.

* * * *

John Dunsford was having equally troubled thoughts as he sat huddled over his beer in his now-darkened living room and looked back across the city walls toward Sarah Bristow's apartment.

Dunsford's apartment at the edge of the Laiki Yitonia tourist district was old; the heat was not sufficient; the pipes grumbled; the wiring could not take the load of many appliances; the bathrooms were a sight; the neighbors and street activities were noisy; and there was no elevator. But this was a world that he'd become accustomed to from his many years in the Soviet Union and Eastern Europe, and it was one that gave him comfort. The apartment was old and tired, just as he was. He was thinking just how tired he'd become of the game when, at great length, his telephone rang.

"Good, I'm glad you're there. We must talk."

"I'm not really up to talking at the moment," responded Dunsford morosely. He had his revolver in his hand. He'd been sitting

239

there with it in the dark, contemplating taking full control of his future.

"We really should meet, John. Did you know that Chamberlain has been implicated in a couple of murders on the Turkish side and that both he and Mehmet Tosun are on the run?"

Dunsford sighed and placed the revolver on the table. "What do you mean 'on the run,' Sarah?"

"Tosun seems to have disappeared into Turkey, and Chamberlain has returned to Brussels."

"Yes, that's right," Dunsford said. He did not seem even slightly interested in the topic, however.

"You knew? How?"

"Yes. That's what people in my business do for a living, you know. We know things before other people do."

"And did you know that the police are hot on Chamberlain's tail and that they think he might be the key to the NATO case? John, I need to see you. We need to resolve a couple of things. This just keeps getting more and more tangled."

"Yes, of course you're right, Sarah. You're always right. How about lunch tomorrow?"

"Sorry, I can't. I have to go to Limassol on business at the Episkopi sovereign base. How about dinner instead?"

"Fine," answered Dunsford. "I'll meet you at that new Georgian restaurant in Laiki Yitonia at 9:00 PM."

"Yes, that would be fitting."

"Yes, very fitting indeed," murmured Dunsford, as he slowly returned the receiver to the cradle. He picked up the revolver and turned it over a couple of times in his hands. Not yet. It was not yet time for this. He sighed and replaced the weapon in the torn and soiled trench coat that hung over an adjacent chair. He returned to his seat and poured another glass of beer and resumed staring out of the window of his darkened apartment.

The closing session of the bicommunal police seminar was tomorrow. Well, to hell with that. He had better things to do. He wondered whether he had chilled enough beer—and then, with a dry laugh, whether he had remembered to put bullets in the revolver.

* * * *

It was sometime later that evening. Sarah Bristow had retired to her own room shortly after dinner, and Takis had left only some ten minutes previously to return to his office for a final check before going back to their repaired house for the night. Caitlyn was finishing washing the glasses and turning the lights off in the living room and kitchen before retiring herself. A persistent ringing from the garage entry seven stories below broke the silence.

It must be Takis. He must have forgotten something, Caitlyn thought to herself, as she reached for the door release.

But a strong, firm grip arrested her hand in midmotion. The ringing continued.

"I think it's Takis," explained Caitlyn.

"It's always best to check," responded Sarah as she turned on the flood lights above the entry on the street below and switched on the surveillance camera.

In the second it took the camera to adjust focus, the figure below had managed to turn and fade back to the fringe of the light. Caitlyn could discern enough to tell that it was not Takis. But, beyond that, she couldn't tell anything about the figure other than it was not a creature of the light. For the light had scared it away. The doorbell did not ring again that night.

Chapter Eighteen

The Canadian high commissioner ground to a halt, almost in midsentence—certainly in midthought—as if his batteries had given out. It didn't seem to the seminar attendees that he had intended on giving this talk. John Dunsford hadn't shown up at the Friday morning closing session of the bicommunal police seminar. Takis Koniotis supposed that Dunsford's absence and the high commissioner's lack of preparation and barely concealed irritation reflected cause and effect. For his part, Koniotis was delighted when the diplomat wound down to a somewhat hesitant "So, there it is, then." This provided the opportunity for him and Safa Ziya to go off in the corner and compare notes. He looked over at Ziya. She quite obviously felt just as he did.

The Canadian diplomat sat down with a bewildered look, a red face, and a smattering of polite applause to be replaced by one of the professional seminar leaders. The latter's duty was to review the basic points that were supposed to have been brought out in the seminar and to make everyone believe these were, in fact, the very points brilliantly surfaced at one time or other by the participants themselves.

As if by signal, Takis Koniotis and Safa Ziya rose to refill their coffee cups and, upon reaching the coffee urn, slipped as quietly as possible beyond the folding doors and into the darkened auxiliary portion of the Treaty Room.

The two were followed by a distressed and sweating Canadian high commission underling, who suddenly had unpracticed and unwanted responsibility thrust on him by Dunsford's absence and the high commissioner's displeasure. Ignoring his presence, Takis and Safa quickly briefed each other in whispers on what they'd come to accept was a shared investigation.

They agreed that Chamberlain was to be the main focus of their current investigation, although Ziya did so reluctantly. And in tacit recognition of Ziya's inability to quickly bring the investigation process beyond the embargoed borders of northern Cyprus to bear, Koniotis volunteered to spearhead the international search for the American art broker.

"Chamberlain has flown between the two sectors via Athens and Istanbul, freely trading off identities in the process," reasoned Takis. "There is little reason that someone else could not have done the same."

"I'm sure you're right, Takis," Ziya responded. "But I've been trained to be very cautious and to sift through all of the evidence. We should be getting the records from the Turkish crossing today—I'm really sorry it's taken so long, but you don't know how much red tape our system is able to employ—and I think I'll still have Tansul do an analysis of those records."

"Fine, we do still consider the Russian, Sergey Stepanov, a viable suspect. We don't have any records of him crossing the border, but we do have some reports of him having been seen over there."

"I don't really see how that can have happened," Ziya responded. "I've gone to great lengths to place him on the Turkish side, using the photos and dossier you gave me, but haven't come up with anything. I would find it very hard to believe that he'd gone unnoticed on my side. The Russians stand out quite prominently, and they get very close attention from the Turkish army authorities. There is a lot of animosity toward Russia in mainland Turkey. I'm sure that if anyone had seen Stepanov doing anything even remotely suspicious in the Turkish zone, the authorities would've been quite pleased to tell me all about it. No, I don't think Stepanov had much if anything directly to do with the killings on this side, although maybe Tansul will come up with something from the border crossing records. I am quite convinced, however, that Roentgen—excuse me—Chamberlain killed Peggy Bingham. And she was killed in the same manner Bertelli and Kleist were."

"Ah, speaking of Bertelli," Koniotis persisted, "didn't you say that she was a favorite dancer of a group of Russians. Even if Stepanov wasn't operating on the Turkish side himself, could not another Russian have been acting for him?"

"Yes, that's always a possibility. But the Russians who've frequented Anti's nightclub are in tour groups that usually only visit once. It's really the tour director who chooses to frequent Anti's, not a regular clientele of Russian nationals. But, yes, it's possible that Stepanov is involved and that someone acted for him on our side of the Green Line. But, if so, there's no reason why it would have to be a

Russian. Why can't we both be right? You have connected both Stepanov and Chamberlain with Brussels during the NATO spy ring period. Why couldn't they have been working together?"

"Of course, Safa, that's true!" exclaimed Koniotis loud enough that the progress of the seminar in the other half of the room was halted and all eyes were turned toward the darkened corner they occupied. The two parted heads and sipped at their empty coffee cups, eyes deflected until the seminar regained momentum.

Then Koniotis returned to the discussion. "Most of the victims arrived here under very similar, if not identical, circumstances. As far as we now know, only Eleni Piccard, Justin Chamberlain, Sergey Stepanov, and Mehmet Tosun were connected with the NATO scandal—or at least were in Brussels at the time—but arrived here under different arrangements from the others. Eleni Piccard almost certainly made the arrangements for most of the victims who came to the Greek side. Her position on the island and her control of a shipping company were probably what made Cyprus the natural location in which to salt away this nest of blown spies. My surmise is that Mehmet Tosun made the arrangements on the Turkish side. And then, if Justin Chamberlain was also in the inner circle, with the original job of pointing to the information to be collected from the representatives of the other countries, based on what he could glean from his father's activities. . . . And they were all controlled by the KGB through Sergey Stepanov . . ."

Koniotis's discourse came to a halt as he noticed that Ziya's smile had frozen and then melted from her face and she was now shaking her head.

"What's wrong with that scenario?" asked Koniotis.

"Nothing. It may be close, but it's not complete."

"What do you mean?"

"There's a fallacy back at the beginning of your construct." When Koniotis looked quizzical, she continued, "Those were not the only four who were connected with NATO and Brussels and who arrived here outside the pattern. Both Sarah Bristow and John Dunsford fit that description, as well."

"I know you've needled them about a possible connection to this, but surely you don't seriously think—"

"In our business, it is dangerous to assume too much, isn't it? Why would you discount them and not any of the others?"

"No, of course you're right, Safa. And I must admit I haven't felt the answer in my bones on this one as I usually do. There still are some unknowns. But I feel so close to the answer."

"Yes, I know what you mean about not being comfortable with a solution as yet," Safa responded gently.

"But there is something I'm sure of, Safa."

"And what is that?"

"That we must go on meeting. We can solve this one together. I know we can."

"Agreed," Safa's face was suddenly almost beautiful with the most dazzling smile Takis had ever seen.

They then concluded their discussion with the agreement that they would approach the Canadian high commissioner together at the end of the session and request that he set up regular coordination meetings between the two police departments. They thought that meetings every two weeks in the Ledra Palace Hotel would be the most useful. They also agreed they each would campaign strongly to be their community's representative at these meetings. Even when this investigation was solved, they thought they should continue to meet to discuss mutual problems.

"At least that should put a smile on the commissioner's face," said Ziya, with a mischievous glint in her eye. "That alone should validate his seminar and give him a victory message he can send back to Ottawa."

The high commissioner was especially pleased that the ensuing request from Takis and Safa to sponsor regular coordination meetings between the Greek and Turkish Cypriot police officials had come directly to him rather than to Dunsford. The official thought it was quite fortunate that, because he was too "under the weather" this morning to take charge of the concluding session, Dunsford was not present to take credit for the step forward in Greek-Turkish relations.

"A hangover more than likely," the diplomat said to his aide, with a sniff. "John seems to be falling apart at the seams. Odd. I'm told he once showed such promise. Well, he isn't doing us much good here. He's gotten erratic and sloppy. That's the kiss of death in his business."

* * * *

Jean Valery strode confidently out of the Hotel Metropole and onto the Place de Broukere. The Friday morning weather was dismal, windy, and cold. And Valery loved it and loved being back in Brussels. His fondest memories were of this intimate, yet highly cosmopolitan city. He breathed deeply and clutched his precious little package ever closer to his chest as his luggage was being wedged into the trunk of the taxi. He knew that they would most likely have been looking for him at one of the more renowned hotels, such as the Hilton

International or the Royal Windsor. But even there it would've taken longer than just the night for them to look for him by any other name than Chamberlain or Roentgen.

He was sure that his French passport in the name of Jean Valery was not yet compromised. However, he couldn't have stayed anywhere but here at the Metropole, not only because good taste dictated it, the Metropole being one of the best surviving examples of the Art Nouveau style in Europe. He had to stay here because this was where they'd met and had conducted their relationship during those golden months of intelligence intrigue and sexual exploration. He sensed that he was at some sort of turning point in his life, a fact that excited him rather than scared him as it might a different sort of person. It had become a fetish for him to touch base at the Metropole during these transitions.

As he saw Sergey Stepanov rushing down the walk toward him, he stepped adroitly into the cab and gave the destination to the driver: "To the Gare du Midi train station please."

Stepanov had almost reached the vehicle when it pulled out into traffic. Instead of pretending not to see the Russian, however, the American art broker rolled the window down, smiled saucily, and called out: "Bruges, the Hotel d'Medici. Appropriate, no?" Then he laughed, gave a royal-family-on-parade flick of the wrist, and turned away to enjoy the cruise down the wide Boulevard Anspach.

Neither the American nor the Russian, however, saw the third figure, who had been watching the proceedings from beside the hotel's entrance. When Chamberlain's taxi was safely into traffic, the third figure turned back into the hotel in search of a telephone booth.

* * * *

The same Friday morning was gracing the stalwart fifteenth-century keep of Kolossi Castle, once home to the Knights Templar and location of the first vineyard on Cyprus as well as one of the world's oldest wines still in existence, Commandaria.

It wasn't wine or the neat rows of propped-up vines radiating from the castle keep that Willie Hamilton was thinking about, though. He was trying to catch his breath, as he huffed up the narrow winding stairs to the castle battlements at three-quarters past eight. He wanted to win a strategic vantage point for his coming appointment. As sure as clockwork, the first tourist buses from the Limassol beachfront hotels would start arriving a few minutes before 9:00 AM. They would stop here for a brief photo-opportunity en route to a full morning's tour of the nearby widely dispersed Curium Greco-Roman ruins complex.

Hamilton was going over and over in his mind what he had to say—all in a gamble to make Ginger invulnerable to renewed attack. He figured that when he saw the Knife approaching, he would descend and remain in the protective vicinity of the groups of tourists that would arrive in waves for the rest of the period of daylight. This should give him enough time and opportunity to convince the Knife that he had constructed a protective wall that would come tumbling down if either Ginger or he himself were harmed. If only he'd actually had time to write up that protective document and safely deposit it. That would've given him more courage to face these negotiations.

When he got to the roof of the keep, he was surprised to see three other people there. One couple was looking toward the east, over the peninsula that was now taken up by Akrotiri, one of the huge British military bases over which the United Kingdom had maintained sovereignty when Cyprus gained its independence from British colonial rule in 1960. They weren't actually looking at the sights. They were wrapped up in each other's arms, whispering to each other and giggling in their own little world. The third figure, in a bulky blue wool coat and flowered scarf, was turned away from the rest and was gazing intently off to the west, toward the cliffs of Curium and yet another British sovereign base area, Episoki, beyond Curium.

Apparently put off by the appearance of the others at the top of the keep, the couple moved, still entwined, toward the small covered staircase to descend to the interior of the castle below. Here they could find a place to themselves for a few more minutes before the first tourist group surged into the building.

Hamilton walked over to the south end of the keep's roof and positioned himself where he could see the parking area and the approach past the ticket hut and into the ruins of the courtyard below. Besides his own Mini, there were only two other vehicles in the parking area. One was a car marked as a rental by its red license tag. Next to it stood some sort of SUV he hadn't noticed when he'd driven into the lot but that looked familiar to him. This vehicle was pulled up close to some bushes at the far end of the parking area, so Willie couldn't see it very well.

Hamilton found he was standing over the walled-in open grate immediately over the entrance to the keep two stories below. This entry to the keep was reached by ascending a stone staircase rising one story above ground level and crossing a drawbridge through a high doorway and immediately into an impressive hall. The "welcome" grate he was standing on was typical of protective medieval vantage points from which slops and more lethal substances could be dumped on unwelcome callers at the front gate several stories immediately below. The grating was meant to shield the defender at least somewhat from the slings and arrows employed by those below who didn't much appreciate such a welcome.

Very interesting. I've never actually seen one of these, Hamilton mused, as he started to bend down to take a closer look.

But then, without warning, he was taking a much closer look at the grate than he'd intended, as he was knocked to the stone floor by considerable force being applied from behind. His face was being literally ground into the grating, and his throat was being throttled mercilessly. The pressure was unbearable. He couldn't breathe. The choking was momentarily relieved, only to be replaced by a sharp pain in his side.

As the stranglehold on his windpipe lessened, Hamilton let out a scream. What normally could've been quite a display of lung power by the former regimental commander, however, was reduced to a weak cry and a gurgling noise. Before he could get enough breath to call out again, the strangling grip at his throat was resumed with a vengeance.

Chapter Nineteen

The young couple walked out of the main entry of the Kolossi Castle keep onto the drawbridge and into the blinding sunlight. Their immediate reaction was to retreat back into the shadows of the doorway and burrow their faces into each other's shoulders. This instinct was closely followed by the urge to kiss and grope. While in the doorway and in a pleasantly suffocating embrace, they heard the hum in the near distance. It was 8:53 AM. Right on schedule, the first of the buses from the Limassol hotels pulled up to the ticket hut, began disgorging its vacationers, and a wave of tourists was lapping through the garden gate and toward the castle keep.

Struck with the reality that the peace and calm was coming to an end and the jostle of the crowd was about to reach them, the young man broke from the clutch. He waved his camera, backpeddled across the drawbridge, and coaxed his girlfriend out of the shadows at the entrance for a last-chance photo opportunity. After a bit of pressure to loosen up for the photo, which was given urgency by the approaching thundering horde, the girl flung her arms out theatrically in an I'm-the-queen-of-all-I-survey pose and turned her eyes heavenward.

A short cry and a gurgling sound from above made her adjust her gaze from the blue sky to the battlement grate directly overhead. What she saw there was not heavenly, but it certainly seemed to be turning blue. A face of a man, smashed into the metal framework, grotesquely contorted, eyes bulging, and tongue grossly distended out of the mouth and through the grating. He appeared to be trying his best to scream, but he just couldn't manage to find the breath for it. So the young girl screamed for him. And she continued to scream as her boyfriend reached her side, looked up, and sprinted past her and into the building. She was still screaming when the wave of tourists, which had initially been arrested by her first outburst, flowed ever faster toward her and around her.

* * * *

That afternoon John Dunsford turned his Izuzu Trooper onto Byron Street and into the grounds of the large Victorian British colonial-style villa that shared a tree-lined block with the Greek embassy and that served as the Canadian high commission. His depression had now cleared, and he looked nearly fit, handsome, and ready to face and conquer the world. The trip he'd taken out of the city instead of attending the closing session of the bicommunal seminar had gone a great distance toward restoring his confidence and purpose. The burden of this NATO case and of his own entanglement with it had weighed him down for a decade. He'd never been able to recover from the blunders that had been made and the unfinished business that had not been resolved. He'd once had every confidence in his abilities. He had been the best, and he and almost everyone else had known that. Brussels had cast a pall over all that.

254

Well, it was all being run to ground here and now. Win or lose, he was ready to cast the die. And there would be no more weak-kneed blubbering over an easy way to end the frustration and pressure. This was not the time for cowardice or sentimentality.

The high commissioner was on patrol in the old mansion's front hall. But, although Dunsford had expected his nominal boss to be visibly livid at his failure to chair the closing police seminar session, the man looked nearly as satisfied as the bird-swallowing cat. Dunsford could almost hear the man purr as he spoke. "Feeling better are we, John?"

"Yes, I am, Sir. Quite. The extra half day fixed me up splendidly. Did you manage the seminar closing all right?"

"Yes, thank you. It was quite satisfactorily concluded. Just what was needed; a little word of encouragement from the high commissioner. I've already sent a wrap-up cable. A copy should be on your desk. You do plan to carry through with the bicommunal cocktail party for the participants next week, don't you? No more anticipated illness, I trust?"

"Of course I'll coordinate the cocktail party," Dunsford responded. "And, no, I'm sure I've quite recovered."

"Yes, you do look far better than you did yesterday." The high commissioner sniffed. "In fact, you look far better than you have in the few months you've been here. You know, I've been worried about you, John."

"Well, I'm sure you need not worry any longer, Sir. I'd been having some second thoughts about how to resolve some of my business. But I think I'm beginning to see my way to clear sky now."

"Yes, well," the mission chief answered with a lingering note of suspicion and a gaze down a long, thin nose. "I've often seen this when those in your line have gotten too close to the personalities involved. Distance. Objectivity. That's what I always say."

Dunsford had used the cover of this lecture to get far enough down the hallway to grab up a stack of telephone messages from his secretary's desk, to smile thankfully for the "highly valued" advice, and to slip into his commodious corner office.

"Twit," he murmured as he moved toward the centrally positioned desk. He wasn't about to let his stuffy superior ruin his good mood. He threw a bag containing the disguise paraphernalia he was returning to the classified storeroom on the overstuffed leather sofa and plopped down into his swivel chair. The room was right out of a prewar colonialist movie. The ceiling was high. The wainscoted walls were painted in a cream color that had been enriched with the patina of age and the lacing of blistered paint. The wooden plank floors were hard scrubbed and polished by generations of pacing boots. The two large floor-to-ceiling windows, on separate walls, were outfitted with dark green shutters on both the inside and the outside. Steam heaters huffed and puffed on three of the walls. Brass wall sconces brought almost adequate and well-defined pools of light into the room. And a ceiling fan lazily rotated over the desk. Dunsford loved this room. He didn't think he could face the prospect of ever returning to the rat maze, plasterboard wall cubicles of the service's headquarters in Ottawa.

A copy of the high commissioner's cable was on the desk. Cheeky of him to take advantage of my absence to send the wrap-up cable himself, thought Dunsford. The high commissioner undoubtedly had used the opportunity to take full credit. Oh, well. It couldn't be helped. And it now mattered not one zot to Dunsford anyway. He scanned the cable and made an unpleasant guttural sound when he reached the paragraph about the intention to set up a permanent police information link between the Greek and Turkish communities.

Irritated, he pushed the cable aside and concentrated his attention on the telephone messages from his operatives.

At the bottom of the pile—Dunsford always read in what could be presumed would be chronological order—he found the expected report. Sergey Stepanov had reentered Cyprus through Paphos Airport but had left again soon thereafter from Larnaca airport. Then came the jolt. The message went on to report that the agent following Stepanov had met up with another one of Dunsford's agents at Larnaca airport—the one who'd been watching Justin Chamberlain's apartment, waiting for him to slip back into the country. The two agents had met at the airport, because Stepanov and Chamberlain had taken the same plane. The message stopped there.

After a long pause over this message, Dunsford exhaled, having found that he had been holding his breath since the search for the destination had begun. "The two of them together? I should have known," he muttered aloud. He had no choice. He would have to go straighten this out himself.

Dunsford lifted the telephone receiver and rang directly through to the travel agency he used for his personal travel. That done, he rang Sarah Bristow's office, only to be told that she had not returned from her morning appointment at the Episkopi base near Limassol yet.

"Would you like to leave a message?"

"Yes, please. This is John Dunsford of the Canadian high commission. Please tell her that I called to let her know I was suddenly called out of town for a few days and cannot have dinner with her this evening as we scheduled. Tell her that unless we can touch base for firmer arrangements, I'll meet her at the International Fair in Makedonitissa Tuesday evening. I know that we both have commitments to drop in at exhibits there that evening. We can go on to dinner from there."

As he hung up, he was considering whether Sarah might have stopped off at home and could be reached there.

No, I'd better not try, he thought, as he replaced the telephone receiver. Caitlyn Koniotis was staying there. She and her husband had already gotten too deep into this investigation. Dunsford knew he couldn't chance having her answer the telephone at Sarah's apartment. But he also knew that Chamberlain had spoken with her just before leaving for Brussels. And he wondered what Caitlyn had told Chamberlain to make him bolt like that—and what Chamberlain had told her. She certainly seemed to know a lot about what was going on.

The telephone rang. It was the agent who had been following Chamberlain. He had managed to book onto the plane to Brussels at the last minute and had stuck with Chamberlain. He'd been trying to call Dunsford every half hour since early that morning.

"Yes, I see that," admitted Dunsford as he sifted through the messages he had picked up at his secretary's desk. Then he proceeded to praise his agent and to ask about Chamberlain's whereabouts.

"I lost him outside the Hotel Metropole. . . ."

"Of course," Dunsford interrupted. "Where else could he have gone?"

". . . But I heard him say he was going on to Bruges. Something about the Hotel d'Medici."

Dunsford thanked the agent, complimenting him highly on his work, and told him to come back to Cyprus.

"Come back? You don't want me to follow?"

"No, that's not necessary now. I know what I need to know."

After disconnecting, Dunsford stood, quietly calculating, his thoughts returning to Caitlyn Koniotis. There was danger in her staying with Sarah. "Sarah, Sarah," his whispered as he stood at the window, watching the normal world go happily by. "Why does it have to be you? Could you not just have left it alone? I was willing to. But you're forcing my hand."

But then he went into action with the determined statement, "No, there's always time to get to Caitlyn Koniotis after I've returned from Belgium. Sarah shouldn't be able to see how this is all closing in yet."

Dunsford made one telephone call, grabbed the bag off of the leather sofa, and headed for the door, giving a definitive concluding twist to the lights and the ceiling fan as he departed.

* * * *

Takis Koniotis was pacing the floor outside the emergency room of the Limassol General Hospital. Dr. Savvides, an old family friend of the investigator's, emerged from the surgery and stripped the rubber gloves from his hands. He was frowning, his face reflecting deep concern.

"I must, Marius," Koniotis declared in a way that indicated this was a continuation of an intense exchange. "Too many people connected with this have died already. Hamilton would want to talk to me no matter what. I know he would."

"Hamilton is in no position to talk to you, Takis," the surgeon answered wearily.

"He's not—"

"No, and he should fully recover—eventually. Constitution of an ox. I'm still worried about the possibility of shock, however. No, he can't talk to you because his voice box was bruised in the throttling. It will be a day or two before he will be able to make any sound at all. He is very lucky to be alive."

Indeed he was. The couple had made their way to the Kolossi Castle keep entrance and looked up at the grating overhead just in time to save Willie Hamilton's life. Hamilton's thick clothing had apparently prevented the attacker from knifing him to death. There'd been one stab wound in the side that had failed to be lethal only because the Britisher had been wearing two heavy sweaters and a coat. Those who'd tried to piece the crime together had surmised that the attacker—someone the couple said they "sort of" saw at the top of the castle when Hamilton had arrived, someone so bulked up with a coat that it could have been either male or female—had waited for the couple to start down the stairs and then had attacked Hamilton.

Hamilton must have sensed the approaching attack, because the first knife thrust apparently only sliced through material. The attacker may have realized that Hamilton's bulky clothing gave him too much protection for a deadly blow to be struck before he could give the alarm. That was probably why the newspaper reporter was strangled—so that he would slip into unconsciousness and be unable to fight a resumed knife attack. The attacker had switched back to the knife from the chokehold too soon, and Hamilton was able to make enough noise to attract attention when the pressure on his throat was first released. Then, when the young girl screamed, the attacker panicked and fled the roof.

Which for her—or him—had been a self-preservation instinct, as there was only one, narrow circular staircase in the castle. Once the braver of the souls below started rushing up this staircase, there was no way the attacker could descend without having been trapped and caught.

There had been one fallacy to this scenario, however. There was a central level, with two separated rooms between the entry floor and the roof. There was also a ground floor level with a separate entrance underneath the drawbridge that led directly into the castle ruins and garden. Evidently, the attacker had managed to reach the central floor and hide in a side room while the first wave of rescuers rushed by to the roof. Then in the lull that separated the onslaught of the first wave from the more deliberate approach of the less brave, the attacker had quickly descended the stairs. Once past the entry level, he—or she—could exit the castle keep at the ground level and merge with the milling groups of tourists that were arriving in the garden area.

In any event. The murder had been foiled—although the perpetrator probably had no idea as yet that the attack had not been successful. The outcome had, indeed, been touch and go for a while. A less wiry and feisty man than Willie Hamilton probably would be dead now.

Takis Koniotis, who'd managed to get to the hospital early enough to have orchestrated the release of information on the attack at least for now, had no intention, for the present, of publicly acknowledging that Hamilton was alive.

"Let the killer and public think he's dead. The only one who could be distressed is Ginger, his wife, and she's still in a coma herself. In fact, Willie will probably get a kick—and a good newspaper article—out of the reaction to the premature news of his passing. But, I do need to try to communicate with him as soon as possible. There may be other lives at stake."

The doctor was too tired to hold his ground. "Oh, all right. You can communicate with him as best you can as long as he's conscious—which, I warn you, will not be for long. He needs a long rest and as little stress as possible. It'll probably help him recover, I suppose, if he realizes that he has identified the attacker for you."

Willie Hamilton looked far smaller and older in the vulnerable surroundings of white sheets and quiet hospital conditions than he managed to convey through his bulldog personality when he was on his own two feet. His face still had a blue tinge to it—at least what could be seen of his face through the bruises and the bandages. His eyes, though, were wide and were darting around the room. When Takis Koniotis came into view, they focused on and bored into the investigator. It was quite evident that Willie Hamilton would very much have liked to talk to Koniotis.

He started to move his right arm in a struggle to bring himself up in the bed and toward Koniotis, but he winced and fell back in excruciating pain from the knife wound in his side.

"No, Willie. Relax. Don't exert yourself. We need to let you tell us as much as possible before you tire yourself."

Hamilton tried to speak but couldn't. A frustrated tear formed in an eye and rolled down underneath the puffy white dressing covering his cheek.

Koniotis leaned his face down closely to Hamilton's ear. "Relax, Willie. Here, I'll hold your hand. I'll ask you a few questions. If the answer is 'yes,' don't do anything; if the answer is 'no,' then squeeze my hand—but don't overdo it. Do you understand?"

Hamilton squeezed the investigator's hand with a continuous and unbelievably strong grip and gazed imploringly into his eyes until Koniotis got the message.

"Ginger? You're concerned about Ginger?"

The grip eased.

"Ginger is fine. They expect her to be conscious at any time now. And we're keeping a guard on her. We haven't told anyone, but she was moved to another hospital right after I heard you'd been attacked. Almost no one knows. No one but the police and the chief medical staff and my wife Caitlyn, of course. I was with her at Sarah Bristow's flat when the call on the attack came in."

There was a sudden pressure on Koniotis's hand, Hamilton's eyes began to roll back into his head and Hamilton lost his grip altogether.

A nurse pushed a button, setting off a loud, piercing alarm. Dr. Savvides rushed into the room. Koniotis was shunted aside, and Savvides started to yell instructions to a medical staff that was gathering from all corners. After the initial, life-stabilizing assault on Hamilton, Savvides turned to Koniotis and said: "Shock. It was a high possibility that it would settle in at any time. There's no telling what set it off. Often it's inevitable and just delayed for no known reason. He should be all right, but we've got to move him to intensive care now. He won't be conscious again for some time."

"Understood," Koniotis said in a clipped tone that barely covered his frustration and disappointment. "But, I'll have to insist on a full police guard. And if you want him to live, you will have to impress on your staff that they are not to mention this patient to anyone. No one must know Hamilton has survived."

Koniotis headed for the door to make the necessary arrangements, and the sounds in the room began to return to the steady, rhythmic, soothing beeps that had predominated before the quickly aborted interview.

Chapter Twenty

Sergey Stepanov was sitting, cooling his heels, in the small reception hall of the Hotel d'Medici in Bruges. The quaint, late Saturday morning scene of medieval stepped-roofed buildings on Speigelrei Street across the tree-lined canal had not cheered him. Neither had the colorful paintings displayed around the public rooms of this small, fashionable hotel, tucked into an old neighborhood within the confines of the formerly walled and wealthy trading city.

The hotel staff had been extremely cordial to him, particularly considering he was insisting that either a Mr. Chamberlain or a Mr. Roentgen had checked into the hotel and had summoned Stepanov there. Of course no such person was registered at the d'Medici. But the bearing and dress of Stepanov had clearly marked him as both respectable and formidable. Therefore, they had politely offered him the opportunity to wait for his party on the small sofa across from the reception desk and had plied him with bottomless cups of coffee and wrapped Belgian chocolates—knowing that at some point he would give up and go away.

The watcher in the small Opel parked across the lane, next to the canal, had not been accorded any such coddling. The irritation of having to slowly leaf through his paper for the hundredth time—and he couldn't even read Dutch—in a cold, cramped automobile was only enhanced by being able to see through the hotel's plate glass entry doors. He could clearly see Stepanov sitting on a comfortable sofa, sipping coffee, and enjoying Belgian chocolates. But then, just as the watcher was contemplating changing his vantage point, he saw Stepanov rise and go to the telephone at the reception desk.

The caller was Chamberlain. He had described Stepanov to the discrete and nonplussed hotel receptionist and had been connected with no delay.

"Hello, Sergey. I trust the d'Medici has been treating you well."

"Good Christ, Chamberlain. What sort of games you playing? I thought you were staying at this hotel."

"Maybe I am, Sergey," Chamberlain chuckled. "Maybe I am, but just maybe I'm not. Speaking of games, though, what are you doing here? Why are you following me? We had agreed to keep our lives entirely separate now."

"I must see you. I have something for you. You can't be Justin Chamberlain or Helmut Roentgen anymore. Everyone's looking for you. And I bet you don't have any other good identity set up yet."

"And you'd do all that for me just for old time's sake, Sergey, dearest?" responded Chamberlain, his voice dripping with sweetness.

It took a while for Stepanov to answer. "No, not really for old time's sake. But for money I would. I'm sure you have money. I don't need much, but I, too, need to pull out of this problem. Arrest would not help you or me."

"I quite agree." Now Chamberlain was all business. "Meet me by the gate to Number 17 at the Ten Wyngaerde Beguinage at 3:00 PM. Do you think you can find that?"

"I will find it, and I will be there. But no more funny tricks."

"No, I quite agree," answered Chamberlain, "all of the humor has drained out of this one."

The Russian returned the receiver to the hotel clerk and flashed an everything's-coming-up-roses smile at the attendant. The clerk, in turn, thanks to many generations of expert training in discretion in the Belgian hotel trade, returned an open, innocent smile, which was not altered in the least when Stepanov had passed a huge tip and hurried out the door.

As he trundled his way down the Sint-Annarei and across to the Hoogstraat, a route that would take him into Market Square, a small Opel pulled out into the street and slowly gained on the Russian, who was concentrating on being seen as a tourist.

* * * *

Safa Ziya had gone through Turkish Cypriot police headquarters like a buzz saw. No one had been able either to stand up to her or to placate her. Her office mate had long ago snatched up his box of tissues and slunk out of the door. Tansul was in hiding, and even the department chief had left early for the protection of his mountain home.

It was the new case that had set her off. Not that she did not expect to be getting new cases before she had cleared her desk of her current cases. She readily recognized that her small country did not have enough senior investigators for her to expect any rest. But it was what she had found out when she opened the thick new case file she found on her desk when she arrived this morning that had set her off.

The case concerned the rise in crime as a result of the slow but insidious filtering in of the Russian mafia. The case file indicated that much footwork had already been done elsewhere in the department. However, this case had now become so politically sensitive that it was being turned over to Ziya, because much of that earlier footwork had begun to lead to the doors of a small group of senior mainland Turkish army officials.

Ziya was not surprised about the rise in Russian mafia-related crime. She'd been haranguing her superior for months that the Russian tourist ruble would not come without its problems for northern Cypriot society. Better to have continued to develop tourism by the Israelis, who, if generally pushy, demanding, stingy, and impolite, at least kept to themselves, eventually paid their bills, and did not travel in the company of trouble. No, since the Russian tourists had arrived, the incidences of public drunkenness, assault, prostitution, vandalism, road accidents, and absconding without paying restaurant and hotel bills had risen dramatically. In Ziya's opinion, the newly awakened Russians had yet to learn to live by rules. Their recent liberation from the oppression of an extreme socialist system had left them with no structure of fair play or concern for the rights of others in which to operate.

She wasn't at all surprised that a protection racket had grown in northern Cyprus, under the control of the Russian mafia. For the first time ever in their lives, shopkeepers and restaurateurs were having to pay "preventative insurance" to keep their establishments from being destroyed and themselves and their families safe from harm.

Ziya was not much more surprised, now that she thought about it, that some few military officials within the occupying Turkish army were helping the Russian mafia in its shocking activities—if only by looking the other way. It was in the nature of all occupying forces to feather their own nests, and the pickings in northern Cyprus had always been quite slim. It stood to reason that there would be at least a few greedy officials who would be willing to overlook their traditional suspicion and hatred of the Russian bear to help the mafia fleece the unprotected northern Cypriots.

But she had been shocked and angry to have seen the name that kept coming up in the reports of the increasing activity of the Russian mafia over the past several months. Her own renewed inquiries had only turned up two, seemingly natural and innocent visits to the north by the Russian businessman Sergey Stepanov. These reports, however, documented innumerable incidents in which Sergey Stepanov and several of his thugs were involved in intimidating major businessman, restaurateurs, and hoteliers. They also had been setting up illegal strip clubs, gambling dens, and houses of prostitution in the northern zone. And both his charter planes and freighter had made innumerable landings on northern Cypriot soil without benefit of port clearances.

All of these trips and all of this activity in her jurisdiction without her knowledge! The corruption of the military authorities had permitted nearly all of Stepanov's crossing into northern Cyprus to be erased from the records. Well, she knew the first thing she had to do. This changed everything in the thinking she and Koniotis had been doing on the Brussels spy ring case. Yes, this case would be a very difficult one—difficult to handle now that the mafia activity had gotten so out of hand and difficult to close down and to document since elements of the powerful occupying army were involved. But first the NATO spy investigation would be closed, and then she and Koniotis would tackle the Russian mafia together. These gangsters had thought, with plenty of reason, that the division of Cyprus made it ripe for their activity. Well, the Cypriots would not put up with that.

She picked up the telephone and called the British high commission office located on the Turkish side. She asked that she be put into contact with Alec Stuart as soon as possible. She needed to establish a quick link to Koniotis. Yes, she was angry and frustrated, but she was beginning to let her very intelligent brain take over. And she no longer felt alone. She and Takis Koniotis could face this one down together. She was also angry at herself that she was calling the British high commission rather than the Canadians. When she and Takis Koniotis had set up Canadian sponsorship of their communications link, they had not taken into account that the Canadians didn't have a high commission office on the Turkish side.

* * * *

Justin Chamberlain strode out of Bruges's Die Swaene Hotel and onto the Steenhouwerskdijk just to the northwest of the Fish Market. Although he did, indeed, like the small discrete Hotel d'Medici that had been built in recent years on the other side of the old city center, his sense of adventure and danger had led him to The Swan. In the event—which he did not for a minute believe—that his race had just about run its course, there was no reason why he should not be enjoying the best of life. And Die Swaene, named after the legendary swans of Bruges to which the Archduke Maximilian of Austria had condemned the burgers of the city to care for in perpetuity for having killed one of his servants, was the best.

Chamberlain was now taking the short walk from his hotel along one of the canals and to the Fish Market, which bordered one of the lakes and which now, although an outdoor fish market was still located nearby, had become one of the major restaurant districts of the town. The sun was uncharacteristically shining on the water to his right, and the temperature was not nearly as cold as it had every right to be in December.

He kept one hand on the precious package within his sweater and began to decide what he would order at the quaint t'Dreveken restaurant that now occupied a portion of the Huidevettershuis. This building, once the guild house of the tanners, was suspended out over a particularly picturesque, broad bend in the major canal.

Perhaps he'd order the Gratin d'Huitre d'Ostende—creamed oysters and shrimp in shells—for a start, followed by his favorite, the Waterzooi a la Gantoise—a Flemish chicken in lemon cream soup. Yes, he had always thought of that as the ultimate last meal request to be thrown back at the jailers before skipping off to the guillotine. But why were such morbid thoughts surfacing?

But then he was at the restaurant and all morbid thoughts were dispelled. His Belgium broker was there. A package of miniature icons was quickly exchanged for a package of British sterling notes, and this was almost as quickly followed by Justin's dream meal.

It was close on to 2:30 PM before Chamberlain could break himself away from the table and the view out over the canal. He walked with long, elegant strides down the Gruuthusestraat, taking a left turn at the Church of Our Lady, and then hurried, without appearing to be hurrying, down the Katelijnestraat toward the beguinage.

* * * *

Justin Chamberlain's finely honed and convoluted sense of humor had always shown through as a delicious embellishment of his actions. It was thus that he'd stayed at the Hotel Metropole, scene of the trysts that had originally brought him into his current troubles, and it was thus that he'd picked the Hotel d'Medici—named after the legendary Italian family of intrigue and double cross—as his initial rendezvous with Sergey Stepanov. It was also thus that he'd selected the Ten Wyngaerde Beguinage on the Minnewater—the Lake of Love—for what he intended to be his last meeting ever with the Russian who had been a significant, but not superfluous, part of his life. A "beguinage" was a uniquely Belgian medieval-period institution where unprotected woman banded together in a living compound sealed at night as sanctuary from the designs of men.

Chamberlain was hurrying toward his goal because he wanted to be inside the beguinage and in place before Stepanov arrived. He knew he was cutting his schedule close as he crossed the drawbridge over the Lake of Love and entered the serene world of sanctuary. The large inner yard of the thirteenth-century beguinage was lovely and stood in striking contrast to the busy narrow city lanes outside. The Convent of Benedictine nuns took up much of the northern side of the central enclosure. The fourteenth-century Beguinage Church of St. Elizabeth, the only brownstone building in the enclave, was located on the south wall. The rest of the enclosing buildings, as well as the buildings in the adjacent enclosures that had been added on in succeeding centuries, and the convent building itself, were of stark

272

white-painted brick topped with steep red-tiled roofs. The central yard consisted of a large lawn dotted by regimented rows of majestic towering trees, which, with wonderful effect, all leaned from the wind at a slight angle to the southwest. When the wind blew into the courtyard, all of the trees swayed and sighed in unison.

Each of the houses was set off from the central yard with its own private postage stamp-sized entry garden, hiding behind its own tall, white, red tile-topped wall. Identical arched wooden doors pierced these walls, giving access to the private gardens and houses.

It was the privacy of these individual gardens that had given Justin his idea. The houses of the Ten Wyngaerde Beguinage were now being used to house elderly couples. Woman as a class had long ago asserted their individual power and capability to stand on their own within established society. As Justin had already ascertained, house Number 17 was currently unoccupied and its gate was unlocked. Justin was amused by his plan to be inside the walled garden of that house when Stepanov arrived for their appointment and to pull the unsuspecting and unprepared Russian into the secluded garden and to free himself forever from Sergey.

A rather clever plan, but Justin Chamberlain, despite his own high opinion of himself, was not the only clever person on the face of the earth. In the end, the joke was on him. As he approached the gate to Number 17, he was himself pulled into the isolated garden. A knife flashed, banknotes floated to the ground, and a gust of wind blew into the central courtyard, causing the trees to sway and to sigh in unison.

Chapter Twenty-One

Monday morning the Knife was slicing through the traffic on the road between the Larnaca airport and Nicosia. Here the chalky soil of the coast had given over to the redder earth of the Troodos foothills. When the Larnaca highway met the Limassol highway for the last dip into Nicosia, it turned into the sand and dirt combination of the central plain. The small, conical hills, with their tiered sides and reforested slopes, passed in never-ending parade, a parade that was broken occasionally by small church-dominated villages in the folds of the hills. Over it all, including the hills, the road, and the Knife's automobile, arched an all-encompassing, brilliant blue sky.

It was regrettable, of course, but it had been necessary for the Knife if not for the Russians. It had been such a long, tiring nightmare. The sad memories had been and were now almost too debilitating. At times there had seemed to be no reason to go on. But just one more loose thread and it would be over, and the other life would be waiting. Just one more, waiting in Nicosia. But that wasn't true. There was also Caitlyn Koniotis now. The Knife wasn't sure how aware Caitlyn was that she now had several pieces of the puzzle—and there was no telling what Eleni had told her. But she obviously knew too much for comfort, and some of her behavior had been provocative, as if she knew all and was playing a game. Why didn't she just tell her husband all that she knew? Was she thinking of blackmail as that bumbler Hamilton had or as that effete art smuggler Chamberlain had? If so, it wouldn't work for her either. No, there wasn't just one loose thread left. A grim smile of determination formed.

A sleek red BMW convertible pulled up on the tail of the SUV, itself cruising along a good 50 percent over the posted speed limit. A flash of lights, and the convertible was neatly drawing around the larger vehicle and was slowly pulling away. It's taillights were now framed by the panorama of Nicosia and the Kyrenia Range, which was just beginning to emerge from the horizon in the distance. Gears were meshed, the accelerator was floorboarded, and the SUV leaped into action. The race was on.

* * * *

Caitlyn and Takis Koniotis were sharing what these days was a rare leisurely breakfast. They sat across the table from each other in the breakfast room in Sarah Bristow's penthouse apartment. The room, glass walled on three sides, jutted out onto a veranda on the western façade of the apartment. Caitlyn's view beyond her husband was to the north and took in the old walled city of Nicosia, backdropped by the Kyrenia Mountains. Takis's view behind Caitlyn was of the eastern end of the Troodos Range and of the morning traffic entering the urban area from the direction of the southern coast.

Takis was tense and despondent but was trying hard not to reveal this to Caitlyn. Caitlyn, of course, could discern all at a glance and was trying hard not to show her own concern. Takis had been

275

spending the nights with Caitlyn since Sarah Bristow had left suddenly for a meeting in Paris the previous Friday night. Neither Takis nor Sarah wanted Caitlyn to be alone in the apartment, even with its tight security.

"You know you are just shoving that egg around your plate, Takis. We can bring up a sandbox for the balcony if all you want to do is play."

"Sorry. It's this damn case. It's unusual for us to go this long with an investigation without being sure of our ground. If only we could be sure the killing has stopped."

"I thought that the Hamiltons would be able to provide the key."

"Yes, very likely. But Willie's still unconscious and in shock, and Ginger is still in a coma. The doctors keep saying that either one of them could regain consciousness at any time. But this waiting is murder."

"Not the best choice of words, dear," Caitlyn said as she took up her coffee cup and moved over to a south-facing window. The various village clusters Caitlyn could see off toward Limassol appeared so peaceful from a distance. They shone, clean and sharp featured, reflecting the strong rays from the sun. Native stone and white and ocher stucco predominated, all covered in red tile, and contrasting with the interspersed foliage in a riot of colors.

"Is Ginger in trouble, Takis?" Caitlyn turned and looked at her husband, still hunched over the breakfast table and toying with his food. "I rather like the Hamiltons. It's sad to think they're tied up with all of this spy business."

Takis stood and joined her at the window. "Maria's research did, I think, uncover Ginger's link to the Brussels NATO scandal, and, we'll just have to see how deeply she was into it. Her husband at the time she was in Brussels, a Colonel Bertram Remington, was the deputy to the British NATO representative during the period of the spy operation. He was never officially linked to the loss of British secrets in this operation, but he asked for a transfer home— presumably thinking that Ginger was involved—and subsequently died in a hunting accident that was generally accepted to have been suicide."

"How awful. But what would make anyone think Ginger was involved?"

"We're pretty sure that Sergey Stepanov–probably with the help of your friend, Justin—was the linchpin of the operation—and of the retirement of the agents here, aided by Eleni on the Greek side and Mehmet Tosun on the Turkish side. Sergey was a KGB agent in Brussels at the time, and this pretty clearly was a Soviet operation. That he recently came back to Cyprus and the retired spies then, one by one, started to die violent deaths indicates he's been reactivated by whatever replaced the KGB in the Russian system to clean up an operation that could become an embarrassment to the new Russian state in its attempt to cozy up to the West."

"Yes, I can understand that Sergey could do this," Caitlyn said in a troubled voice, "but it's still hard for me to accept that Eleni, or Justin, or Ginger could've been involved in something as cold blooded as all this."

"Well it's still all theory," Takis said. "Nearly everything can now be theoretically and logically traced to the doorstep of Stepanov, either operating alone or in consort with other people. And I'm sorry to say that the evidence indicates that these people include Eleni, who is now dead herself; Mehmet Tosun, who may or may not be alive; Ginger, who is very lucky she isn't dead; and Justin, who could now be dead or in grave danger if John Dunsford hasn't managed to catch up with him before Stepanov does."

"What do you mean if John hasn't managed to catch up with him?"

"He flew off to Belgium after he found that Justin and Stepanov had left for there by the same plane. He had his office notify me that he was afraid for Justin's life."

Caitlyn leaned her head against the glass of the window as if the weariness of the world was just too much to bear.

"Damn!" Takis left Caitlyn's side and strode back to the table. "There's still something about this case that doesn't track, but I can't trace what it is."

"Your famous intuition playing?" asked Caitlyn. "Like my occasional visions of connections with people in the past—my visions that you make so much fun of?"

"No, nothing like your visions. Mine are just subconscious hunches based on years of experience with human nature. What you have is something entirely different, something I'm trying as hard as you are to figure out. But at least I'm now beginning to accept that they work as well as my hunches do."

Caitlyn came back to the table and sat down. "Takis, the visions that connect me to the past didn't really start until I came here, and I could feel the strong connection with this island for months before I found out that my ancestors had, in fact, come from Cyprus.

Takis, there is some real connection between me and my ancestors, something that is emphasized when I'm here. Something I haven't asked for and don't fully understand myself, but you know yourself that it's there. How could I have found the archeological sites here without this ability?"

"And you felt such a connection to Eleni Piccard, didn't you?" Takis asked in a quiet voice.

"Yes, I did—and I do. I still do. It's as if we were connected in past lives as much, if not more, than we were connected in the present life. I guess that's why I am taking her death so badly and why I almost feel she's still here, watching over me, and warning me of something."

"Well, I certainly hope her murderer doesn't know you're still in connection," Takis said softly. "That would put you directly in the line of danger. And that brings us back to the Hamiltons and to how frustrating it is that neither one of them has regained consciousness."

Takis balled his hands into fists and brought them down on the surface of the breakfast table. Caitlyn looked up at him in sympathy and covered both of his fists with her own hands. The tension started to drain out of him, and he smiled sheepishly and in appreciation at his wife.

It was at that moment of shared intimacy between husband and wife that the alarm went off. Someone had entered the garage below. Both Takis and Caitlyn headed for the foyer and instinctively threw open the front door, oblivious to all the security mechanisms that would keep them safe from assault as long as they remained behind locked doors.

The elevator was huffing up the floors. It reached their level about the time they realized their vulnerability and started to retreat back into the apartment. The elevator door opened, and Sarah Bristow struggled out under a pile of luggage, a grim smile of determination on her face as well as an apology for letting the alarm go off. After helping her into the apartment and dispensing with pleasantries on the weather in Paris and whether or not her flights had been crowded, Takis grew more serious and reopened the inquiry on Brussels.

"Sarah, I must talk with you again concerning the years in Brussels during the NATO scandal."

"Sorry, I can't talk now. I've got to be at the embassy in a half hour. I just stopped by to drop my luggage and to get a quick shower and change," she said and she was through her bedroom door, which she firmly shut behind her.

Takis was not deterred. Putting his head to the door and raising his voice, he said, "We found out that Ginger Hamilton was the wife of Colonel Bertram Remington, who was attached to NATO in the service of the UK during that period. I suppose you didn't know that, did you, Sarah?"

There was a pause and then, from the other side of the door, a muffled, "Yes, I knew that."

"But, why didn't you—?"

"That's classified, Takis. Look, I really do have to get in the shower and to work. What I was working on in Paris is important and needs to be followed up immediately."

"But I really do have to talk with you, Sarah. I'd rather not make this formal and make you appear at police headquarters. How about dinner with Caitlyn and me tomorrow night? Otherwise, I'm afraid it will have to be in my office."

The door opened, forcing Takis to take a quick step backward, and a berobed Sarah Bristow stuck her head out. "I'm not trying to avoid you on this, Takis. It really doesn't bother me in the least to tell you whatever doesn't have a classified seal on it. And it doesn't bother me in the least, either, not to tell you whatever is classified until and unless my superiors tell me to. And I'm not going to promise not to pursue the case myself within the mandate that's been given to me by my government. A meeting is fine, even though, as you well know, I have diplomatic immunity, so I don't have to talk to you. But dinner tomorrow isn't possible. I have to attend an opening of an exhibit at the International Fair, and I have a dinner engagement with John Dunsford. He's meeting me at the fair. I wasn't able to get hold of him right before I left Friday to make any other arrangements. Your office, Wednesday morning at 9:00. I'll be there, I promise." She disappeared back into her bedroom and the door snapped shut.

Takis was back on the attack as he returned to the closed door and declared in a loud voice, "Then you don't know Dunsford has gone to Brussels? He's in pursuit of Justin Chamberlain and Sergey Stepanov, who undoubtedly are up to their separate and combined necks in this NATO business and who left here on the same plane Wednesday afternoon."

There was no answer from the other side of the door, only the sound of a suitcase heavily hitting the floor, a prolonged moment of silence, and the rush of water being turned on full blast in the shower.

281

Takis shrugged his shoulders, kissed his wife, and headed for the door. He'd had enough of Sarah Bristow for at least the morning. He could feel the cream he had laced his coffee with curdling in his stomach. It was going to be a long day.

* * * *

The reflection off the slowly revolving ceiling fan flickered shadows across the morose little group of people hastily gathered around the desk at the Canadian high commission. It was twilight of the same evening. Takis Koniotis, Sarah Bristow, and Alec Stuart had been summoned to John Dunsford's Byron Street office to receive the disturbing debriefing of his unsuccessful and tragic trip to Brussels in pursuit of Justin Chamberlain and Sergey Stepanov.

In sad, defeated tones, Dunsford told how he'd picked up the track of the two from one of his agents who'd managed to catch the same plane the two had booked from Larnaca. The agent had reported in when on Friday in Brussels he overheard Chamberlain tell Stepanov to meet him the next morning at the Hotel d'Medici in Bruges, Belgium. Dunsford, with the knowledge and cooperation of the Belgian police, had proceeded to take up the hunt from there. He had been outside the Hotel d'Medici that morning when Stepanov had taken a call at the reception desk and then had departed on foot toward the historic center of the old city. Dunsford tried to follow, but, because he was in an automobile and Stepanov was walking, the Russian soon lost him by turning up a one-way alley. By the time Dunsford had parked and followed, Stepanov had disappeared in the maze of cobblestoned streets in the old city.

Dunsford hadn't thought that Stepanov actually saw that he was being tailed. Thus the Canadian searched methodically through the network of streets around Market and Town squares well into the afternoon before he had given up the hunt and called the Bruges police for assistance in the search.

What he had heard when he contacted the police, however, had chilled him to the bone. They said they'd been trying to find him. They had to pass on the information that one of the men he had said he was tracking, Justin Chamberlain, had just been found in the secluded garden of an empty cottage in the Ten Wyngaerde Beguinage. It was almost a fluke that he'd been found. The victim had been carrying identification under multiple names, including the two that had been provided them. The house had been empty for several weeks but was inspected late that afternoon by an elderly couple that had just been given the opportunity to move in.

Although it was quite obvious Chamberlain had been killed just inside the cottage garden gate—by multiple stab wounds—his body had been moved to a corner of the garden that could not be seen from the gate. A few British pound notes were found on the ground in the area.

"I presume you're responsible for the quick identification, Alec?" Dunsford broke off his monologue to interject the question.

"Yes, Takis told me that you had taken off in pursuit of the two, and I assumed that you hadn't had time to take files on the two with you. So I faxed some background information on the investigation and suspects to the Belgian authorities."

"Thank you. That sped up the process significantly. I hadn't, in fact, been able to provide more than very sketchy descriptions of the two to the authorities."

"So," Dunsford concluded glumly, "I was too late. Chamberlain is dead, and Stepanov has vanished. The Belgian authorities are still looking for him, but they haven't found a trace of him since he left the Hotel d'Medici. My guess is that he's gone back to ground in Russia, and we'll never hear from him again. The case here in Cyprus seems to be solved, although it can hardly feel satisfying to close the books when all of the players are dead or effectively out of reach. But what is most galling is that the Russians seemed to have again managed to completely cover their tracks on the NATO spy ring scandal. They're now likely to press for membership in NATO even harder. Isn't the world just a barrel of laughs?"

But no one was laughing. Alec Stuart sat, looking sad, his chin dropped on his chest. John Dunsford was sitting forward in his swivel chair, hunched over his desktop and making slow-motion stabbing gestures at his fingers with a letter opener. Sarah Bristow was staring, seemingly mesmerized, at the slowly revolving ceiling fan. There was no telling what she was thinking. The expression on her face couldn't be described as either a smile or a frown. It was more like a slightly disturbed grimace. Takis Koniotis was looking more contemplative, his eyes glued to the slowly moving letter opener in Dunsford's hand. A stubborn expression crossed his face, and he spoke:

"There is one question. . . ."

Everyone looked at the Cypriot investigator, but he didn't have time to voice the question.

The telephone on Dunsford's desk rang. It was Maria Solonos for Takis Koniotis.

"Good, you're still there. Willie Hamilton regained consciousness, but—"

Koniotis didn't hear the last word, however, as he was already excitedly passing the information on to his colleagues. All exclaimed in surprise, as none had known Willie had survived the attack at Kolossi Castle.

"No, wait, Takis," Maria called down the line. "Hear me out. Hamilton regained consciousness, but then he disappeared. He's no longer in the hospital, Takis. We've put out a search order for him."

Koniotis passed on this word as well, and, without further conversation, the four officials quickly scattered to their individual battle stations.

It was only after he was on the now-dark highway to Limassol, en route to the hospital where Hamilton was last seen, that something nudged at Koniotis's mind. It was when he had reported Hamilton was alive and awake. Not all of the initial reactions in the room had been what he would've anticipated. "Now what was out of step? Think, Takis, this is important."

But he couldn't concentrate hard on this issue and maintain complete control of his automobile at the same time. This became self-evident as an SUV, its high-beamed lights blinding, roared up behind him in the murky night. The larger vehicle very nearly—and seemingly purposefully, thought Takis—sideswiped him as it swept around him and charged out at maniac speed toward Limassol.

Chapter Twenty-Two

Safa Ziya was hobbling as fast as her uneven legs would carry her away from Government Square, across the remains of the ancient city walls, past Mehmet Tosun's tightly shuttered shop, down Memdoluh Asaf Street, and toward the American embassy's Turkish Cypriot zone office on Tabak Tervish Street. She was making quite a spectacle of herself, not least because her colleague and assistant, Tansul, was shuffling along beside her, flapping at her with her arms, and trying to reason with her in a quite loud tone.

"Ms. Ziya, Ms. Ziya. Wait. It's too long of a walk to the Americans' office. I ordered a car for you. Why didn't you wait?"

"I wanted to go today," Safa wheezed out tersely. She wanted to save as much of her breath and energy to help her get to the embassy's office as quickly as possible.

"I could've gotten you a hire car. Come, let's turn here. There's often a hire car down by the checkpoint."

"That would take even longer. Ouch. Get out from in front of me. Either walk off to the side or go back to the office. You're making this more difficult."

"But why are you going to the Americans? And why must it be so fast? Why can't you just wait until the bicommunal party they're going to hold for the police seminar and talk with Mr. Koniotis directly? And I thought you'd set up a deal with the Canadians to act as a go-between for you to on these cases."

"We're here now, Tansul." They stopped at a small gate in front of what looked like any other small bungalow in this part of the town that had once been a Greek suburb just to the northwest of the old city walls but that had suffered some of the heaviest house-to-house fighting when the Turkish forces overran this section of the city in 1974. The Greek owner of this house, who'd had no means to get to his property for twenty years, had been delighted to rent it out to the Americans to serve as their embassy's outpost on the Turkish side of the island. All of the neighboring houses now housed Turkish refugees who'd fled their own homes in the southern, Greek-dominated portions of the island in 1974—and did so without any compensation going to the Greeks who still formally owned the properties.

"Well, are you coming in with me or not? This is all your doing, you know. And very good work it was."

As Safa walked up the pathway and entered the building, Tansul, basking in the praise offered by her friend and superior, hesitated only briefly before scurrying up the walk. She didn't trust these Americans, who always acted so superior and who'd given little help when the Turkish Cypriot families were being massacred by the Greeks, but she did trust her friend Safa implicitly.

Although the Turkish employee who coordinated American interests in the north was quite willing to help Safa, who he said he was honored to receive on a personal visit, she was doomed to disappointment.

"I'm afraid Mr. Conte isn't in country at the moment," he reported after having spent several minutes on the static-belabored line, albeit nearly the only telephonic link sanctioned and in existence between the Turkish and Greek sectors. "They ask if there is someone else who might be at the embassy who might help you. Or—I think he's still here. The driver for the defense attaché was back in the kitchen a few minutes ago. If you have a note you'd like to send, I think—"

"No, no. None of that will do." Safa had recoiled as if the mere thought of talking to anyone else at the embassy or trusting the embassy's driver with a note was terrifying.

"Can you get through to any of the other embassy's on this line?"

"Certainly. It's a regular telephone line. It's just that it's one of only a couple that link to the other side at all. But I don't think I could let you call just anyone, especially not any of the Greek authorities."

"Not even the British high commission? Couldn't you try to get their political officer, Alec Stuart?"

"Well, a connection to Mr. Stuart should be all right. Perhaps some sort of clearance from your police chief—"

"Screw my chief! There may not be much time before someone else dies."

"Yes, screw my brother, the police chief, and all those men wrapped in red tape," Tansul joined in exuberantly. "Here, give me that phone. What numbers do you push in?"

* * * *

288

"She's awake! Takis, Ginger Hamilton's regained consciousness."

Maria Solonus just about smacked Alec Stuart with the office door as she rushed into the room. He'd just stood aside so that Takis Koniotis could get at his office telephone.

"That's great, Maria," Takis answered. "I don't think she'll have much to add that we don't already know, but we'll go almost straight over there anyway. Hold just a minute."

Takis picked up the phone and dialed. He nervously dug at his desk top while he impatiently waited for a connection. "Caitlyn. Good, I caught you. You have to get out of Sarah's apartment immediately. Collect whatever you can't get along without—but quickly—and wait by the door. Don't let anyone in. No, don't ask questions. Just go do it. We're on our way."

He hung up and started for the door. "Come on, Alec. No, just Alec, Maria. I need you to muster up the team and get over to the International Fair grounds. Safa and her assistant have broken the case for us. They've analyzed who crossed over into the Turkish zone at times relating to the murders over there, and it all fits now. We've been so off base. Alec, Caitlyn, and I will check with Ginger in the hospital and then join you."

* * * *

Darkness had enveloped the city and lights were beginning to glow in the surrounding houses when Takis Koniotis stormed out of Ginger Hamilton's hospital room. He hurried over to the nurses' station, flashed his police credentials, and reached for the telephone. Caitlyn interceded before he could take the call.

"Ginger. Is she—?"

"Yes. She's going to be fine, and what she had to say pretty much jibes with what we've already put together. Just let me take this call, then I'll drop you off somewhere safe and Alec and I'll be on our way."

"That's what you think. You can't lose me now. And Alec has already started over there."

"No time to argue just now. That's the office calling. Hello. This is Koniotis. Who is this?"

"Androulla here. We have William Hamilton on the line. He insists on speaking only to you, Mr. Koniotis. Here, I'll transfer him through."

"Hello, Willie, are you all right?"

"Yes," came the haltingly husky and alcohol-slurred reply. "I just had to get away to think what I should do. I'm ready to talk to you now. I—"

"Just a bit too late, Willie," Koniotis cut in impatiently. "Thanks for the decision to cooperate, however," he continued somewhat more gently. "We know the important parts already, and I need to get moving on follow up. You need to get over to Makarios Hospital in Nicosia immediately. Ginger is awake and very much in need of a husband. Room 121. I'll instruct the medical staff and guards to let you in." And then, only because it had been a long haul and he couldn't resist: "If I were you, I'd be the first husband she sees."

Without waiting to hear Willie's reply, Koniotis returned the receiver and headed for the exit. But then he stopped in his tracks, and Caitlyn almost tripped over him in her haste to keep up with his pace.

"What is it, Takis?" Caitlyn asked.

"Well, it doesn't matter now," Koniotis responded. "But I just remembered whose peculiar reaction I saw when I broke the news to the others at Dunford's office that Willie Hamilton was alive and had regained consciousness. I certainly wish I had been able to remember what I saw at the time." But he just shook his head and headed once more toward the exit, a very determined Caitlyn in train.

"Where to? And don't even think of trying to stash me someplace, as you say, safe."

"You're right. There's no time for that now. You keep complaining that I never take you to the International Fair. Well, tonight's the night."

* * * *

The Cyprus International Fair covered several acres on the Makedonitissa valley floor adjacent to the grounds of the Makedonitissa Monastery and across the road from the Makarios Stadium and the national sports facilities. The exhibit facilities consisted of a series of large, flat-roofed warehouse-style buildings sheathed in colorful panels. The buildings were connected by palm tree-lined pedestrian streets, and the grounds were dominated by a gigantic replica of a Carlsberg beer can on a platform that raised it above the rest of the grounds.

The complex typically housed four major exhibitions a year. This was the quarter for the annual electronics and computer technology fair. The permanent U.S. pavilion was featuring defense communications systems, which accounted for Sarah Bristow's prominent presence at the Tuesday night opening of that country's exhibit.

The combined British and Canadian computer components exhibits had opened the night before, but both John Dunsford and Alec Stuart had signed up to help push the goods during the second evening—or at least to put in a sympathetic appearance.

Sarah Bristow came by the British and Canadian pavilion at about twilight and broke into what looked like the start of a heated conversation between Dunsford and Stuart, whom she'd seen arrive just before her.

"Have you just arrived, Alec? I thought you were planning to be here earlier this afternoon."

"Listen, Sarah. Now that you're here, I need both of you to stay right here until—"

"Please, Alec, I don't have time for this. John, we have to talk."

"We're very busy here at the moment, Sarah. I'm sure it can wait for dinner."

"No, it can't wait for dinner. We have to talk before then."

A visitor to the pavilion pulled on Dunsford's arm, quite evidently wanting to ask a question about the computer they were standing near. But, Sarah would have none of that. She pulled Dunsford back around. "All right. If not right now, within ten minutes on the back porch of that deserted Russian log house from last year's exhibit."

"Isn't that a little off the beaten track?" Alec asked nervously. "Is there some reason you need to meet on Russian ground? Couldn't you both just stay here for—"

"Oh just butt out, Alec." Sarah said and stomped off through the swirling crowd.

At the appointed time, Dunsford moved despondently toward the back of the Russian house. A strong arm reached out of the shadows, spun him around, and slammed him up against the logs. The wind knocked out of his lungs and the roughness of the logs sending fingers of pain radiating from his side, Dunsford turned an expression of surprise and hurt on Sarah Bristow.

Bristow backed up a step and clicked the safety off her nasty-looking service revolver.

"Why, Sarah? Why . . . ?"

The vicious backhanded slap across his face effectively curbed his question and jerked him back onto the rough-hewn logs.

"You couldn't leave well enough alone, could you, John? I loved you, you know. All of this because I loved you."

Dunsford had straightened up. He put his hands in his pocket and moved gingerly—not directly at the angry woman scorned, but in a little semicircle that brought him ever closer to her and to the gun she held loosely in her hand. He was trying to appear to be intently listening to what Sarah was saying, but all of his inward attention was focused on the swaying revolver.

Bristow's torrent of words continued. "It's time to bring the truth about the Brussels operation into the open. This wasn't Justin's or Sergey's operation, and it hasn't been the Russians that have been killing off all of the spies retired from that operation. Sergey's a false lead and it isn't going to take Koniotis much longer to figure that out. We don't have much time now that Willie Hamilton is on the loose and Ginger is probably close to regaining consciousness. You know, I should've killed you first. But I loved you. I still should—"

Dunsford made his move. The two grappled, a slow-motion dance of death that was suddenly caught in the beam of an approaching flashlight.

Having illuminated the death struggle with his flashlight, Alec Stuart yelled and hurled himself on the couple from the shadows of the pathway. There was a flash of metal in the light, an explosion of gunfire, and a bloodcurdling scream. And that was just the beginning of the end.

Chapter Twenty-Three

The lights had been turned on in the Russian log house and everyone had been dragged inside. Some folding chairs and a folding table had also been obtained from somewhere on the fair grounds and brought in. The cheery buzz of sound from the nearby lighted exhibition halls indicated that the drama at the side of the Russian house had not even fazed the festivities just steps away.

Alec Stuart was hunched in a folding chair in one corner of the log house's living area and was applying ice to various parts of his anatomy.

"Here, drink this coffee," Caitlyn said as she tried to minister to his needs. "It's cold and terribly strong, but I think you need it."

"Thanks, Caitlyn. I've always considered myself a fair scrapper, but I wouldn't try to take on Sarah Bristow again under any circumstances. That is one tough soldier."

John Dunsford was crumpled in a chair in the most isolated corner of the room. He had his head in his hands and was refusing all attempts at communication. He had initially been making little grunting and gurgling sounds, but now he was silent.

In contrast, Sarah Bristow stood in a belligerent stance in the center of the room and was sharing her thoughts and views in loud tones with anyone who would listen. Takis Koniotis, accompanied by Maria Solonos, notebook at the ready, was quite pleased to listen to the tirade.

"Not only do I have diplomatic immunity," Mr. Koniotis, "but my embassy is also claiming jurisdiction over this Brussels spy ring investigation—and you are impeding my work."

"Let's just cut the theatrics, Sarah," Koniotis broke in with a matter-of-fact business-like tone. "The game is up. Just tell me this for now—I pretty much know how most of the other details fit. When did you first suspect John Dunsford was behind the killings?"

Bristow's balloon was deflated. She sank into one of the folding chairs and answered, a great weariness having descended, "I knew something terrible was eating at him the first time I saw him here in Cyprus. He'd changed so much in so little time. You should've known John in Brussels. He had such vitality and charisma. No one could resist John. I certainly didn't."

She lifted a hand to her face and shuddered. She threw a pitying glance toward the Canadian but drew no response from that quarter. Then, her face set in an expression of resignation and determination, her back went ramrod straight, and she continued, "I guess I first really suspected what he was up to when that soprano was murdered at the Famagusta Gate concert. I recognized her as soon as I saw her in the exhibition hall as having been connected with Brussels. John should've recognized her, as well. But he kept saying he didn't remember her until I wouldn't drop the point, and then he pretended to suddenly recognize her for the first time. I told John that we'd have to corner her as soon as possible after the concert, but he'd been unreasonably lukewarm to that idea. Until she appeared on stage, I had no idea she was one of the performers.

"Just as we reached our seats before the concert began, John said he needed a smoke and headed for the exit door. I became suspicious and left the hall just before the lights went down. But the only person out front was Alec Stuart, and he said he hadn't seen John come out. And then there was that shot and all that pandemonium. When I finally caught up with John, he said he'd gone to the men's room instead. It sounded plausible at the time, especially since I wanted to believe it. But, in conjunction with everything else, it became just too much of a coincidence."

"But why didn't you do or say something before now, Sarah?" Koniotis gently probed.

"I guess I just couldn't bring myself to face reality. I loved him. I guess I still love him." She cast another glance at Dunsford; still no connection. "And I was mesmerized by him. Look at him. You wouldn't know by looking at him in his present condition, but he once had the power to mesmerize people. And he somehow has maintained the power to mesmerize those he once touched. It wasn't until I was on the plane to Paris that I started objectively assessing the situation. I'd always thought it was me he loved in Brussels. But he didn't love me. He wanted to use me, just like he used the others. But I was too blinded by love to see what he was up to, and," she laughed bitterly, "I was too naïve in love to even recognize his attempts to change the relationship to one of spymaster and agent. Ha, that must have frustrated him. I was too dumb even to distinguish between endearments and a pitch to spy for him."

"OK, Sarah. I guess that's enough for now."

Koniotis turned to Dunsford, who was still slumped over in his chair.

"No use keeping up the silence, John," declared Koniotis as he approached. "Ginger Hamilton has already fingered you as the spymaster. Come on, sit up John. You might as well tell us the rest."

But John Dunsford could not sit up. John Dunsford was far, far away.

The cursory search by the policeman hadn't revealed the extra knife Dunsford carried in the lining of his rumpled trench coat. Dunsford's hands had found the knife and had exercised one of the two options that he had been struggling so hard with the last couple of weeks—whether from a natural instinct of self-preservation, to keep killing everyone who could link him to the Brussels spy ring or just to give it all up and do away with himself.

In the end, he had largely exercised both options.

Epilogue

The final cocktail party for the Canadian high commission's bicommunal seminar that Friday evening had almost been canceled for fear the exposure and death of the program's coordinator would throw a wet blanket over the event. But, in fact, this notoriety had just the opposite effect. The reception, held on the hotel's decaying terraces surrounding the crumbling swimming pool, was the best-attended bicommunal gathering the Ledra Palace Hotel had hosted in years. All officials—and their spouses—from both sides of the Green Line and from the press and diplomatic corps who could claim any connection with the seminar or police business were there. Black tux and glittery sequined dresses covered the terraces and spilled out into scraggly rose beds. The air was electric with titillation at the delicious rehashing of events of the previous four weeks.

Takis Koniotis of the Greek Cypriot police and Safa Ziya of the Turkish Cypriot police were sitting at a table just inside the French doors to the dining room. Just as had been the case during the seminar itself, both had detached themselves from the event, lost in their own shared world of note comparisons. At the same time, the two senior police officials were the center of attention from all sides.

The two investigators were not alone at the table. Caitlyn Koniotis had accompanied her husband, as had Maria Solonos. And, as a reward for her help, Safa Ziya had brought along the research assistant, Tansul, who was somewhat cowed by her very first venture across the Turkish Cypriot border in nearly thirty years. Alec Stuart of the British high commission and Paul Conte of the American embassy rounded out the small group at the table.

Sarah Bristow had been invited to join them at the seminar finale, but she had declined. She was bolted away in her secure penthouse, packing and preparing to return to her country under less than victorious conditions. She was not being charged for her approach to the case—she had been trying to bring the Canadian spymaster in alive—but the U.S. army would look a little dimly on the emotionalism that had clouded her judgment and paralyzed her action for so long.

Paul Conte had just that afternoon returned to the island, so the others were filling him in on how the case had been wrapped up.

"Ginger Hamilton was able to tell us that John Dunsford was the spymaster in Brussels, but she herself seemed to be too muddleheaded about what was going on to realize how serious it was," Takis explained. "She hadn't actually spied for Dunsford. She probably frustrated the hell out of him in his attempt to recruit her. Up until the time the scandal broke, she was concentrating more on getting him into bed. Even after the whistle was blown, she didn't realize that her husband's embarrassment had been what sent him to suicide. She probably didn't realize how much trouble she was in as well as Willie did."

"So Willie was involved, as well," said Caitlyn. "I'm sorry to hear that."

"No, not really," said Alec Stuart. "He only caught on when Ginger noted in passing that she recognized several of the people who were being popped off around the island from the period of her brief years in Belgium with NATO. Even then she hadn't been able to add up what was happening and to conclude that she, too, might be in danger. Willie thought he could get Ginger disentangled from it all without getting her into trouble with the authorities. But he was way below Dunsford's league in intrigue, and he almost died because of it."

"So, Ginger broke the case for you," Paul Conte said.

"Not really," answered Takis. "We'd already figured it out before Ginger regained consciousness. Safa broke the case for us."

"No, not me," said Safa. "It was Tansul who did all of the comparisons of the border crossing records with the timing of the killings in the north. And, if she hadn't bullied her brother and his cronies, we would never have gotten accurate records. John Dunsford's border crossing records fit, and, as you know, Takis, I never ruled him out as a suspect."

"I understand that Eleni was involved, along with that Turkish merchant, in locating the spies here, but I hate to think she condoned all those murders."

"I'm sure she didn't, Caitlyn," Takis said. "I'm sure she thought she was protecting those people by helping to move them here. But I'm sure John knew where this would lead all along—or at least he knew as soon as he saw that the Soviet empire was collapsing and that records of old spy operations undoubtedly would fall into the hands of the Western allies."

"Even then," Takis continued, "Dunsford must've foreseen that he would eventually have to, as they say, 'retire' his salted-away agents 'with prejudice.' Otherwise, it would have made more sense to disperse them throughout the world rather than go to the trouble of having them all conveniently available on one small, water-encircled island. And this wasn't an operation of the Russians trying to clean up after themselves. It was simply John Dunsford trying to protect his own hide for past sins. Everyone else was just a pawn—most controlled by sex, including, I'm afraid, even Justin Chamberlain."

There was more than one gasp around the table. But not from Caitlyn.

"I guess I already knew that," she said.

Koniotis registered surprise.

"After I had learned that Justin was dead," Caitlyn continued, "I went to Andriko Visiliou and made him tell me why he and Justin had suddenly become so bitter toward each other back at the university. Andriko told me that it was because Justin had made explicit—and persistent—passes at him. Andriko had rejected them all and hadn't told anyone about it, but he finally violently rebuffed Justin. Their relations were hopelessly strained from that point on. And in retrospect I saw that that was why Sarah Bristow had been so catty in her apartment the other evening about Justin having shown up and included himself in activities she'd planned for herself and Dunsford alone. It was pure sexual jealousy surfacing. I'm not even sure she realizes why she reacted as she had. But something inside her must have realized that Justin was competing with her for Dunsford's attention and affection."

"I'm afraid Justin was involved in far more than the spy ring case," continued Koniotis. "His affair with Dunsford in Brussels taught him to crave danger. He set up his own antiquities forgery and smuggling racket here, blackmailing various of the other retired spies into involvement in that operation. It was he, not Dunsford, who killed Peggy Bingham—and he would've killed Mehmet Tosun and his nephew if he could've caught up with them—and assuming that he didn't after they'd all left the island."

"The relationship between Dunsford and Chamberlain was also what was behind what bothered me about Dunsford's explanation in his office the other night of his hunt through Belgium for Stepanov and Chamberlain."

"Yes, I meant to ask you about that," Stuart chimed in. "You were about to ask a question at that meeting when the telephone call came through about Willie Hamilton's disappearance."

"I was initially disturbed that Dunsford called the detective who had followed Chamberlain from Larnaca to Brussels back to Cyprus after he reported Chamberlain's departure from the Hotel Metropole for Bruges just as Stepanov showed up to the hotel."

"I don't understand," said Conte, speaking up for the first time that evening.

"Well, first, why, after the detective had already successfully followed Chamberlain half way across Europe, did Dunsford call him off the hunt? Even if Dunsford wanted to take up the pursuit himself, why wouldn't he welcome the extra manpower already in place? In hindsight, it obviously was because he didn't want anyone nosing around and getting in the way of what he planned to do to Chamberlain once he'd found him."

"Very perceptive," intoned Ziya. "And the second nagging question?"

"It wasn't too logical, Chamberlain's sense of humor aside, for Stepanov to be huffing and puffing behind Chamberlain around Brussels. If they'd left Larnaca on the same plane by design, why would they have been separated once they got to Brussels? I think Chamberlain must have given Stepanov the slip at the airport— Dunsford's detective managed to keep Chamberlain in sight, but he didn't claim that Stepanov was following along, as well. I don't think Chamberlain told Stepanov where he was staying. I can understand why, once Stepanov found him at the Hotel Metropole, Chamberlain decided on the spot to set up another meeting to do away with the Russian. And I can understand how the detective knew Chamberlain, who was traveling under yet another assumed name, was at the Hotel Metropole—and he followed him there. But I didn't understand how Stepanov knew Chamberlain was at the Hotel Metropole if he was only getting around to finding him there two days after they'd landed in Brussels."

No one around the table stirred. A smile began to form on Ziya's lips.

"It turns out that the Hotel Metropole had been both the center of Dunsford's spy operations and the venue of his trysts with Chamberlain," Takis continued. "This was obviously known by Stepanov, as he was handling the support arrangements for the operation. Thus, what was just a nagging question when Dunsford was describing what happened in Belgium, turned out to be a logical contradiction of what Dunsford was trying to conjure. Stepanov eventually thought of checking the hotel where it had all began, and, because of Chamberlain's perversity, that was where Stepanov located him."

Koniotis sat back and worried a cigarette out of a pack that was in front of him on the table. He felt around for a match but didn't seem to be finding any. Instinctively, Caitlyn reached into her purse, drew out a silver lighter, and handed it to her husband. Koniotis looked at her in surprise.

"There's that lighter again. You don't smoke, Cait—and God knows you've tried hard enough to get me to stop. What are you doing with a lighter?"

"Oh, it's Justin's lighter. He left it at my office at the museum when he steamed off after hearing that Eleni had been murdered. What's wrong?"

Koniotis had been reading the inscription. "Did you read what's written on this lighter?" he asked tightly. Everyone leaned forward to see.

"Part of it," responded Caitlyn. "Something about 'all my love' and . . . 'Brussels.' Oh, no, would that have been some sort of clue?"

"You didn't read the rest—the initials?"

"No, it was too dark in the office, and then I got involved in my work and forgot to check the initials when I got home. What are they?"

"J.P.D."

"Oh," she said weakly. "John Dunsford, no doubt."

"And John has seen you with that lighter before. And he also knew you were very close to both Eleni and Justin, the two people who knew the most about what he'd done. No wonder you seemed to have been living under a threat the last couple of weeks—even you yourself said you felt Eleni was trying to reach and protect you from beyond the grave."

Everyone sat morosely, boring their gazes into the table top for a few minutes. After a short interval, Paul Conte cleared his throat and changed the topic by way of a new question, "So what about Sergey Stepanov? I suppose—and I suppose I hope—he is floating in some Belgium canal."

"I'll bet not," responded Safa with a laugh. "He's the type who knows how to swim too well. When Dunsford caught up with him, he probably just sold the information on where he was meeting Chamberlain and then blissfully flew off to Moscow."

"And I bet we haven't heard the last of Sergey," chimed in Alec Stuart.

"At least he's no longer here and stirring up trouble with his Russian mafia gang. The others in his bunch may not be gone, but they are far weaker in his absence. Which reminds me, Takis. I know exactly where we need to focus the cooperation between our two police forces now—on the Russian mafia problem that is growing on both sides of the Green Line."

Takis assented readily and started to talk strategy.

"Not just now, my eager friend," said Ziya cheerily. "Right now I refuse to be sad about whatever fate has befallen Stepanov or to worry about this Russian mafia. I'm celebrating."

"Yes, Ms. Ziya has every reason to be happy tonight," blurted out Tansul, working up the courage to speak for the first time that evening. Beyond being in awe of the company, her English was not quite as good as that of the others.

Tansul was now the focus of everyone's attention, and her face had turned beet red. But she resolutely continued, "Ms. Ziya can be happy because she was promoted today."

"Promoted?" Caitlyn exclaimed, reflecting the good will of all present. "Congratulations!"

"Yes, congratulations," Koniotis chimed in. "I presume your superiors recognized your vital contributions in this NATO spy ring investigation?"

Ziya and Tansul burst out laughing and looked at each other in a conspiratorial manner.

"No, I'm afraid not," Ziya wedged between the giggles. She dug into her purse and briefly brandished a rubber stamp on high before dropping it back into her bag. "I got promoted for solving a serial rapist case three years ago. Sorry that we laughed. We can't explain, really. It's one of those Turkish Cypriot bureaucracy jokes."

The frivolity of the two Turkish women lightened the atmosphere at the table and in the vicinity considerably. But, just before the group moved on to happier topics, Koniotis raised one last serious note.

"Alec, we really do need to start working together on this Russian mafia problem. Could the British high commission see its way clear to set up a regular periodic meeting between the two police services—at least one between Safa Ziya and me—so that we have regular access to each other on shared issues? We had already asked the Canadians to do it, but in the wake of what we've learned about John Dunsford, I'd really rather have someone else sponsor our meetings now."

"Of course, I'd be delighted. We can call them the John Dunsford Memorial Meetings," Stuart quipped. "In our review we saw that Dunsford had done everything he could to keep the two of you from getting your heads together in unknown pursuit of his crimes. And yet he'd worked himself into a box, as the seminar was his brainchild to start with. Initiating this contact was probably the biggest mistake he ever made. We'll get this started next week."

"I'll drink to that," declared Safa Ziya as she raised her glass, a twinkle in her eye. "And I'll drink to you, Takis Koniotis." And then, without thinking, she pronounced the Greek drinking toast "Stin I yassu, skol, Takis!"—Health to you, Takis.

Smiling broadly, and fully knowing what he was doing, Takis shot right back with the Turkish drinking toast "Sihhatine, Safa!"—And health to you, Safa.

Caitlyn was glowing inside. It was a start. Not necessarily a giant step to reconciliation between the communities, but a good start nonetheless.

Gina Drew:

Gina Drew is a retired American foreign service officer who specialized in investigating and countering international crime and espionage and who still travels the world in both the imagination and in fact.

Koniotis Mysteries Series

Each book in this series stands alone, but they are also all connected in various ways and form the different parts of one story.

www.cyberworldpublishing.com

www.ingramcontent.com/pod-product-compliance
Lightning Source LLC
Chambersburg PA
CBHW070223260626
47160CB00002B/669